The Awakening

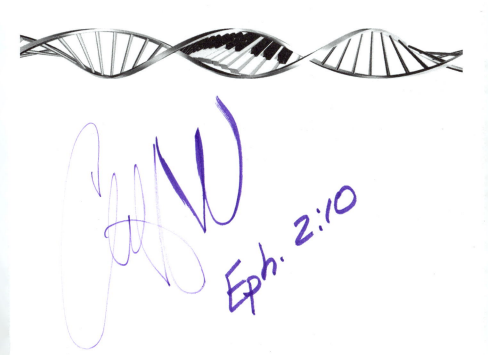

Cliff Warden

THE AWAKENING by Clifford Warden
Copyright © 2009 Clifford Warden

Cover design by Jeron Moe, www.jeronmoe.com

This is a work of fiction. Names, characters, places, and incidents either are the product of the author's imagination or are used fictitiously. Any resemblance to actual persons, living or dead, events, or locales is entirely coincidental.

All rights reserved. No part of this publication may be reproduced, stored in a retrieval system, or transmitted in any form or by any means—electronic, mechanical, photocopying, recording, or otherwise—without the prior written permission of the copyright owner(s).

International Standard Book Number: 978-0-578-03205-4

The Awakening

BY CLIFFORD WARDEN

1

Snowflakes Are Dancing

ART STOOD TO BOW for the thunderous applause. He was the final performer for the Hawthorne Academy Prep School Winter Holiday Concert. He had started his performance by playing two of his original compositions; he then played a traditional religious Christmas carol and ended his performance with his own arrangement of *Snowflakes Are Dancing* by Debussy.

The Boston Globe had recently heralded Art as the nation's top teen piano virtuoso. As a seventeen-year-old high school senior, he was being courted not only by the most prestigious universities, but also by the major symphony companies all over the world.

As he raised his head, Art gazed out into the standing crowd, the women adorned in red and green holiday dresses and the men in expensive suits, all applauding. It was overwhelming, and he let his vision blur to make them look like a field of flowers blowing in the wind. He wondered why he felt so empty, why he could not enjoy his success. He felt pleasure in his music, but he also felt robotic, as if he could not help but watch his fingers run up and down the keyboard, almost without volition. He snapped back to reality, mechanically bowed again and quickly exited off stage to the smiling faces and thumbs-up of his fellow student performers and music faculty. He did not stop to soak in the praise, but continued his brisk pace out the back door of the auditorium to the outdoor commons area.

Although Hawthorne Preparatory Academy was only fifteen years old, it had quickly become the premier Ivy League Prep School. The new captains of commerce who emerged just after the dawn of the twenty-first century had financed Hawthorne and populated it with their children. Seeking the legitimacy and feel of a top-notch Ivy League feeder institution, the founding board/financiers had purposefully designed the campus with an English Gothic architectural bent. They wanted the campus to have an Oxford ambiance that would hopefully translate into a feeling of hundreds of years of history and tradition. The only things it lacked were the black and white class photos from the early 1900s. The outdoor commons areas were perfectly designed to compliment the buildings, adorned with mature spruce and fir trees that looked like they had been there for over one hundred years.

Art embraced the twenty-degree air, taking in a large breath of relief. The cold air filled his lungs and helped clear his head. He closed his eyes and listened as the wind hummed its chorus through the tops of the fir trees. After a big gust, he opened his eyes and noticed that it had begun to snow giant flakes. He watched as the flakes meandered down to decorate the fir trees. As they intensified in number and size, Art raised his head and hands upward as if to welcome the white cleansing from the heavens. He thought to himself that the ice crystals were so beautiful, all different, floating down to their destiny, mingling with the others. With his eyes, Art selected a falling snowflake and attempted to follow it to the ground. He was pleased with this peaceful yet invigorating encounter with nature. He wondered if this was the feeling

Debussy was trying to express when he wrote *Snowflakes Are Dancing*.

Art's nirvana was shattered by the sound of his own name.

"Art, Art, come on, or you'll miss the receiving line and you know how Professor Silverman will feel about that. Besides, we need to get you through that line so we can catch our flight to Arizona. The sooner we're done here, the sooner we can be catching rays and checking out babes in Scottsdale."

The plea was from Chris Taylor, considered by most to be the top dog at Hawthorne. Chris had it all. He was a triple threat at Hawthorne, being the school's best athlete, number one in his class, and extremely good looking. He was about six-foot-two with sun-streaked sandy blond hair and muscles perfectly proportional to his height and weight. He was every girl's dream and the envy of every guy at Hawthorne.

Art quickly jogged back inside with Chris, brushing the snow off his tux and shaking it out of his hair. He knew what to do—smile, be gracious and praise the Hawthorne benefactors for their generosity in providing him with the incredible opportunity to study and hone his skills in an ideal setting with the top instructors in the country.

Chris and his family were waiting for Art just off the main receiving line. Actually, it looked as if Chris's father, Eugene, was running a second receiving line of his own. As soon as the Hawthorne benefactors had congratulated the student artists, they immediately went over to greet Eugene Taylor. Mr. Taylor had been on the Hawthorne board for the last ten years and for the last two years had been chairman of the board. The Hawthorne benefactors lined up to receive Eugene's recognition and praise while the parents of students lined up to pay homage in an attempt to assure a continued seat for their child at the academy.

Art had no parents to "kiss the ring". A natural gas explosion had killed both his parents when Art was eight months old. The closest thing Art had to a parent was his trustee/guardian from Boston Mercantile Bank & Trust. For as long as Art could remember, he had been in some sort of foster care, day care, boarding school or summer camp. He received visits from Mr. Jason M. Alexander, his designated trustee, twice a year along with "official" visits around his birthday and during the Christmas holiday season.

The hardest time for Art emotionally was at Christmas. For as far back as he could remember he felt as if he were the pathetic Christmas charity project of some family of a student where he was attending school. Some of the holiday visits with families were warm, inclusive and wonderful, with Art really feeling a part of the host family and their holiday traditions. Some of the holiday experiences were horridly awkward, spent with the families who couldn't seem to emotionally allow Art in on their family traditions, leaving Art as a spectator—feeling odd, an outsider, and aching for his own family, the family that he never knew.

One of his worst Christmas memories was from middle school. Art was invited to spend the holiday break with Johnny Webber's family. Every night at dinner, the Webber family children would light Advent candles and open a wrapped box containing a portion of the Christmas story. Art made the mistake of reaching out to light one of the candles. Mrs. Webber immediately grabbed his hand and informed Art with a firm voice and a stern look that the candle lighting was only for the Webber children. Not only did this embarrass Art, it reinforced in the deepest part of him that he was a second-class citizen, an outcast, a social leper.

Art had come to hate the winter breaks. When everyone else was full of excitement and anticipation for the holidays, Art dreaded the approach of Christmas, becoming withdrawn and quiet and going through a pre-grieving process where he would mourn his lack of family, tradition, and belonging. Even if his host family was wonderfully inclusive, deep inside he knew they were not his family, and these were not his traditions. Internally, he longed and ached for the day when he would have his own family with his own traditions where he could truly know that he belonged, not just allowed to follow along or merely observe someone else's intimate family traditions.

This year he was told that he had hit the jackpot. He was to be the guest of Chris Taylor's family. The Taylor's were not only the envy of the Hawthorne crowd; they were the envy of the social, intellectual, political, and monetary elite of the east coast. They were the "blue chip" family.

As soon as the receiving line was finished, Art and the Taylor family bolted for the limo for the twenty-minute ride to TEI's headquarters and private airport. TEI—Taylor Enhancements, Inc.—was a company started by Eugene Taylor and his wife, Virginia Taylor, in 2007. Mr. Taylor had been one of the pioneers in youth and longevity research and pharmacogenomics. Mr. Taylor's timing was perfect, matching his product line with the insatiable desire of the aging "Baby Boomers" to look young, feel young, and live forever.

The plane was waiting for them on the runway, fully stocked and ready to head to the private Scottsdale, Arizona Airport. The Taylors owned a southwest getaway home in the Boulders Resort in Carefree that they frequented quite often during the winter months.

Mr. Taylor maintained a lucrative consulting contract with the basketball and baseball professional sports teams in the Phoenix area. He specialized in helping sport franchises modify and control personality issues such as anger and fits of rage in troubled players. Ever since the steroid, HGH, and blood doping scandals years ago in football, baseball, and cycling, all non-prescription substances had been highly monitored. Gene Taylor was known as the best in the business at working with doctors, league officials, and players to "legally enhance" positive, healthy personality traits and performance.

Mr. Taylor had been on his phone ever since leaving the winter concert and was still talking nonstop as he boarded the plane. Virginia dutifully and patiently followed Mr. Taylor wherever he went, with a distant but pleasant look on her face. The only time her expression had changed was when Chris introduced Art to his mother. Art felt strangely awkward as Mrs. Taylor appeared to look at him as if she were seeing a relative she had not seen in a very long time, a kind of "so this is how you've turned out" look. Art tried to act normal and gave his usual adult greeting, "Very nice to meet you, Mrs. Taylor. Thanks so much for including me on your family's vacation. This is quite a treat for me; I have never been to the desert before."

Mrs. Taylor snapped out of her unsettling stare and came back with the equally polite, "Art, it is our pleasure to have you with us. I hope you will feel comfortable and part of our family. If there is anything at all that you need, just let me know and I will make sure things are taken care of for you."

They all boarded the corporate jet. Mr. and Mrs. Taylor occupied the private cabin near the front of the plane while Art, Chris, and his younger sister, Elisha, were given the rear portion of the plane. This area was a virtual in-air entertainment center with instant access to any and all entertainment available via satellite transmission.

Chris and Elisha immediately grabbed the video goggles and began searching through their options. Art, who had never been on a small private jet before, thought he would just take in the reality around him, sink down into the large leather seat, and admire the expensive wood trim and the fully-stocked kitchen area. This was nothing like flying on a commercial flight. It made first class look like a bad bus trip.

The best part of the flight for Art was the opportunity to stare at Elisha without being noticed while she was wearing movie goggles. Elisha was a freshman at Hawthorne and extremely beautiful. Art was amazed at her incredible looks, especially after seeing her parents who were not exactly characterized by their good looks.

Mr. Taylor was about five-feet-ten inches and extremely thin and lanky with long, thin, bony fingers. His shiny, straight, jet-black hair was combed neatly back. His most distinguishing feature was his very narrow, long, pointed nose. He was in his mid- to late-forties, but looked much younger, with smooth unwrinkled skin and not a hint of gray hair anywhere. He presented himself as rich, powerful, and successful.

Mrs. Taylor was petite, standing barely five-feet tall. She was not what you would call thin, but she was not overweight either. She had short legs and a long upper body, making her look disproportional and imbalanced. Her natural hair color was a mystery. Her current hair color was light brown highlighted with blonde and cut to fall just short of her shoulders. She had piercing hazel eyes with dark brown eyebrows. She dressed rich, but she could not match the powerful, successful presence that exuded from her husband. If dressed differently, a person could easily imagine her to be an ordinary mom shopping at the grocery store.

Elisha, however, had perfect proportions, right down to height, weight, cheekbones, and eyes. She was about five-feet-eight inches tall with a small waistline and long legs. Her long, flowing blonde hair came halfway down her back, which she enjoyed flipping around to draw the attention of the opposite sex. Her most striking feature was her dazzling green eyes that had a kaleidoscope quality to them. She was perky, she was witty, she was stunning, and she carried herself like she knew it.

Art felt he was jet-setting with a supermodel. For a few minutes, Art fantasized what it would be like to have Elisha as his girlfriend, holding hands and walking through the Hawthorne grounds with Elisha gazing into his eyes in an adoring way. He bolted back to reality. Who was he kidding? He was five-foot-six, a little pudgy, with unruly black hair that was already starting to recede. He was not part of the elite popular group at Hawthorne and he didn't come from a family with status or wealth.

After they reached cruising altitude, Art put on the headset, found a great music channel, and pretended he was in his own private jet, flying to his next performance with his entourage—including Elisha. Before he knew it, they were landing in Scottsdale. The plane had chased the sun westward, arriving just in time for them to witness it setting over layers of dreamy-looking silhouetted mountain ranges. As Art got off the plane, he immediately noticed the warm breeze on his face and the swaying date palm branches. The change in three hours from snow to palm trees made him feel special, wealthy, and important. He decided this might be his best winter break ever. They loaded into the waiting limo and headed north through the mass of red tile roofs to the Taylor's home in the Boulders where they would settle in for the evening.

Virginia showed Art to the guest bedroom and told him that there was nothing planned for the next day so he could sleep in as long as he desired. This was welcome news, as the fatigue of finals and the pressure of the winter concert had brought him to the point of exhaustion. Art unpacked his bags, brushed his teeth, folded down the bed, turned the television to music videos, and fell asleep within five minutes.

He awoke the next morning to the sound of a car door slamming. He looked at his watch; it was 8:05 A.M., which he quickly computed to 6:05 A.M. Arizona time. The guest room had only a partial view of the driveway and by the time he got to the window, he caught just a glimpse of the back of a man carrying a square brief case. It was still dark outside and hard to see, but Art thought the man looked vaguely familiar. His fatigue kept him from mentally pursuing the connection as he stumbled into bed and fell back asleep.

Virginia's Discovery

VIRGINIA AWAKENED TO THE SOUND of Gene showering. She rolled over and looked at the alarm clock on the table beside her bed. *Why is Gene getting up at five-thirty when we are on vacation?* She rolled back over and tried unsuccessfully to go back to sleep. She was wide awake and her mind was the clearest it had been in a very long time. After seeing Art again, she had decided to purposefully stop taking her specially formulated daily enhancement packet designed by Gene to regulate her mood, emotions, and disposition.

Taylor Enterprises was known for gathering vital information from a client and using it to formulate a personalized combination of psychotropic drugs to produce what TEI called "the best version of you." In Virginia's case, Gene had tweaked the formula to create his vision of what or who Virginia should be. In fact, he had concocted nine different formulas for Virginia designed to fit special occasions or circumstances, ranging from being the very perky, social extrovert in order to work a crowd, to being the calm, mellow, book reader on a rainy day. Virginia had literally been his "puppet on a string" via Taylor Enhancements for the last eighteen years. Sometimes Virginia wondered who she was, but she did not possess enough confidence in herself to challenge Gene and the Virginia whom Gene wanted. However, seeing Art again triggered something in Virginia to cause her to forego the enhancements. It was time to get in touch with her true self again.

Virginia listened intensely as Gene left their bedroom and jogged down the hallway toward the front door. She heard the front door open and two sets of footsteps come back down the hall and veer off into the adjacent study. She wondered who would have come over to the house at this time of day. She got up out of bed and tiptoed over to inner door separating the master bedroom and the study. Slowly and quietly she sat down on the cold tile floor. The gap under the door made it easy for her to overhear the conversation.

She heard Gene lash out at the visitor in a disgusted tone. "I thought I told you to park outside the security gates and walk in from the north side of the house!"

The visitor quickly apologized, "I'm sorry, Gene. The guard at the gate said he would not allow me to enter on foot and that I would be required to stay in my vehicle until I arrived at my destination. I probably should have called you and let you know the situation."

"Yes, a phone call would have been much better than a car door slamming."

"Sorry, sorry, did he wake up?"

Virginia recognized the visitor's voice immediately. She wondered what in the world Eric was doing in Arizona? She reasoned correctly that it must have something to do with Art.

Gene continued to pummel Eric with questions.

"Did D.H.E. agree with the plan? Are you still going to run your final battery of tests? Did you get all of the other records sealed?"

"Whoa, whoa, what question do you want answered first, Gene?"

"Sorry, Eric, tell me what D.H.E. thought of my plan for Art's 'coming out'?"

"They are extremely nervous about how all of this plays out. No one contemplated all the possible scenarios eighteen years ago. They are very excited about the possibilities of this whole project. However, the overriding message they repeated ad nauseam was that Art's successful transition to a productive adult life without incident is critical to whether this program can continue. As we both know, out of the four brothers, Art is the greatest risk because of his talents and inevitable exposure to public acclaim and scrutiny by the press. When and if he becomes famous, and it looks like he is well on his way, the press will dig into his background for the human-interest story. Which means either the plan we drafted for his life eighteen years ago better hold up to public scrutiny or we need to change it now, and quickly."

"Okay, okay, Eric, but what did they think of the plan?"

"They are willing to go with the plan as long as it looks like Art is buying into it one hundred percent and accepts who he is and what he has been designed for. If it appears that he is the least bit hesitant to embrace the whole concept and the course of his life, D.H.E. or D.A.R.P.A. will perform a removal."

"A removal," Gene said in a startled voice. "What's a removal?"

"They were not specific, but various scenarios were discussed. One that was shared with me was to place him into the isolation program with the other brothers, create a new identity through modifications, drug therapy, and relocation; or if we are totally unsuccessful, a tragic accident resulting in elimination. The D.H.E., as well as D.A.R.P.A., the C.I.A., N.S.A. and the Oval Office view this as a matter of national security.

If the real story on Art comes out prematurely, it won't take much imagination to speculate how this technology has been adapted and secretly used for other purposes. Even though we have come a long way, the nation and the world are not quite ready to embrace positive eugenics to the extent we have taken it. There are still those around who only think of Hitler when the word eugenics is mentioned. Gene, the good news is that you have been officially approved to start the first phase of your transition plan. I just wanted you to know in advance the climate and concerns of the board."

"What about the records? I'm not even starting this process unless all of the records are sealed and outside the reach of the Freedom of Information Act."

"Gene, it's all been classified as a matter of national security and cannot be accessed without the very highest security clearance."

"Okay, Eric, the story we've created must be without credible challenge until the political and moral climate is such that the general public readily embraces this vision of the future."

"Gene, I'm glad you brought up the timing issue. One of the bigger issues debated among the board members was the question of why Art, or anyone else, ever needed to know the mysteries of Art's origin and design."

"I thought they all understood and agreed when I explained it at the briefing in September. Why did we do any of this if we didn't intend to implement our success? This is the future of controlled human evolution. It's critical that Art eventually know his origin and design and fully embrace the benefits. If we ever want to mainstream positive eugenics, Art must become an enthusiastic advocate of what has happened to him. If he doesn't, it has the appearance that we have forced this on an unwitting and unwilling subject. If the perceived benefits are great enough, no one will really care that an embryo had no ability to consent. However, if Art does not enthusiastically embrace his design benefits, all the public will see is a living, breathing person who objects to what has been done to him without his consent. If this is ever going to work, we must win the battle of hearts and minds, and Art's is the first heart and mind that must be won. He is the key to this battle."

"Okay, Gene, you're the master of behavior modifications, and the board is counting on you to do your magic. About the tests, I intend to once again show up as Jason M. Alexander, Trustee of Boston Mercantile Bank & Trust to oversee the medical exams that I have been conducting since Art was four. You will be credited as the benevolent host who, at your expense, agreed to fly me out to Arizona so the tests could be accomplished in a timely manner. I have leased an exam room at Mayo for tomorrow morning at ten o'clock. We are also flying in the Jenicks Project psychiatrist to be part of the exam. This guy is really good and he is very excited to see and talk to Art after having monitored the three other brothers for the last sixteen years."

"Eric, do you think our project is still ahead of the nanoheads?"

"I think so. It appears that the board is still freaked out from that nanotechnology speech you gave about how, if left unchecked, the machines would take over and we would cease to exist. The whole non-human approach really played well to their fears."

"That's great news. We can't afford to lose to the nano-heads. We have way too much time and money invested to let them horn in on our future. Okay, let's get this show on the road. You need to get out of here before Art wakes up. Come back around three this afternoon. Get another car, one without government plates. It needs to be a rental car. Also, wear your bank clothes and remember that you have never met me before, and I'll make sure to address you as Mr. Alexander. I'm counting on you, Eric. You've acted the part for fourteen years, and I'm looking forward to another wonderful performance."

"Yes sir, Mr. Taylor."

"Why thank you, Mr. Alexander."

Their conversation ended and Gene quietly escorted Eric down the hall and out the front door. Virginia quickly scampered back over to the bed and arranged herself under the covers to look like she was sleeping. She listened as Gene walked back down the hall and opened the bedroom door. There was silence for about five seconds and then she heard the door close and Gene walk back down the hall toward the kitchen. She was devastated about what she had just overheard. Gene had not kept her in the loop about Art or the Jenicks Project. Until now, she was unaware of how Gene intended to use Art to accomplish his plan and vision for the future. The thought of Art possibly being subject to a "removal" if things did not go well made her sick to her stomach.

J.M.A. or D.H.E.

ART WOKE UP AGAIN around noon with a vague memory of getting up and looking out the bedroom window earlier that morning. He showered and put on shorts, a t-shirt, and flip-flops. He was pleased to be free of the Hawthorne uniform for the coming week. He headed downstairs toward the kitchen where he heard Chris and Elisha debating what to have delivered for lunch. Chris turned to Art and quickly said, "Pizza or Thai food?" Art had heard Elisha arguing for Thai food on the way down. Maybe he could score some points. Art acted as if he were debating in his mind, "Well, I can get pizza at Hawthorne anytime, so I say Thai food."

"Yes," squealed Elisha, as she gave Art a wink and a smile. Chris put his head on the counter and said, "I'll be hungry again in an hour." Art was extremely pleased with Elisha's response. Score a big one for me, he thought. The bad thing was that he was now going to have to pretend he liked spicy Thai food, and that would not be easy for a guy with a notoriously weak stomach.

While they were talking, Mr. Taylor walked into the kitchen and attempted to crack a joke about sleeping in. He bungled it, and the three teenagers just stared at him. Mr. Taylor shook it off and immediately changed the subject. "Art, I didn't have time to talk to you about this earlier, but when we arranged this trip with Hawthorne, one of the conditions was that we meet all the requirements of your trust. To make sure we complied, I agreed to fly in your trust officer for a couple of days for his semi-annual meeting with you."

"Whoa! I mean, thank you for going to that expense, Mr. Taylor."

"Not a problem," said Mr. Taylor. "Your trustee, a Mr. Alexander, will be coming by around three this afternoon to meet with you for about an hour."

Art was used to his meetings with Mr. Alexander. Art would smile, be polite, review his grades, and answer a bunch of questions about how he was doing. Once a year, Mr. Alexander would have Art go through a fairly extensive physical check-up. Apparently all these tests required by the trust were put in place by his parents before their death, to help insure his well-being and growth—both physical, and intellectual.

Virginia, Chris, and Elisha left about two-thirty to go shopping for some sunscreen and summer clothes. Art sat waiting for Mr. Alexander, surfing through the channels on the television, killing time until three o'clock.

The doorbell rang and Mr. Taylor opened the front door, greeting Mr. Alexander in a loud, forceful tone, "Welcome. You must be Jason Alexander. Did you have any problems finding your way here from the airport?"

"No, the GPS pretty much makes it impossible to get lost unless you fall asleep at the wheel." Both men laughed mechanically. "This place is sure different from Boston, so spread out and wide open." Again they both laughed artificially.

When Art saw Mr. Alexander, he turned off the weather report he was watching on the television and politely stood to greet Mr. Alexander with a nod, a smile, and a handshake. Mr. Alexander never changed much. He seemed to always wear the same black suit with a white shirt and red print tie, and he consistently reeked of cheap cologne that gave Art a headache. Art always thought Mr. Alexander looked like a small overweight clown trying to disguise himself as a banker. He was about five-foot-three with a giant shiny bald spot on the top of his head. He sported an enormous bulbous nose and a very large mouth. What sealed the clown look for Art was Mr. Alexander's enormous feet that occupied what looked like gigantic black clown shoes. Even though Art had been meeting with Mr. Alexander for as long as he could remember, not even the slightest relationship had ever developed between the two. Their meetings were always very polite, but strictly business, with Mr. Alexander mechanically asking only the questions on the sheet in front of him and filling in Art's answers. Art sometimes wondered why Mr. Alexander never broke from the script to ask an unimportant personal question like, "what was your favorite thing to do at camp" or "what's your favorite book" or "have you seen any good movies?"

The two of them sat down and Mr. Alexander began. "You are looking good, Art. I am not used to seeing you in the shorts and sandals look. Well, are you ready for your last set of checkups?"

"My last?" Art replied with a questioning tone.

"Yes, Art, the terms of the trust only require the six-month exams until you reach the age of eighteen, and you'll be eighteen in April. Congratulations! This is the last time you'll have to go through this prodding, poking, and questioning."

Art smiled, "When do we get started?"

Mr. Alexander looked at his watch and smiled in return. "Well, let's get through the paperwork today and hit the medical stuff tomorrow." He pulled his leather folder out of his travel case. Art couldn't help but notice the initials D.H.E. on the leather folder. D.H.E.—shouldn't it be J.M.A. for Jason M. Alexander, he thought, or maybe BMBT for Boston Mercantile Bank & Trust? Art decided not to prolong this part of the exam with a time-consuming question to his trustee. He wanted the questioning to be over as soon as possible so he could enjoy his holiday break. Mr. Alexander zipped through all of the compulsory questions, thanked Art, and was on his way in less than an hour.

Examination & Indoctrination

THE NEXT DAY WENT PAINFULLY SLOW for Art. There he was in warm, sunny, Arizona, and he couldn't believe he was stuck inside a medical office being poked, prodded, and at times provoked. He kept stealing glances outside whenever he got a chance. He loved looking at the palm-tree-lined parkway leading up to Mayo Clinic. He couldn't believe that even the hospitals in Scottsdale looked like resorts.

Art was less than thrilled by the addition of a psychiatrist named Dr. Mendelssohn. Dr. Mendelssohn fit all of the stereotypes. He came in wearing a white doctor's coat, peering at Art like he was a rare specimen in a zoo. His scraggly salt-and-pepper hair pointed in all different directions on his head, and his thick, bushy eyebrows were in need of a major trim. He sported a patchy beard that matched his hair in color and lack of uniform direction. Every breath through his giant banana nose sounded like the jets taking off at the Scottsdale airport.

Dr. Mendelssohn worked his way through a set of psychological tests and questions that Art felt were bordering on being an invasion of his privacy. Art did the best he could to conceal his discomfort and embarrassment at times. He had a hard time believing that his parents' will would really have called for such a detailed exam. He almost objected a couple of times, but thought it would just slow down the whole process. He just wanted it over, and to be outside, enjoying the beautiful warmth of Arizona.

In this last examination, Mr. Alexander also threw in a bone scan of Art's left hand to determine whether Art had reached his maximum growth, check joint health, and also rule out possible premature arthritis. He informed Art that he wanted to find and eliminate any potential problems that could be devastating to his career as a concert pianist.

Five grueling hours later, all of the exams were finally finished and Art felt as if he were being released from his torturers. Upon arriving back at the house, he was invited to take a swim with Chris and Elisha. Wow, swimming in December with the beautiful people. He thought he might just be able to get used to this kind of lifestyle. After a little water volleyball they all took a nap on the side of the pool and let the sun's warm rays soak into their skin. The warmth ended quite abruptly when the sun went down behind the mountains and it felt like the temperature dropped thirty degrees in thirty seconds. They immediately ran in, showered and met back in the kitchen for a wonderful Mexican feast prepared by Juanita, their housemaid for the week.

Mr. Taylor arrived back at the house at about eight o'clock after his golf game and dinner with the Phoenix Sun's coaching staff. He walked into the media room where the kids were watching the wall screen. He gave Chris and Elisha a look indicating that he wanted to be alone with Art. Both kids politely found separate excuses to go elsewhere in the house. This made Art more than a little uncomfortable and nervous. He had never really spoken with Mr. Taylor before other than to say hello, and now it appeared that Mr. Taylor wanted to engage him in conversation.

"Art, what do you think of your trip to Arizona so far?"

"I like what I've seen of it so far, other than the hospital, of course."

Gene laughed at Art's comment, which put Art more at ease. "Well I hope we can broaden your Arizona experience a little more tomorrow. First thing in the morning, we are going on a hike in the Superstition Mountains that I think you will really enjoy."

"Sounds great!" replied Art.

"You're just about ready to turn eighteen, aren't you, Art?"

"Yes, Mr. Taylor," Art replied politely.

"Mr. Taylor—that sounds pretty formal. Please, just call me Gene. Art, you're a very talented young man with an exciting future ahead of you. Would you consider yourself happy?"

Art thought the question was a bit strange, but he shrugged and replied, "I think so."

"What do you think is the key to happiness? What conditions do you think need to be present for a human to be truly happy and fulfilled in his or her life?" Gene continued on, not waiting for an answer. "I remember my dad telling me that if I truly found something I was good at, and that I liked doing, I wouldn't have to work another day in my life. Now that I'm considerably older, looking back on it, I think he was absolutely right. I have made a study of older people, those who were very happy and satisfied with their lives and those who were unfulfilled, lost and even bitter. You know what I found to be the distinguishing feature between the two?"

Art, now curious, raised his eyebrows and shook his head.

"The main difference is that those who were happy and fulfilled discovered what they were good at or, you could say, that they discovered what they were made to do, and pursued it with a passion. As a result, they were fulfilled, useful, and happy. The unfulfilled, or the lost, as I like to call them, were never able to figure out what they were made for, or, for other reasons, economic, social, family, religious, etc, were never allowed to pursue what I call the 'Best Version' of themselves. I have talked to numerous adults living with regrets because by the time they discovered what they were made for, it was either too late or they were saddled by obligation and social restrictions that prevented them from pursuing the 'Best Version' of themselves. Take a look at the average parent. They are frantically trying to determine where their child will be successful and be happy. Their searches are usually evidenced by countless hours of wasted time running their child to art lessons, music lessons, sports practices, acting lessons, space camp, you name it. Most of their attempts are based on the parent's desires, dreams, and wishes for their child, not on their child's gifting or predispositions. You know what I'm talking about. You've seen the kids at piano lessons or on the soccer field who look like deer caught in the headlights, frozen with fear, over their heads, with no aptitude or desire whatsoever. What a total waste of time, energy, and money leading to feelings of frustration, inadequacy, and failure for both parent and child."

Art was thinking about the dilemma being presented and wanted to show Mr. Taylor that he could engage in meaningful dialogue with an adult. "I see what you mean, but unless it is so clear at an early age what a child is good at, how does a parent avoid this whole scenario? Isn't this what any loving parent would do, even if most of it is considered a waste?"

Gene looked at Art with a big grin, nodding his head in approval, "Ah, a very astute question. This is exactly where my passion, my life's work, comes in. I see my life's work as making it possible for individuals to become happy and fulfilled in their life pursuits without wasting precious time and money."

Art, desiring to continue to participate in the conversation asked, "How do you go about doing this, and how can you be certain that you are picking the right areas for each person?"

Gene again smiled at Art, "Another great question, Art. There are a couple of avenues to accomplish this. First, we make it possible for individuals to become the 'Best Version' of themselves. This takes some real time and effort, but not nearly as much time and effort as it takes for a person to stumble across this on their own. We at TEI have put together a pretty sophisticated system where we combine an extensive physical, mental, and psychological profile to narrow down the possibility of what we call your Personal Life Course. Once the individual assents to their Personal Life Course, we then take their natural physical building blocks and work to enhance their capabilities in these areas. At the same time, we provide a psychological conditioning path or regimen that reinforces the physical enhancements to be undertaken. This whole process allows individuals to find, and realistically and honestly believe in, their 'Best Version' of themselves."

"Is this what you do with pro athletes?"

"Pro athletes, actors, teachers, doctors, etc. . . . The client's chosen life course dictates our assistance for the individual to become the Best Version of himself or herself."

"Okay, take sports for instance. Isn't that kinda cheating?" asked Art.

"If I give a player shoes that help him to cut, run, or jump better, is that cheating? No, it's only cheating if the societal norms surrounding that activity say it's cheating. Do they make all the riders in the Tour de France use the exact same kind of bike? Or in the Olympics, do all the bobsled teams use the same type of sled? What person who wants to excel in his field would purposely handicap his ability to achieve by not using the best equipment available? It would be like a pro basketball player playing in flip-flops. Everything we do is closely monitored and scrutinized to stay clearly within the rules and social and ethical norms of whatever profession or field chosen. When norms, rules, and ethics change, we change to give our client his or her best opportunity to compete, achieve, and excel."

"Okay, I think I see what you are saying. It would be like me choosing a little spinet piano to play instead of the best Grand Steinway. I guess it makes sense, as long as it's within the rules of whatever you are doing. Okay, okay, now you have me curious. You said that you pursued this by way of a couple different avenues. What is the second avenue?"

"Art, you keep coming with those good questions, quite impressive for your age."

Art blushed and cracked a slight grin. He liked the feeling of importance and maturity that came with successfully carrying on a deep conversation with someone as important as Mr. Taylor.

"Let me back up a little and put this once again in the context of the parent's role of discovering, nurturing, and guiding their child to a fulfilling life course choice. Almost every parent has desires and wishes for their child's future and will invest in and make sacrifices to bring those desires to fruition. Now granted, some of their desires are just not realistic. A father of five-foot-one and a mother of four-foot-eleven cannot realistically believe their son will be able to play power forward in the NBA. However, within their combined gene pool and their genetic makeup, there may be the building blocks of a brain surgeon. We have advanced to the place technologically where we can, through a process of elimination and identification, use the parents' gene pool to produce a child that is gifted in an area that is in biological harmony with their parents. Now, all of a sudden, instead of years of wasted searching for what their child is good at, the parents know, and can selectively invest assets to provide the environment to release this gift, not only for the child's future happiness, but also for the betterment of society. We end up with healthy, happy and fulfilled humans living out their passion for the betterment of society."

Without really thinking about his audience, Art blurted out, "Sounds a little like playing God, pre-arranging a child's future."

"It may first appear that way, but remember this is all volitional. The parent can refuse and there is no guarantee that the child will follow his gifting. We are not violating free will. We are merely enhancing positive choices," Gene reassured.

"It doesn't seem like the child ever has a choice. Aren't you 'engineering' the child's future without his or her consent?"

"What child ever does have a choice, Art? No child ever asks to be born with his parents' genetic code imprinted on his or her future. It's impossible to give the child the choice before it comes into being. And what better place to leave that choice than with a parent who will want, guide, and nurture the child to fulfillment and happiness?"

"Yeah, I'd never thought about it like that before. But how do you know that the child will be happy with the choice?"

Gene confidently retorted, "Well, we can never say absolutely that the child will be happy, but there're a couple of very positive dynamics going on here that stack the results in our favor. First, we know that people are the happiest and most fulfilled when they are doing what they are good at. Through this process, we allow them to have a much-enhanced probability that they will be good or even excellent at what they do. Doing something well or excellent brings with it self esteem and pride in accomplishment. Art, you are very good at composing and performing on the piano. How does it make you feel when you nail a performance on a piece you have written and those in the audience explode with tremendous praise?"

"Well, really good, I mean . . . great!"

"That's right, you are fulfilled and the audience or society is enhanced and fulfilled by your artful contribution to their lives. The other dynamic is the dynamic of a child naturally wanting to please the parent. I have witnessed men in their forties and fifties still struggling with their failure to live up to their father's expectations, thinking that if they had tried a little harder, maybe they could have been better in chemistry and gone to medical school. If you pull back all the emotional covering, you usually find a father with unrealistic expectations and a son who just didn't have the tools, no matter how hard he tried to pull it off. Wouldn't it make sense to counsel the father in advance regarding the realistic possibilities available to his and his wife's gene pool and then to select and tweak an embryo so that it actually has the tools to live up to 'realistic expectations'? The result is a child who is good at and enjoys what is chosen with the added bonus of parental approval and blessing."

Art thoughtfully replied, "Yeah, it all logically follows. It seems a little contrived and set-up, but you do make a great case that doing nothing can end in kind of a chaotic, disappointing life for all involved."

"Don't get me wrong now—even if we do all the right stuff on our end, it doesn't guarantee happiness or success. We can't control the environment and we still have not unlocked the mystery of personality or what I like to call a person's 'bent' in life. But, we think what we do will give all involved more than a fighting chance for a favorable life outcome."

"Wow! My head is spinning; I have never stepped back and thought about any of this before."

"Very few people ever have or do, but it's good to, as you put it, step back and look at the big picture so that the things we do can be done purposefully and with excellence." Gene reached into his pocket and pulled out one of his TEI business cards and handed it to Art. "Art, this is one of my expanded information business cards. Most of the cards I hand out only have the basic company information loaded in the card. When you get a chance, stick this into your computer and walk through the whole T.E.I. philosophy, process, and business purpose. I think you will be impressed by our vision of the future." Gene smiled, then said, "Well, I think I have probably bored you enough for one night. We need to get some sleep so that we'll be fresh for our hike tomorrow. You are going to love the beauty of the Superstition Mountains."

With that, Gene stood up, wished Art a good night's rest and walked out of the room.

Art went back to the guestroom. As he lay in his bed he tried to process all he and Gene talked about. He was taken in that a powerful man like Mr. Taylor would sit and talk with him about such deep matters. Still, in the back of his mind was a disturbing little thought, a caution flag. He was struggling with the eeriness of tinkering with people to program the future. He remembered reading Huxley's *Brave New World* in his sophomore literature class and couldn't help thinking about the possible long-term effects on the future through the engineering of embryos. Who was right, Gene Taylor or Aldous Huxley?

Art faded off to sleep. He woke up several times that night from what could best be described as sci-fi nightmares where he found himself in the future trying to relate and interact with one-dimensional beings designed to carry out specific tasks beneficial for the rest of society. Each time he awoke, he wondered if Mr. Taylor's 'Best Version' of the future would be filled with beings who looked and functioned biologically as humans, but who possessed no real humanity.

Jumping Cholla

THEY WERE ALL UP and going very early. The Boulders Resort delivered breakfast to the house at six-thirty. They ate and picked up their backpacks already fully packed with lunch, sports drinks, granola bars, and first aid kits. They loaded into the vehicle and took off for the Superstition Mountains just east of Phoenix. As they came into view of the mountain range, Art realized that Mr. Taylor was correct. The Superstition Mountains were incredible, appearing to rise almost straight up out of the desert floor. They were magnificently eerie-looking with their jagged peaks silhouetted against the sunrise. They took the winding dirt road back to the trailhead and began their hike to Weaver's Needle. The early morning air was clean and crisp. They could see their breath as they started up the trail. There were no other hikers on the trail at that time of the morning, allowing them to startle unsuspecting coyotes and quail.

Art was amazed by all the varying forms of plant life in the Arizona desert that he would never see back on the east coast. He loved the long appendages of the Ocotillo plants, and all of the different kinds of cactus, from prickly pear and barrel, to the majestic saguaros with their arms stretching out this way and that, no two exactly alike. He imagined that the saguaros were the sentries of the desert, standing guard over the natural beauty. The sun was now up in full strength and wonderfully bright. The sky was bluer than Art had ever seen it in his entire life.

Mr. Taylor led the group up the narrow trail, followed by Chris and Elisha, and then by Art and Mrs. Taylor. Art would have preferred to be last, but for some reason he felt that Mrs. Taylor was more interested in observing and asking him questions than she was in taking in the natural beauty of the hike. He had caught her starring at him several times already that morning. Art did, however, like following Elisha, smelling her perfume and being hypnotized by her blonde ponytail bobbing up and down with each step she took.

As they started the slow climb up from the valley floor, Virginia Taylor began what seemed to Art like an interrogation session. "Art, are you enjoying your first trip to Arizona?"

Art replied, "Oh, yes, Mrs. Taylor, it is like being in a different world with blue sky instead of gray, different plants, different animals, and best of all, warm weather in December."

"Please Art, not so formal. Virginia is just fine. Don't you think it is interesting how the environment you're in can so dramatically effect your whole disposition, mood, and attitude? I much prefer a naturally-induced attitude adjustment like this than all the things we do artificially."

Art, puzzled by this statement, said, "What do you mean by 'things we do artificially'?"

"Oh, I guess there are a number of examples, ranging from entertainment consumption, to alcohol and chemical use. I just know that when I get out into nature it evokes deep feelings that cannot be duplicated by anything else I do or encounter. Art, do you have anything that you are passionate about, anything that excites you, that you feel energized by, that you're curious about?"

Art thought the conversation had made an abrupt leap from 'isn't nature cool' to 'what makes you tick'. He had never been asked these type of personal questions by anyone and preferred not to answer, especially with Elisha walking only a couple of steps in front of him and likely to overhear.

Art responded jokingly, "Oh, yeah, I'm really passionate about beautiful women and fast cars."

"Okay, Art," Virginia responded in a semi-disgusted tone. "You know that's not what I was referring to. Let me ask in a different way. What types of things motivate you, what are you curious about in life?"

Art, now really feeling pressured and uncomfortable, began to turn red and stammer, "Well, umm, I umm, well, I . . . "

Virginia interrupted, "Am I being too personal? I'm sorry. I was just wondering what inspires such a talented young man like you to produce such awesome musical compositions."

Art stopped walking, turned and looked at Virginia, raising his eyebrows and said, "Well, actually, I really don't know, it just kind of happens. I hear the music in my head and transfer it to paper and then into reality by playing it. It just comes to me, it's kind of like I'm on autopilot when it happens. But as for things I am really curious about, I guess the thing I am most curious about is my past, or I should say, my family history. I feel like I really don't know who I am or where I came from. I have no real history. Everyone else I know has parents, grandparents, great grandparents, family trees, cousins and weird uncles. I have a trust fund officer and a sketchy story with a dead end."

Virginia had stopped walking when Art turned to speak to her. Art felt that her eyes were peering right through him into his deep inner self. When Art mentioned the void he felt from having no family history, the color seemed to drain from Virginia's face, her expression changed from inquisitive and engaged to a look of panic. Art could see beads of sweat emerge on her forehead. She began to lose her balance and started to wobble. Art froze for a second or two, shocked by the sudden change he was witnessing. He snapped out of it and rushed to grab Virginia just when it appeared she would no longer be able to maintain her balance. He grabbed her and gently sat her down on a nearby boulder, calling out to Mr. Taylor who was now about forty yards or so up the trail. When he saw that Virginia was down, he, Chris, and Elisha, ran back down the trail as fast as possible.

Mr. Taylor quickly took charge, giving orders, "Quick, help me lay her down! Chris! Pull the space blanket out of your backpack so we can keep her warm." By this time, it appeared Virginia had passed out. Mr. Taylor pulled an ammonia stick out of his first aid kit, broke it, and passed it a few times in front of Virginia's nose. He also pulled out a dissolvable pill and placed it under her tongue. She jerked abruptly as the ammonia hit her senses and her eyes began to open.

"Are you all right?" Mr. Taylor asked in a soft but firm tone.

Virginia, now sitting up, responded, "Yes, I think so, I just got overheated and clammy all of a sudden. The last thing I remember was that I stopped walking when I was talking to Art. I think the hike caught up with me all at once. Maybe I didn't eat enough for breakfast."

Mr. Taylor, now down on one knee next to her, said, "Let's just take a break here and get you rehydrated and get an energy bar in you and then see how you feel. It's early and we are not in a hurry. If we need to, we can head back from here."

"No, no, no. I should be all right. I don't want the rest of you to miss the hike."

Elisha spoke up quickly, "If mom's not feeling better in a little bit, I'll just stay here with her and have a picnic. Besides, I've seen Weaver's Needle about ten times and it doesn't change. We've only done this hike every year we come out here. That way you guys will conquer your goal for the day and mom and I can get some natural high-desert tanning accomplished."

They all took a break and checked to make sure their "PACA's" were fully powered and working properly. PACA—short for Personal All-In-One Communication Assistant—was a cell phone, short-wave radio, GPS, satellite phone, internet, and emergency network packed into a device that was about one-inch wide and one-sixteenth of an inch thick, and could be worn as a wristband.

During the twenty-minute break, Elisha convinced her mom and dad that she and her mom should just hang out there and tan while the guys finished the rest of the two-hour round-trip hike out and back to Weaver's Needle.

"Okay," said Mr. Taylor, "I guess we should get going so we can conquer the hike and return. We certainly want to live up to Elisha's expectations." Everyone responded with a polite chuckle as Gene, Chris and Art loaded up. "We'll see you in a couple of hours. If you need anything, just call. You each have a first aid kit in your backpack if you need it."

The guys took off, slowly disappearing out of site over the ridge. The only thing that could be heard was the sound of hiking boots crunching on the decomposed granite trail. After the way-weird interaction with Virginia, Art was pleased with listening only to the sounds of nature, and he now could appreciate the incredible views and even pass a little gas from last night's Mexican Fiesta without embarrassing himself in front of Elisha. The fainting episode with Mrs. Taylor was really scary, but he was happy that it provided an escape from the uncomfortable feeling of being under Virginia's magnifying glass.

After a long, hard, uphill climb with multiple switchbacks, they rounded a large boulder field at the crest of a hill. A huge valley opened up in front of them.

"This is amazing!" Art blurted out loud, without realizing he was saying a thing.

"Your mouth is hanging open, Art," Chris said, laughing at Art.

"I can't help it! This is like a view of another planet, it's incredible!"

"This is why we come here every year," said Mr. Taylor. "Why don't we take a break, grab a snack, and get some water. I need to check on the girls. I'm going to head over to that outcropping to try to get better reception."

As Mr. Taylor headed toward the rock outcropping, Chris looked at Art with a sly smile and said, "Art, you want to make a wager?"

"What do you mean?" replied Art with a puzzled look.

"Every time I come up here with my dad, he always talks about two things, the legend of the lost Dutchman's Gold Mine and Chimeras."

"Ka-what's?" said Art.

"It's not important," said Chris. "I'd be willing to bet you just about anything that before we get back down to Mom and Elisha, my dad will talk about the Legend of the Lost Dutchman's mine and Chimeras."

After being gone for several minutes, Gene traversed the boulder field back down to where the boys were lounging in the sun, munching on energy bars. "There she is, boys," Gene said as he was looking down into the valley opening up in front of them. "There's Weaver's Needle, also called the Sombrero and the Witch's Hat." He was pointing down in the valley at what looked to Art like a large rock spine, a mini-mountain rising out of the desert floor. Mr. Taylor continued, "The Needle is the key landmark surrounding one of the biggest mysteries of the Superstitions Mountains, the mystery of the 'Lost Dutchman's Mine'."

Chris caught Art's eye and mouthed the words, 'Lost Dutchman's mine' at the same time his dad said them aloud. Then, he raised one finger, smirked and mouthed "that's number one."

Mr. Taylor went on for another ten minutes or so recounting the legendary events of the last three hundred years of gold and murder, involving Spaniards, Jesuit Priests, Apache Indians, and a German miner in the late 1800s called the Dutchman, and how till this day, the cache of hidden gold has never been found.

Gene was interrupted when his PACA started buzzing. The boys watched as he reviewed the information. A concerned look came over Gene's face.

"Is everything okay?" asked Chris in a concerned tone.

"Yeah, just to make sure your mom is okay, I had the lab run a quick blood panel from the BF-1 chip that your mom has implanted. I don't think there is anything to worry about. Everything looks fairly normal. There are a few anomalies, probably from not getting enough to eat before the hike, or possibly failing to take her daily vitamin packet. She'll be fine; nothing really to be concerned about."

Gene's verbal reassurance, along with a little smile at Chris, broke the tension that Gene had created with his concerned look.

"What is that bright glow down over to the right?" Art asked, pointing down the hill.

"I'm not sure," said Chris, "but it looks like a group of Jumping Cholla."

"Jumping what?" said Art.

"Yep, that's Jumping Cholla," Gene piped in. "They're cactus with lobes containing thousands of little closely-grouped needles. When the sun hits them just right, they put off a shiny, almost golden glow."

"Why are they called jumping?" Art questioned.

"Well, when you get close to them or step on one of them, they appear to jump up and attach themselves to your clothes, skin, shoes, or whatever's close. They don't really jump. They are spring-loaded and when you come in contact with them, they release a kind of hinge that allows them to jump or pop and attach themselves to anything and everything that's close by."

"I'd love to get a closer look," said Art, looking quite fascinated.

"We'll meander off the trail on the way down to the Needle and take a look," said Gene, "but try not to get too close to them. The needles are like tiny fish hooks, and if they get into your skin, you have little choice but to yank them out, skin and all."

The desire to take a closer look at the Jumping Cholla excited Art. He took the lead as the group headed down where they could go off trail and check out the Jumping Cholla. Art got to the place that appeared best to him to go off trail to get a closer look. He turned to talk to Chris and Mr. Taylor and realized that he must have been jogging down the trail because Chris and Mr. Taylor were now about forty to fifty yards behind him. Art yelled back to them, "I'm going to head down to the Cholla from here. I'll see you down there."

Mr. Taylor yelled back, "Go slow and stay away from them."

Art's excitement would not allow his pace to slow as he scampered down the hill toward the stand of Cholla, jogging back and forth between and around creosote bushes, barrel cactus, and an occasional saguaro. As he approached the Cholla, he noticed that there was an abrupt twelve- to fifteen-foot elevation drop right in front of where the stand of Cholla started. He stopped momentarily, mentally picked the best route and started making his way down to the Cholla. Never having spent any time in the desert before, he failed to appreciate the effect that decomposed granite would have on his ability to stay on his feet. He lost his balance, slipped down on his left side and continued sliding down the hill. He attempted to stop by putting his hands down, but the small granite rocks shredded his hands and caused him to spin sideways and then start rolling. The rolling did not stop until he was face up, wrapped in Cholla balls, lying in the middle of the stand of Cholla.

Art tried to yell for help, but all he could muster was a little bit of air pushed out of his lungs making a sick moaning sound.

Gene and Chris took off running in the direction of the moaning. They came to the top of the hill where Art had slipped and fallen. From there they saw him, lying flat on his back covered with Cholla balls.

"Art," Gene yelled, "just lie still. We'll be right down."

Art half-spoke and half-moaned as he whimpered an okay, not daring to move for fear of increasing the pain. He could make out Gene and Chris slowly traversing their way down the hill, holding on to each other in order to keep their balance. Once they reached the bottom, they carefully picked their way through the Cholla to get to Art. When they finally reached him, he was breathing in short breaths, punctuated by short moans each time he exhaled. Art could feel beads of sweat breaking out on his forehead. His arms, legs, and side were covered with Cholla balls. What was worse, on the right side of his neck three more Cholla balls were firmly imbedded in his skin.

Chris pulled a pair of leather gloves out of his pack, put them on, and attempted to remove the Cholla balls from Art's pant legs. One of the looser balls came off Art's pants, but now Chris couldn't get the Cholla ball off his glove. He finally bent over and stepped on the ball with his hiking boot and pulled his glove away. Gene pulled a multi-tool out of his pack that he configured to work like a pair of pliers and attempted to pull out the Cholla balls without getting stuck.

Art yelped, "Eeow!" The needles had penetrated right through Art's pants and attached to his leg.

By this time, Art could feel his breathing becoming labored, and the pain became excruciating. As if from a distance, he heard Chris yell, "Dad! He's turning grayish-green and I think he's passing out."

"Art! Art!" Gene said firmly. "Listen to me! You need to start taking deep, slow breaths." Gene began demonstrating to Art how he should be breathing. "Chris, I want you to keep Art taking deep breaths while I contact some help."

Gene walked away from the boys and pulled out his PACA. When he returned he informed the boys that he had made contact with the emergency room at Mayo. They were very familiar with cactus incidents and had ordered an air evacuation to fly Art to Mayo. Gene then called back to Virginia and Elisha, told them what was happening, and instructed them to hike out on their own as soon as Virginia felt up to it.

"Hey, Dad, I think Art's doing a little better. His breathing has slowed down and he's regained a little of his color. I was thinking that Art would be fine if he were one of those Chimeras with Armadillo skin that you used to always tell us about when we were on this hike."

Out of nowhere, Gene looked as if he were going to explode. He gave Chris a stern look, furrowed his eyebrows, and shook his head. "This is no time to talk about imaginary, mythical creatures. We need to stay focused on what we need to do to help Art."

"Sorry, Dad, it just came to my mind. You said the technology was in existence to make one of these multispecies creatures," Chris argued.

"Chris!" barked Gene, now almost shouting, "Not now, just drop it, okay!"

In the meantime, Art managed to get his breathing further under control and the feeling that he was going to lose consciousness was beginning to wane. Trying not to move anything but his lips, he asked Chris, "What's going to happen now? How am I going to get out of this mess?"

Before Chris could answer, Gene piped in, "Art, it's going to be okay, I called in a top notch desert rescue unit and they should be arriving here any minute. They know exactly what to do in your situation. The best thing you can do now is try to lay still, breath slowly, and relax."

Art shifted his eyes to look at Gene, "Mr. Taylor, I'm really sorry! I screwed up this whole day. I feel really bad. I know this is a special family hike for you guys and I really ruined it."

"Are you kidding? These hikes are usually pretty boring. This is the most excitement we have ever had on one of these. You didn't ruin a thing. Don't even give it a second thought."

They started to hear the faint sound of a helicopter. In the distance, they spotted a sleek-looking air-evac chopper approaching from the west. The chopper circled a few times and found a flat area to put down about fifty yards away in an area with no Cholla. The rescue team jumped out wearing bright optic yellow jumpsuits and toting giant gear packs on their backs. They slowly picked their way through the Cholla to get over to Art. After assessing the situation, they pulled out what looked like a quilt of plastic bubbles and carefully rolled Art up in it very slowly, while Art tried to still the feeling of panic flowing over him. It felt eerily like a burial, and every little jostle brought more pain. They then picked up each end of the quilt and placed Art onto a portable stretcher. The whole group, including Gene and Chris, slowly walked the stretcher over to the chopper, loaded Art, boarded the chopper, and headed west to Mayo Clinic.

They made it to Mayo in about ten minutes and were received by a medical team that immediately took charge of getting Art to a secure treatment room. Art thought he caught a glimpse of Mr. Taylor talking to his bank trustee. *What is Mr. Alexander doing here, and why is Mr. Taylor talking to him?* He thought about it for a minute. His trustee flew back to Boston yesterday and there was no way he could have found out about what happened and got back to Arizona in an hour. Art mentally dismissed it, thinking that he must be a little delusional from the painkillers they had given him. Or, maybe Mr. Taylor was talking to a man who just looked like his bank trustee.

In the ER, the team of doctors and nurses went to work on Art. They assured Art that they had seen quite a few cases like his over the years and had developed a very successful heat process that was effective in causing the hook-shaped cactus needles to straighten for easier removal. Art was very relieved to hear that the result of his carelessness was treatable. As he lay on the operating table he slowly faded away, being overcome by the combination of pain killers and sedatives.

A New Game Plan

VIRGINIA AND ELISHA CAME RUSHING into the emergency waiting room. Gene just started to bring them up to date on what had taken place when a doctor from DHE came out to report on Art's condition. He informed Gene and Virginia that everything was going well and that Art should get through all of this with no long-term effects—other than bad memories. He advised that Art should probably stay in the hospital a couple of days, until the swelling went down and they were certain that there was no risk of ancillary complications from the accident.

Virginia was relieved by the news, but she could see that something was still bothering Gene. After the briefing from the doctor was concluded, Virginia motioned for Gene to go with her into one of the private family waiting rooms.

"What's up, Gene? Art should be okay, so why are you still so upset?"

"Why shouldn't I be upset? This has been a day from hell, a day where everything I've been around has seemed to spiral out of control."

"How so?"

"Well, first I have you passing out in the middle of nowhere and I find out that you haven't taken your daily enhancement packet. Was that just a mental lapse or are you trying to really mess yourself up again?"

Virginia just stared at Gene, while inside she wanted to scream. She decided she would not answer the question and just rolled her eyes at Gene in disgust, "What else has refused to cooperate with your universe today?"

"Real funny, Virginia," replied Gene sarcastically. "It just seems strange that after all these years I've spent worrying about something bad happening to Art, and after all of the procedures and safeguards I've put in place to keep Art safe, it was while Art was in my care that things went wrong. Then, to top it all off, Chris mentioned chimeras in front of Art. I know it was innocent from Chris's perspective, but I really don't want Art knowing about or investigating Chimeras until the proper foundation is laid out for human-non-human species. I am hoping that with all the trauma, today's mention of Chimeras will be lost forever in the fog."

"Anything else you want to tell me about? I was kind of shocked to see a doctor from DHE here, and I saw Eric as I was walking into the emergency room. He tried not to notice me. What's he doing out here in Arizona and why is he here at the hospital?

"I called in for the doc from DHE and Eric is just out here performing his pseudo-Bank Trustee duties."

"Oh, I see," Virginia replied sarcastically. "You two aren't cooking up anything else, are you?"

"No, what do you mean by that?"

"Nothing, I'm just always wondering what you and the DHE are up to. Is there more at stake here with Art than you are telling me?"

Gene looked back at Virginia with a puzzled look. "I have no idea what you are talking about."

With that comment the conversation was over and Gene and Virginia walked back out into the waiting room to find Chris and Elisha.

Virginia was determined that she would stay at the hospital until she knew the needle extraction procedure was completed and Art was okay. Gene and the DHE doctor assured her that Art's condition was not critical or life threatening and that Art would be heavily sedated until midday the next day so he really wouldn't know if anyone was there or not. With that assurance, Virginia reluctantly agreed that they all should go back to the Boulders for the night.

Virginia was vitally concerned with Art's short- and long-term safety. Based on the doctor's assurances, she was fairly confident that he would fully recover from the cactus accident. However, based on the conversation she had overheard between Gene and Eric, she was intensely worried about Art being able to live up to the plans Gene had for him.

Once the Taylor family was back at their home at the Boulders, Gene announced that he needed to have a family meeting tomorrow to discuss the family's ongoing interactions with Art. Chris and Elisha looked puzzled by the announcement, but were too exhausted to probe further. Virginia, however, knew what was at stake with Art and was very concerned with what Gene may be planning. She had seen Gene scheme and maneuver to get his way and she knew that once he set his mind on something, he was ruthless with his tactics. She feared for Art, for her children, and for her own sanity. She also knew that Gene had probably figured out by now that going off her drug regimen was intentional on her part. She was not yet ready to have the conversation she knew was coming as to why she had deviated from Gene's "ideal chemical balance" for her.

Virginia got up at six in the morning and started getting ready to go see Art at the hospital.

"What are you doing up so early?" Gene whispered in a groggy voice.

"I'm going to see how Art is doing. It would be horrible for him to wake up alone in a hospital room after what he went through."

"You are really fascinated and taken with this kid, aren't you?"

Virginia turned abruptly, looking Gene straight in the eye with a piercing look. "Well, when you design and program a life, you really become concerned eighteen years later about whether or not you did the right thing. When you actually see him almost fully grown, standing right in front of you, you realize that you've been playing with a person's life, and then you want to do what you can to reassure yourself that you've done the right thing or can do the right thing from here on out to somehow rectify what you've done. Do you know what he said to me on the hike? He basically said he's a person without a past, without a family, without a sense of belonging. I'm not sure exactly what we created, but I do know this, we created an orphan, a lost soul, and it bothers me greatly because I am the one responsible for the condition in which he now finds himself."

Virginia didn't want, need, or wait for a response from Gene. She abruptly turned and briskly walked out of the room to head for the hospital.

The timing on Virginia's arrival at the hospital was perfect. She was hoping to be there when Art woke up and to her delight, she was. Prior to entering Art's room, she met with the DHE doctor. He informed her that Art was doing well and that he had set the new hospital record for number of cactus needles removed from one patient. He also informed Virginia that Art would be pretty swollen for a few days and that they would treat him for inflammation and watch him closely for any signs of infection.

Virginia walked into the room and pulled a chair over near Art's bed. His face and exposed arm reminded her of the old Pillsbury Dough Boy commercials she remembered seeing as a little girl. Had she not known it was Art, she would not have recognized him. Art was starting to stir. He had been heavily sedated and was floating back and forth between sleep and waking. He finally managed to keep his eyes open but it was obvious that his brain was still in quite a fog. Virginia leaned over his bed, staring at him with motherly concern and asked, "How are you feeling, Art?"

Art, looking down at his puffed up arm with a half smile, said, "I'm feeling kind of fat right now, but that beats how I was feeling yesterday afternoon."

Virginia smiled back at Art. "Well, I'm glad to see that your sense of humor wasn't deflated by all of those cactus needles. How are you really feeling, physically speaking?"

Art blinked, opened his eyes very wide and attempted to stretch his face. "Well, other than feeling puffy, I don't feel that bad at all—although I am really hungry."

As Virginia pressed the call button, she replied, "Hunger is a very good sign coming from you and one problem we can easily deal with."

Virginia spent the rest of the morning at the hospital with Art. Other than detailing for Art his condition and the probable length of his stay at Mayo, she kept the conversation light, commenting and laughing about the news and TV shows, and making jokes about the staff, hospital etiquette, and patient garb.

Late that afternoon, Virginia slipped quietly out of Art's room after his pain medication made him drowsy. Prior to leaving, she had told Art she would be back tomorrow and would do her best to try to get him out early so he could spend as many days as possible in the Arizona sunshine before heading back to the northeast ice box. Art politely thanked her for coming and being there with him. He then rolled over to face Virginia and gave her a gentle smile. Virginia was deeply touched, interpreting the smile as Art's sign of approval.

Virginia arrived back at their home at the Boulders to find Gene anxiously waiting for her arrival so he could conduct his family meeting. Right after dinner, he called everyone into the study and began to weave the tapestry of his new plan. He sat them down. His face was serious and his furrowed jet-black eyebrows and focused eye contact signaled them to pay extra attention, with no room for joking around. He began his speech like an attorney making his opening statement. "You all know that I can be pretty hard charging, to the point of being totally insensitive to the feelings and needs of others. Something has happened to me this holiday break to open my eyes."

Virginia noticed Chris and Elisha looking at each other in wide-eyed amazement, no doubt wondering if they were really hearing this come out of their 'I've got everything under control' father.

Gene continued, "Having Art here for the holiday break has opened my eyes as well as my heart. Your mother shared with me this morning what it must be like to be an orphan, with no family history, and without the support of a family to fall back on, especially during tough times. It has been an epiphany for me to realize that I have been totally inwardly focused all these years. Sure, I've been involved in a lot of community and charity activities and I have the resume to prove it, but if an activity wasn't going to be of benefit to my family, my business, or me, it was not realistically considered. I also know that, unfortunately, I have modeled that for you and probably kept you from reaching out and extending yourself for the benefit of others who are truly in need. Quite confidentially, looking back, I am embarrassed of my egotistical, self-centered lifestyle."

Gene's little speech froze an expressionless gaze on Virginia's face. She heard the words and knew what they meant, but deep inside, her past experience with Gene would not allow her to fully buy into his speech. Her head had been clearing more and more since she had backed off her regimen of psychotropic drugs and mood enhancers. She was starting to see things and think about things she had not thought about in a long time.

Looking at herself and her history with Gene in a different light, she did not like what she saw. Still, Gene's speech was confusing her thoughts. *Was this for real?* Had Gene really had this epiphany experience that he spoke of? Had what she said to him this morning really had the impact he said it did? Was there really hope that the relationship of mutual trust, admiration, caring, and love that she had always longed for with Gene could finally become a reality? Or, was this the same old classic Gene setting up one of his little schemes? Her stomach began to knot up from the thought, but at the same time she was holding on to the hope that it was not the same old Gene.

Gene continued, "So, I have decided that we as a family are going to take on a project—a project that is not in any way public, to show how generous we are. This project will be our family secret. We won't reveal it to anyone under any circumstances, and especially not to the person who will be the focus of our project."

Gene paused, took a deep breath, displayed a look of concern, and then continued, "Yesterday we had a tough day as a family, and I was pretty uptight. I didn't handle it very well, especially with you, Chris. I'm sorry for blowing up at you. But our guest, Art, had an even worse day, which must have been absolutely frightening for him. Here was a young man going through a terribly traumatic experience with no real support system, no family, only acquaintances and strangers helping him through this crisis in his life. Who did he have to turn to for emotional support? Who did he have that he knew he could fall back on no matter what happened? The answer is no one! This morning your mother got up early and went to be with Art. She began filling that gap, and that's when I realized what we should do as a family. Without fanfare and without saying a word, we are going to step in and be the family this young boy has never had."

Chris shrugged his assent and Elisha nodded approval. Virginia, however, remained fixed in a dead, frozen stare, wondering if Gene's proposal was out of real heartfelt concern for Art. Or another plan to further his goals for the program?

Gene looked directly at Virginia and delivered his summation, "I don't know exactly how we are going to do this. We'll have to take it one day at a time. A lot will depend on how Art reacts and responds to us reaching out to him. We will need to be patient with him and keep our expectations modest. He may never embrace us as his family. But, regardless of his response, we will be there for him. What do you think? Are you with me on this? Are you willing to commit to this undertaking?"

Gene looked at each of them again. Elisha nodded her head up and down and said, "Sure, sounds good to me." Chris likewise agreed without hesitation. Gene then turned his attention to Virginia. She bit her bottom lip as if in deep thought and then spoke, "I think this would be a wonderful thing for our family to do. I want us to do this because we really care for him as another human being who has real needs that we as a family may be able to fulfill." Virginia looked straight at Gene with a stern, determined face. "I don't want this to be like a science project where we measure everything and are constantly looking for a certain response. I want us to honestly develop true relationship with Art."

Before anyone could really digest what Virginia said, Gene stood up and announced, "Looks like we're all in."

Chris, looking a little confused, asked, "Well, what are we supposed to do now?"

Before Gene could open his mouth, Virginia responded immediately, "I think we all just start by a change in attitude toward Art. If we do that, our hearts will tell us what to do next."

Gene nodded in agreement and added, "Chris, I think there are practical things we can do to show our genuine interest in him. Let me ask you this. Back at Hawthorne, who does Art hang out with?"

Chris looked up, tilted his head back and then closed his eyes to think. "This is going to sound pretty bad, but I really don't know. I mean, we don't do the same kind of things and so I hardly ever see him. He doesn't ever hang out with any of the people I do. My guess is that he probably hangs out with either the music people or the tech-heads. Now that I think about it, I know I have seen him hanging out with that jerk tech-head kid that everyone calls Dizz. I don't know if he still does though."

Gene chuckled and half smiled. "In my day the jerky tech-head kids were called 'geeks' and 'nerds'. I know, because I was one of them. Let me ask you another question, one to which I think I already know the answer. Would you say that the kids you hang out with at Hawthorne are the most popular kids?"

Chris shrugged, "Well, yeah, I would have to say they probably are, but we don't have anything against the tech-heads or the music people. We just don't relate to them very well and them to us. It's just not a . . . uh . . . natural fit. Does that make sense?"

Gene nodded affirmatively, "Yes, it makes sense. How hard has it been for you to hang out with Art during this vacation? Has it been really awkward for you to be around him?"

Chris tossed his blond hair out of his eyes. "Nah, it's been fine. Art's okay to be around. He's not really, really weird, just a bit artsy and stuff. What are you getting at, Dad? I feel like I'm being set up to have to buddy up to him."

"Well, part of what we want to do with Art is to be accepting and inclusive, and at the same time help him build his self confidence. If just every once in a while he were included in some of the activities with you and your friends, he may start seeing himself differently—you know, more important, more confident of his social skills. Chris, this project won't be free; it will cost you something. Every good thing you do will cost you something. So, what do you say, do you think you could gradually start integrating Art into just a few of your activities from time to time?"

Chris took a deep breath and then let it out slowly, closing his eyes. "Okay, yeah, I'll figure something out. This may be tough though."

"Chris, come on, you've got to be the most popular kid at Hawthorne—if you include him, the rest will go along. Wouldn't you say you are one of the most popular kids there?"

"Well, yeah, but I'd kinda like to keep it that way if possible."

"I don't think your social status will be in jeopardy if, once in a while, you include a young man who will probably become world famous for his music."

Chris's eyebrows shot up. "I hadn't thought about it that way . . . maybe this has some potential."

Gene, looking pleased with Chris' response, added, "Good. I think you will find this to be beneficial for both you and Art. After you are back at Hawthorne awhile, I'll check in on you to see how you are doing and offer any help or suggestions. Chris, I want you to know I really appreciate your willingness to jump in and be a part of this project. This really shows some maturity on your part. Oh, and one more thing that applies to all of us, I think we should keep Art's accident with the Cholla our family secret. It would be really embarrassing for Art at Hawthorne if a story like that got out."

Gene then turned to Elisha, "Tell me, Elisha, what do you think about our little family project?"

Elisha shrugged her shoulders. "I don't have any problems with it. I think it's a good idea. I don't know how we are really going to do this, but it seems like a good thing to do. You know, focus outside ourselves, help someone else out, and maybe make a positive difference in Art's life."

Gene nodded his head in affirmation of Elisha's statements. "And have you started to think about how you can personally contribute to our project?"

Elisha stared sideways at her dad, her sharp green eyes mirroring his own. "Contribute? Do you mean what am I going to do?" Gene nodded, and Elisha sat up and folded her arms across her chest. "Well, I guess I'll just be nice to him." Gene laughed out loud, then caught himself.

Elisha cocked her head to one side, "What's so funny, Dad?"

Gene smiled. "I hope you have already been nice to him. What do you mean by 'be nice to him'?"

Virginia noticed that Elisha looked a little embarrassed as well as piqued. "Okay, Dad, here's the deal. I've caught him more than a few times just staring at me, and I didn't want him to think I like him or anything so I have been purposefully ignoring him."

Gene leaned back in his chair and grinned. "Oh, I see, and has this evasive action deterred Art's interest in any way?" Gene leaned forward and made direct eye contact with Elisha. "How bad would it really be for the most talented seventeen-year-old piano player on the planet to have a crush on you? Don't take me wrong, I'm not trying to set up anything, but if he's going to like you, he's going to like you. You don't have to reciprocate, but the arrangement may prove beneficial for both of you."

Virginia forcefully interrupted, "Gene, I really do not like what I am hearing here. It sounds like the deliberate manipulation of a young man's emotions."

Elisha's eyes brightened as she abruptly sat up straight, ignoring her mom's statement. "I'm curious," she said, "How would you see it being beneficial?"

"Gene, I don't like where this is going," protested Virginia again.

"Just hear this out a little before you judge too quickly," responded Gene. "Elisha, I can see it being beneficial to Art in a couple of ways. First, to have the attention of a beautiful young lady like you will naturally build his self-confidence and help him to be at ease around the opposite sex. This will be very important for his people skills as he becomes more and more famous and encounters the 'beautiful people' among music aficionados. Secondly, it will make him more popular to other members of the opposite sex. You know how it is, if you appear that you have a girlfriend, other girls become interested in you. Nobody goes after the guy who hasn't had a girlfriend for a while.

"Now, as for you, Elisha, you are very outgoing and like to be in the limelight. Right?" Elisha barely nodded a yes. "In the next year Art will more than likely go from high school senior to international phenomenon. Anyone with him will be noticed. Anyone who is really close to him will undoubtedly have a certain amount of influence over him and over his music. It doesn't mean that you would have romantic feelings for him. It also doesn't mean you should purposefully lead him on. All I am saying is that if he is going to like you regardless, you both might as well benefit from it."

"Gene!" Virginia protested again. "I will not be having you instruct my daughter on how to lead a boy on just for her own benefit!"

"Virginia, I think you are missing what I am saying. Having Elisha's attention will be of great value to Art. It will help him mature socially and help him learn to handle popularity. All I am saying to Elisha is that her being nice to him will also naturally benefit her because of Art's eventual standing in the world as a great musician."

"But, Dad," interrupted Elisha "I think you're telling me that it's okay for me to maybe kinda lead him on, but not really. If I am just nice to him, he will probably misinterpret my niceness as being interested in him. However, I really should treat him nicely because it's the right thing to do. I can't help it if he misinterprets my actions. Am I on the right track?"

Gene nodded affirmatively, "I think you pretty much got it, but remember, Elisha, you're walking a fine line between just being nice and leading him on, and your mother is right that you should not lead him on."

With that, Gene announced an end to the meeting stating that he was greatly encouraged by their willingness to take on this project. It didn't take long for the encouraging mood to wane as Virginia gave Gene a cold stare and mouthed the words, "We need to talk, now." Gene nodded and followed Virginia down the hall into their bedroom.

Once in their bedroom, Virginia spun around with fire in her eyes and let her pent up fears and concerns shoot out of her mouth like arrows at an enemy. "This better be the real deal, Gene, because if it's not, you're not just playing your little manipulation mind games with the public or your subordinates at work, you're playing with the hearts, minds, and emotions of your own children. I've seen your brand of manipulation wrapped up in a package that feels and looks like concern. I've seen your need for absolute control sold as protection, and I've seen the way you exploit people and disguise it like you're their savior, providing them with opportunities. If I find out that this is all just another one of your little 'game plans', I'll shut this little façade down and blow you right out of the water with the DHE."

Virginia could not remember ever going after Gene with such anger and force before. In the past, she had always allowed

Gene to nudge her in the way he thought best, if not emotionally, then chemically. Virginia knew that because of her desire to be loved and accepted she had gone along with whatever Gene thought was best. But something had caused her to snap. She guessed it was being around Art and coming to the stark realization that she was responsible for forming and controlling the destiny of a real live human being, not just a genetic experiment with a hypothetical outcome to be analyzed in the lab.

Gene calmly responded, "Virginia, all I can say is, based on my past and what you've had to live through with me, I totally deserve your doubt and the skepticism. I really meant what I said in there to Chris and Elisha. Being with Art these last few days has really had an effect on me, too. For one thing, I am now convinced that we made a terribly huge mistake having him grow up exclusively in institutionalized settings without a mother and father or some sort of family system. I know why we did it from a project and security perspective, but it was a glaring mistake from a nurturing and sense of belonging perspective. If I could go back and do it all over, I would adopt him myself. Even though it is too late for a meaningful adoption, I would like to try to make it right by being a family for him now. I don't know what else I can say that will convince you, but I am willing to start proving it with my actions."

Virginia looked back at Gene with a silent, hollow, expressionless stare. She finally broke the silence without changing her expression, "I'll be watching and waiting for the proof."

Gene quickly responded, "That's all I can ask for, Virginia."

7

Nagging Questions

THE NEXT MORNING, Art was ready to get out of the hospital and enjoy a few more days of the radiant Arizona sun. He was surprised when the whole Taylor family showed up for his release and check out. He was even more surprised that everyone was so cheery and nice to him, especially Elisha. Art reasoned that they all were probably just feeling bad that he had been injured on the hike.

Art got his prescriptions and his final release instructions. He was still tender and puffy in places, but the only permanent injury he suffered was embarrassment. They finally left the hospital and Art and the Taylors spent the last few days of their holiday relaxing back at the Boulders Resort.

The time in Arizona had proved mysterious and dangerous, but at the same time emotionally invigorating for Art. His trip with the Taylors was nothing like he had imagined it would be. He was taken by the Taylor's interest in him, from the interesting discussions with Mr. Taylor to the motherly attention he was receiving from Virginia. He had started seeing Virginia as someone who genuinely cared and was concerned about him. All of his life he had wondered and fantasized about what it would be like to actually have a mother. He knew that if he had a mother, she would have been right there with him at the hospital, just like Virginia, worrying about him, making small talk, and making sure that he was receiving proper care.

While he went back to Hawthorne feeling like he was cared for, he could not get a few strange thoughts out of his mind: his trustee Jason Alexander and his leather folder with DHE on the outside, Virginia's early probing and staring, Mr. Taylor being so upset with Chris about mentioning chimeras, whatever that was, and being pretty sure that he saw his bank trustee talking to Mr. Taylor when they were taking him off the rescue chopper. Even with the accident and the lingering questions, he decided this was the best holiday break that he had ever experienced.

Art cringed at the thought of coming back to the cold stone buildings of Hawthorne after being in warm sunny Arizona. As the limo drove under the words HAWTHORNE ACADEMY carved into the massive stone archway entrance, Art wondered if he would soon be the joke of the campus. Especially with news of having cactus needles pulled out of his butt. He imagined his new name at Hawthorne would be "Porcupine boy" or "Cactus Butt." However, to his surprise and relief, Chris and Elisha told no one about his embarrassing accident.

The next couple of months were unlike any other he had spent at Hawthorne. Prior to the trip to Arizona, Art's life at Hawthorne was somewhat mundane. His days were spent attending class, studying, usually eating his meals alone, and composing and playing piano. On the weekend his social life consisted of watching movies and hanging out with his friend Dizzy. Since getting back from Arizona, his association with Chris and Elisha instantly propelled him into the "popular" group of kids.

To his amazement, he was actually being invited to do things or even to just hang out with Chris and his friends. It was a little awkward at first, but they tolerated him pretty well.

He also felt like he was making some headway with Elisha. She actually sought him out to talk to him and would occasionally come and sit by him and eat lunch. Elisha had also started taking an interest in his music and would ask him to play some of his original compositions for her. He also noticed that the other girls in his class who had never paid any attention to him before were making an effort to talk to him. Things were really going well.

Even though he felt like his world was coming together, Art continued to be haunted by questions that one way or the other he would have to figure out. Once he turned eighteen, where could he go to find out more information about his parents? Could there be some long lost relatives somewhere that he could connect with to find out more about his ancestral past? Why did his trustee Jason Alexander have a leather folder with the initials D.H.E. on the outside? Who, or what, was DHE? Why was his trustee at the emergency room? Why was Mr. Taylor so upset when Chris mentioned Chimeras, whatever that was?

Art continued to be mentally plagued by his questions. He decided he would do a little research and start with his trustee, Jason Alexander. He went online to the Boston Mercantile Bank & Trust site. He perused through the listings of all of the trust officers and found it strange that there was no entry for a Jason Alexander. He then went to the "Contact Us" section and entered the following message:

My name is Art Jenicks. Your bank oversees a trust that my parents set up for me. My trustee at your bank is Mr. Jason Alexander. I would greatly appreciate it if you would have him contact me at his earliest convenience.

He looked at what he had typed and thought about it for a minute. What would he say if Mr. Alexander called? If he really wanted to contact Mr. Alexander, he could do it through the method that was set up through the school office. What he really wanted to know now was whether Mr. Alexander was really employed by the bank. He deleted the email and wrote down the main number for the bank. He walked over and stared out the small arched window of his dorm room onto the common area covered in thick white snow. He punched in the phone number and waited. He worked his way through all of the prompts until he finally was able to speak to a live person on the line. "Hello, yes, I am trying to get a hold of a bank employee in your trust department by the name of Jason Alexander."

"Just a minute, sir, and I will search our directory." Then, after a brief pause, "Sorry sir, I don't show a Jason Alexander in the trust department. Would you like me to do a search of all bank employees to see if I can find him?"

A shock went through Art's system. He swallowed hard. "Yes, please." After waiting for what seemed like five minutes, he heard what he most feared. "I'm sorry, sir, I don't have an employee by that name and our records show that we have not employed anyone by that name for at least the past two years. Is there anything else I can help you with?"

Regaining his composure, Art thought he needed to dig a little deeper. "Yes, can you put me through to your trust department?"

"Yes, sir, I will transfer you over to our trust department."

Art started to work his way through the department prompts, but began to realize that even if he reached someone to talk to, they probably could not give him any information over the phone about his trust. Art hung up. Again he stared out the window, searching his mind for another way to figure this out. He went back online and entered a search for Jason Alexander. The search returned about sixty or seventy individuals named Jason Alexander, from doctors to a sit-com actor from the 1990s. He carefully went through every listing, looking for any connection to the bank. He found none. Frustrated, he entered DHE into the search. It yielded over two thousand results. Discouraged by the daunting quantity, he nonetheless began a slow examination of the results. His problem was that he had no idea what he was looking for. He fought the feeling that he was wasting his time. What else could he do to try to figure all this out?

Art had been reading through what seemed to him mostly nonsense, when something caught his eye—a listing for www.DHE.gov. He selected it and up came a government site for the Department of Human Enhancement. When he went to the site map index, the system froze. He hadn't ever seen this happen before at Hawthorne, which bragged about always being on the leading edge of technology. It must be a problem with the government site. He went to a couple of his favorite music sites and the system worked fine. Trying the DHE.gov site again, the system froze a second time. Now extremely frustrated, Art closed the connection and slammed his fist against the wall.

Then it hit him: Dizzy would know how to help him find information.

Dizzy was one of the first guys Art met four years ago when he came to Hawthorne as a freshman. They quickly became friends. It didn't take long for both boys to recognize that they were not "normal" Hawthorne material. They did not come from wealth or fame, they were not particularly good looking, and they both had unsolved mysteries in their family tree.

Dizz's mother was lower middle class and spent most of her time working two jobs to make ends meet. Dizz's biological father was known only as donor # 27214 from a sperm bank over in Newton. His mother and her husband had been unable to have children and finally decided to have a child through a sperm donor. Six months into the pregnancy her husband couldn't deal with the thought that the baby his wife was carrying was not his and he disappeared, not to be heard from again.

Dizzy was born with the legal name Edward R. Benson. After his birth, his mother immediately went to work, and Edward went to a daycare facility. It didn't take long for the daycare workers to discover that Edward was not an ordinary child. He talked in complete sentences at fourteen months and was reading at two years of age. He also had a peculiarly strong attraction to jazz music at a young age. He demanded that his mother and daycare workers play jazz recordings over and over. He was especially fond of Dizzy Gillespie. To help the daycare workers, his mother would bring him to the daycare with an IPOD packed with Dizzy Gillespie recordings. The workers used the music to calm him down when he was upset. It didn't take long for the workers to replace his proper name with the nickname "Dizzy".

Once school age rolled around, Dizzy's mother enrolled him in the local public school system. It quickly became apparent that this was not the venue for Dizz's education. His intellect and vocabulary intimidated students and teachers alike. Teachers were unable to teach their normal students and Dizzy at the same time. Most teachers would sequester Dizzy in a corner with upper level textbooks and just let him read and work through them on his own. Dizzy became bored and began to stagnate in the public school environment. Fortunately, his mother and the school district were quick to recognize what was happening, found some grants and scholarships, and were able to place him in a small private school for gifted children. In that environment he flourished. By the time he got to high school, several elite private schools were lined up with a full ride scholarship to pay all of his cost of attendance. His mother chose Hawthorne for a couple of reasons. First, she believed it was the best school for intellectual as well as social advancement. Secondly, Hawthorne's offer of tuition and support included substantial additional funding that could be siphoned off for her own support.

If asked, Mrs. Benson would flat out tell anyone that Dizzy did not get his brains from her. She and Dizzy had both attempted to track down and contact donor # 27214 through as many donor/offspring/parent registries as they could find. Time after time, they came up empty.

Even though his mother hoped that Hawthorne would facilitate his social advancement, Dizz's lack of an upper class background marked him as an "undesirable" at Hawthorne. Kids at Hawthorne were not impressed with brains unless status and wealth backed them up. Dizzy, although brilliant, did not have the coveted "complete package" that made kids popular at Hawthorne.

Since Art also came to Hawthorne with less than the complete package, it was only natural that Dizzy and Art would gravitate toward each other and become best friends during their early years at Hawthorne. As Art and Dizzy progressed through Hawthorne, Dizzy became more withdrawn as Art slowly became more social. Then came Art's fateful holiday trip with the Taylors, catapulting him into the circles of Hawthorne's social elite.

The one skill that kept Dizzy from being a total outcast at Hawthorne was his ability to manipulate technology. Everyone at Hawthorne unofficially knew that if they had a problem that could somehow be solved with technology, Dizzy was the guy to see, whether what you wanted to do was legal or not. It was rumored that Dizzy had been threatened with expulsion because of unauthorized access to the school's computer systems, but that the Hawthorne Administrators could never prove anything.

Both Art and Dizz lived on the first floor of McLaren hall. Their entire class had lived in McLaren since they were freshman with the boys on the first floor and the girls on the second floor.

McLaren Hall was one of four two-story residence halls located in what everyone called the "A side" of the campus. The buildings on campus were positioned so that from the air one would see a large "H A". The A side of the campus consisted of the four residence halls that made up the sides of the giant block A. The middle of the A was a building housing the cafeteria on the left side and student union on the right side. The cafeteria and the student union were separated in the middle by a large gothic archway that allowed access to the landscaped green areas inside the bottom and top of the A. The top of the giant block A was an athletic building housing the gym, swimming pool and locker rooms.

The "H side" of campus consisted of five buildings arranged in an H: three classroom buildings, an administration building, and the performance hall. The middle of the H was the administration building which also had a large gothic archway that allowed access to the landscaped green areas inside the bottom and top of the H.

Directly west of the top of the H, the elevation of the property gradually descended down to the athletic fields and the building housing the recreation equipment. The area west of the top of the A was an elevated wooded area, giving it the feel of a small bluff, especially from the vantage point of the athletic fields.

The giant arched entrance to Hawthorne was located at the southeast corner of the campus just below the bottom of the A. The entire outside of the campus was lined with large red maples and enclosed by a foreboding twelve-foot-high fence constructed of large cut stones and black ornamental cast iron.

Art walked out of his room and headed down the first floor of McLaren Hall toward Dizz's room. He knocked on Dizz's door. The door slowly opened, just a crack. The scent of fresh popcorn wafted out and jazz played in the background. Dizzy peered through the crack. "Hey, wow, I must be dreaming. This can't be the ever popular Art Jenicks at my little door. This must be some mistake. Did you turn the wrong way down the hall and get lost? Are you looking for directions, or did you just smell my popcorn and thought you could weasel in on some of it?"

Art pushed the door fully open and gave Dizzy a disgusted look. "Come on Dizz, that's not fair." He walked into the room and made his way through the clutter and dirty clothes on the floor over to the only clear space on the corner of the bed. The dorm rooms were designed to house only one student per room, so they weren't spacious, but they were private. Each room came with a twin bed, a built-in desk, a closet, chest of drawers, and a small place for a microwave, mini-fridge, and a tiny sink. The bathrooms and showers were shared in common by all the students on each floor.

the awakening   69

Even though it was only eight at night, Dizz looked as if he had just got out of bed. His jet-black hair was matted and pushed unevenly to one side of his head. He was wearing Hawthorne-issued red gym shorts from their freshman year and a badly-faded Red Sox t-shirt with baggy tube socks. Dizz stood a very skinny five-foot-ten. He had a square chin, brown eyes sunk deep under his eyebrows, and a very long, thin, pointed nose.

Dizz placed his finger on his upper lip, squinted his eyes, and studied Art. "Hmm, let me see, this is now late February and the last time you went out of your way to talk to me was, oh, yeah, in December before you scored that dream vacation to Scottsdale with the rich and famous. What brings you down to talk to the little people?"

By now, Art was looking down at his shoes. He knew Dizz was right. He had kinda ditched Dizz for the rich and the famous. It was not entirely intentional . . . he just didn't seem to have the time to spend with anyone else.

Art looked up at Dizz. "I'm sorry. I have no good excuses. I have not purposefully tried to ignore you; I've just been really busy."

Dizzy smiled a broad smile. "Lame excuse, but apology accepted. Come on in, you look like you need some help. So what can I do to help Hawthorne's world famous pianist and composer?"

Art shook his head. "Come on, Dizz, I do need your help, but cut the celebrity crap, okay?"

Dizzy slowly sank down in his desk chair and swung it around to face Art. "Okay, Art, no more crap. What's up?"

Art spent the next hour or so rehashing some old ground that Dizz had heard before about his past, or lack thereof, and some new stuff, unearthed by his Scottsdale trip. He told Dizz about Mercantile Bank & Trust of Boston, his trustee Jason M. Alexander, the initials DHE on his folder, about seeing his trustee at the hospital with Mr. Taylor, and about the computer freezing up every time he tried to log into the DHE.gov site.

Dizzy listened patiently, smiling a lot, like he knew something Art didn't know. Finally Art stopped, looked right at Dizzy and said, "Why do you have that stupid grin on your face? What do you know that I don't?"

Dizzy smiled even more broadly. "Well, I don't have any answers to your mysteries, but I can fill you in on some information that may get you looking in the right places."

Art scooted across the bed closer to Dizz. "I'm listening."

"The first thing you should know is that the technology at Hawthorne doesn't freeze up because of technical problems. They have the best system money can buy. The freeze is always by design. You see, no one has unrestricted access to information at Hawthorne. I guess you could call it Hawthorne's little internal "web of control." The Hawthorne system has broad restrictions programmed in for every user in general and, if they so desire, specific restrictions programmed in for each individual user. I probably have the most restrictions regarding access to information of any student at Hawthorne. Judging from my experience, when the system froze when you tried to access the DHE.gov site, it was because someone here does not want you going there for some reason, which may mean you are on to something."

"Whoa! So Dizz, why are you the most restricted user at Hawthorne?"

"Just out of curiosity, I started researching each of the Hawthorne Board Members. All of a sudden, everything was freezing up on me. Of course, I went to the technical director to try to figure out the problem. At first, he acted like he didn't know why it was happening, but I kept after him and suggested diagnostic tests, fixes, etc. He finally broke down and told me how the system was designed, but he wouldn't tell me who made the ultimate decisions on the global restrictions or personal restrictions to the system. Strange thing, he no longer works for Hawthorne—he just disappeared one day. No one noticed except me—pretty low-profile position. The new technical director that they hired refuses to speak with me and has given me the 'we'll withhold your diploma if you start talking about the Hawthorne proprietary system'."

Art was starting to look very depressed. He placed his elbows on his knees, put his head in his hands and sighed, "It doesn't sound like I'm going to get any answers around here and I really don't know what else to do, Dizz. You got any clever ways around this? After all, you are the 'answer man'."

Dizzy smiled his huge smile again. "Well, my buddy Art, you did come to the right place, but it will take a little time and a little deception to get somewhere we can get remote unmonitored access in order to dig into your little mysteries."

Art began to perk up a little. "How are we going to do that and when are we going to do it?"

"How eager are you to get going, Art?"

"The sooner the better, Dizz, the sooner, the better."

"How does this Sunday look for a start?"

Art grimaced, "I'm supposed to go to a concert with Elisha and her friends on Sunday . . . but, I, uh, I'll figure a way to get out of it."

Dizz grinned, "Are you sure you won't be committing social suicide? We're talking about beautiful Elisha Taylor, daughter of Gene Taylor, the new captain of industry, Hawthorne's main benefactor. What are you going to tell her?"

Art pursed his lips, cocked his head back and then blurted out a quick, "I'll think of something; this I gotta do. I need some answers; this is driving me crazy."

"Okay, Art, meet me at the front gate Sunday morning at six. Make sure you sign out the night before. Just put down you are going to Boston for the day."

"Dizz, where are we really going on Sunday?'

"We're going to Boston, of course. Just be there at six A.M. sharp—timing is important."

It was Tuesday and Art had until Saturday to come up with a good story to feed Elisha. He really did not want to displease her in any way. He liked her attention and he was holding out hope that there might be a chance for the two of them to become a real couple. Ditching out on her was not something that he was looking forward to, but he knew he had to do it. For the rest of the week, he found himself avoiding the places he knew she would be during certain times of the day. When he did see her, he kept his conversations with her short and pleasant, leaving no time to discuss the upcoming weekend concert.

He finished his last class of the week on Friday afternoon. Ever since the Scottsdale trip, he had established a new Friday afternoon routine. Instead of going to his room and taking a nap, he had started hanging out in the student union where Elisha and her friends would come to discuss their social events for the weekend, and of course to gossip about the latest breakups, hookups, and heartbreaks. Art knew that this was the time to let Elisha know he was not going to the concert. He had decided to go with the "moody artist" excuse, needing time alone to work on his latest composition.

Art walked into the commons and went over to the corner where they usually hung out on Friday afternoon. He was relieved to see there was no one there yet. It would give him a little time to mentally review his excuse speech to Elisha a couple of times, and to try to anticipate her reaction and his response. He had just situated himself on the couch when they all walked in, Elisha leading the pack, dressed like she'd just stepped out of a designer's store. Her beauty always mesmerized Art. She gave him a little smile and a wink as she walked over to him. That was enough for Art to begin mentally wrestling with his decision. How could he blow off a concert with this goddess to go who knows where with Dizz? Was he crazy?

Elisha sat down next to Art. "Well, you've been pretty scarce this week. What have you been doing with yourself?"

Art knew that he was going to have to lay the groundwork for a credible excuse, that is, if he was going to actually use it. Art took a breath. "I've been trying to get ahead on all of my course work so I can take some time and work on a new composition bottled up inside of me. I am waiting for some quality time so I can get it poured out on paper. It seems every time I sit down to work on it, I am distracted with assignments tugging my brain in another direction. I figured that if I could take care of all the assignments and even get a little ahead, I could clear some time to do some quality writing. So I've been really working hard this week to clear out all my homework distractions."

Elisha gave him one of her radiant smiles. "Oooh, that sounds extremely responsible and efficient. This new composition must be very important for you to be that driven. Will it be something that I will like, or is this something only the musical elite can appreciate?"

"I'm hoping you'll really like it a lot. I'm writing it especially for you." Art was stunned with what involuntarily rushed out of his mouth. This was not what he rehearsed. How could he have just said that? How would Elisha respond? *How can I come up with a composition for her if I am running around with Dizz?*

Elisha looked a little startled. "For me? Did you say you were writing it for me?"

Art, not knowing if this was good or bad, nodded his head. "Yeah, for you. You have done so much for me the last few months to broaden my horizons and I want to do something musical that somehow captures how I feel about what you've done for me."

A delighted smile came over Elisha's face. Art was relieved, really liking Elisha's reaction. He thought this whole thing could develop into a win-win situation, but then realized he was actually going to have to come up with a composition special enough to impress her.

He decided that the groundwork had been sufficiently laid and that he could go ahead with his excuse for not making the concert. "Elisha, now that I've cleared out this time, I really want to take advantage of it. I'm wondering if you would mind if I didn't go along with you to the Vindicators concert in Boston on Sunday."

Elisha, looking disappointed and understanding at the same time, stuck out her bottom lip in a little pout and looked at Art with sad eyes. "Art, we're really going to miss you, but I understand that this is important to you. I'll try to bring you back a souvenir from the concert."

"Thanks, Elisha. I think you understand me better than anyone else here at Hawthorne. Someone else might have been really upset, but you are a true friend who understands what I need to do."

Art was pleased with how everything worked out. Elisha, of course, let everyone know that Art was going to write something just for her.

8

Aliases with No Freezer Burn

IT WAS FIVE O'CLOCK when the alarm jolted Art from a deep sleep. Art was not happy to be getting up so early on a Sunday morning. He showered, got dressed, and put on his warmest winter coat to meet Dizz at the front gate. He left his room and quickly headed for the outside door. He had officially signed out the night before so he wouldn't have to wake the RA in his dorm.

He opened the door to the outside. It was bitterly cold and deathly quiet outside. There were no lights on anywhere on campus, and with every step he could hear the squeaky crunch of the frozen ice and snow. He looked everywhere for signs of Dizz. Art's irritation mounted as he approached the front gate. *Dizz better be out here or I'll really be ticked*, he thought to himself.

Art swiped his security access card, opened the pedestrian gate next to the arched entryway and walked out into the street. Just as he was beginning to grab his cell phone and text his friend, Dizz's voice broke through the silence, "What took you so long?" Art jumped about a foot in the air. Dizz laughed.

"I'm right on time! Isn't it just six now?"

Dizz put his arm around Art and gave him a friendly hug. "I was just testing to see if you're awake. I hope you're ready for an adventure, because I'm going to take you places today you've never imagined before."

Art shoved his phone back in his pocket and looked at Dizz with a confused look. "I thought we were going to go do some research."

"Oh, we are. We're just not going to go about it in the conventional way."

"Why does that not surprise me?"

"Come on, we gotta hustle to make the train in Concord and we got about a two-mile walk to get there."

The two headed out at a brisk pace. It was one of those mornings so cold that nose hairs froze with each breath. They arrived at the station with just enough time to get tickets and board. There were only two other people on the train—an older couple all bundled up, holding Bibles in their hands probably on their way to an early church service somewhere along the line.

The cabin of the train was warm and toasty. Art and Dizz found a couple of seats where they could lie down and catch a little more sleep. Dizz had Art set the alarm on his PACA to make sure they would be awake for the next connection they needed to make. Art turned to Dizz while he was unzipping his coat. "Where are these tickets taking us today, Dizz?"

Dizz stood up and posed as if he were in a Shakespearian play. "Art, I am taking you to the once grand Essex Hotel in the fine little Boston neighborhood of Roxbury. There we will search out the mysteries of our lives together using names we shall quickly forget. Yes, Art, my friend, I am going to take you down the back alleys of some less than desirable places and show you things in basements that you just wouldn't dream of. But for now, let us enter into a brief period of repose."

"Whoa, quite the little performance, Dizz. How about a translation."

"I estimate we have thirty-five minutes of sleep before the next connection into Roxbury, so goodnight." With that, Dizz laid down on the seat, curled up in a ball, and pulled his black stocking hat down over his eyes.

Art noticed that the older couple looked a little alarmed by Dizz's performance. He gave them a smile and a shrug to let them know that Dizz was just goofing around and things were okay. He continued to watch the older couple as they read their Bibles and talked to each other until he could no longer keep his eyes open. He lay down and quickly fell asleep.

The next thing Art knew, he was being awakened and practically dragged by Dizz through another train station. "Come on, Art, didn't you hear your alarm? We need to hurry to make the connecting train or we'll have to wait an hour for the next one."

They were running full speed by the time they got to the connecting train and were just able to run through the train doors as they were closing. Dizz and Art sat down, breathing hard from the final sprint. Dizz, between big breaths, attempted to shout, "Oh, yeah, we did it, we beat the system!"

Art looked sideways at Dizz. "What's that all about?"

"According to the official train schedules, you're not supposed to be able to make that connection without waiting an additional hour. However, early on Sunday, the train from Concord usually leaves ahead of schedule and the stations are not crowded, so you can sprint through the station to make the connection. It all worked, and we beat the system, and I love to beat the system." The only thing Art could do was give Dizz a fake smile and a nod.

They continued on the train until Roxbury. The sun was finally up in the sky. It was a bright clear February day, but still bitterly cold. Steam was rising up out of everything that was warmer than the air. Bright white snow covered the roofs of the houses, and disgusting, dirty black snow lined the sides of the streets.

Dizz turned to Art. "Come on, Art, we've got about seven blocks ahead of us before we can get out of this cold." They took off at a slow jog in order to keep warm.

The streets of the dilapidated neighborhood were empty except for the parked cars frozen in the snow. Most of the houses were in need of repair. It was not unusual to see entire windows boarded up and broken bottles and cans littering front steps. After about four blocks, Dizz turned and headed down the alley of what must have once been a vibrant commercial area. The alley was loaded with trash, old mattresses, tires and an occasional abandoned car. After jogging two more blocks, Dizz abruptly stopped and walked over to a large black metal door on the backside of an old five-story hotel. On the top floor, Art could see the remnants of a sign with the letters "E" and an "X" as the only remaining vestige of the hotel's sign. Art realized that this must be the "once grand Essex Hotel." He couldn't wait to see the basement.

Dizz pressed the white button at the side of the door and waited. Nothing happened. He kept pressing the button about every thirty seconds. They had kept warm by jogging, but standing and waiting for someone to answer the door rapidly brought back the cold. Shivering, Art appealed to Dizz, "Is there any other way in? What about the front door? Is there a front door?"

Dizz was starting to jump up and down to stay warm. "Nope, this is it for us. Phil will be here in a minute. He always comes, just not ever as promptly as you would like."

About two minutes later they heard a jovial but gravelly voice rattle out of what looked like a rusted out speaker over the door. "You guys want some hot chocolate?"

Dizz, in a perturbed tone, answered, "Come on, Phil, let us in. We're freezing to death out here." The metal door opened to a semi-rotund Santa Claus character in a flannel shirt, blue jeans and unusually wide, large, red suspenders. He was balding on top, but had a full salt-and-pepper beard and mustache. Grinning from ear to ear, he greeted the boys. "Welcome to the Essex, or what once was the Essex."

The boys wasted no time, quickly stepping into the warmth. Dizz introduced Art and Phil to each other. Phil motioned for the boys to follow him down the dimly lit hallway. "Come on boys, let's go to my office and get that cup of hot chocolate."

The three of them continued down the hall toward the front of the building into what used to be the main lobby. Phil took them behind the desk into an adjoining room, which Art learned was his office. Unlike the rest of the building, the office had been remodeled and updated. Off one end of the office was another door that opened into Phil's private living quarters. They followed Phil through the office into the kitchen of his apartment. Art and Dizz took their coats off and sat down at the kitchen table.

Phil took the simmering kettle off the stove and poured hot water into cups filled with instant hot chocolate mix. "Extra marshmallows for both of you? You gotta be having extra marshmallows on a day like today!" The boys grinned at each other, nodded yes and Phil filled the top of their cups with stale miniature marshmallows. The boys warmed their hands on the cups and slurped up hot chocolate and melted marshmallows.

Phil smiled at Art. "So, Art, I hear you want to do a little unrecognizable TPA today."

"TP what?" asked Art.

Phil immediately shifted his gaze over to Dizz. "Dizz, you have explained to your friend Art here how all of this works, haven't you?"

Dizz shook his head to indicate no. "I figured he really didn't need to know before he got here."

Phil's jovial expression changed instantaneously to a stern look of concern. "I thought you told me that you had worked all of this out in advance, including the understanding that what Art sees and does here really doesn't happen. You know the only reason I agreed to this was because you helped me put this all together. But right now, I really need to know that all of this will remain our little secret or back out into the frigid Sunday morning air you go."

"Phil, Phil, Phil, don't worry. We don't have a problem here." Dizz replied with an air of confidence. "Art is one of my oldest friends at school and we have our reasons why what happens here will always remain a deep dark secret. Right, Art?"

Art, now extremely uncomfortable with the conversation between Phil and Dizz, was smart enough to know that he needed to answer Dizz's question with a confident "yes" and go with the flow. Art nodded his head up and down and blurted out a strong "yes!"

Evidently, his 'yes' was good enough for Phil, because his immense jovial grin returned to his face, and he stood and headed for the door. "Okay, as soon as you are finished with your hot chocolate I'll set you up in the computer room."

As soon as Phil was out of earshot, Art immediately confronted Dizz and asked, "What's TPA?"

"TPA is an acronym that Phil and I made up when we set up the computer system here. It stands for third party access. TPA means I access the internet and do whatever I want under someone else's name to conceal the true identity of the person who is searching or communicating. This may sound like conspiracy theory stuff, but I know people out there who get tracked everywhere they go on the internet. In fact, because of what happened to me at Hawthorne, I think I am one of them. It used to be that you could go to the local public library and hop on the internet and search to your heart's content without worrying about big brother watching your every move. Then came terrorism and they discovered the terrorists were using library computers for random messaging. Now everyone at the public libraries has to log on with his or her fingerprint, which of course creates a record of everything you do online. That's what gave me the idea for TPA."

Art, still puzzled, asked, "What do you mean?"

"Well, there are quite a few people out there like me who are, or at least believe that they are, being tracked everywhere they go on the internet. These people still want to use the internet without every little website they go to and every communication scrutinized for whatever reason. Some are more than willing to pay big bucks to preserve their anonymity."

"So how do you avoid the identification issue?"

"Well, it's a little complicated and a little creepy, but here goes." Dizz paused and collected his thoughts. "The complicated part first. Okay, a little history is needed for this to make sense. The largest population group in America is the Baby Boomers. Most of them are in their eighties and nineties now. Right after World War II, the GIs came home from the war with pent up demand to marry and raise their families. Subsequently, about 76 million babies were born between 1946 and 1964. This huge population boom stressed everything in the U.S., hospitals, schools, housing, and most important for TPA, Social Security. You with me so far?"

"Yea, I understand what you're saying, but I don't know where you are going with it."

"It's okay; it'll make sense the more you hear. So in comes Social Security to the picture. When the Boomers got to retirement age, the internet was full blown and operational, but a lot of the Boomers weren't fully on board. The government, for administrative and economic reasons, wanted to get all Social Security recipients online to electronically receive and manage their benefits. This was not a big deal for the retired wealthy, but it was for the poor—especially those in flop houses or low-level social security facilities. The government devised an incentive plan so the operators of flophouses would receive additional revenue if they got their residents to use the internet and set up their social security accounts online. In addition, the operators of low income housing would get paid their monthly fees from social security online, which would be deducted from the resident's account."

"How did you learn about all of this stuff?"

"I owe it to Hawthorne's fine educational programs. There was a whole chapter on this in my Advanced Government and Social Problems class."

"What does all of this have to do with TPA?"

"Well, I've given you the framework for the system, and you know how I like to beat the system. We are currently standing in the office of a low-income social security provider, A.K.A. flop house, of which Phil is the operator. He gets paid extra bucks for each resident he gets up and running on the internet and he gets an extra bonus if he gets a hundred percent of his residents online. To get credited with one hundred percent usage, his residents have to set up their account and go online at least ten hours per month. For about forty to sixty percent of the residents it's not a problem. Phil shows them online gaming sites and sites where they can watch old movies and sitcoms from yesteryears. That leaves about forty percent who are a problem for his revenue stream.

"So how in the world do you get these old farts online?"

That's where I came in with a solution, which again is to the credit of my Hawthorne education. You see, in the section of the book on Social Security and Social Issues they included a little human-interest story about this guy somewhere in the Midwest who kept his dead mom in a freezer for a few years so he could continue to collect her Social Security payments. Well, that got me thinking. How could we keep the non-compliant residents using the internet so Phil could receive the payments without the residents ever really getting on the Internet?

"The solution was really very simple. I had Phil start heavily screening new residents, looking for individuals who had no families or close friends, or who had not had recent contact with family and friends. Once we felt confident they met the criteria, we would sign them up as a resident and obtain, without their knowledge, a scan of their right index finger, which is the finger needed to sign on to the internet. From the scan, we produced an index finger tip cover containing the fingerprint of the resident. We then can use that tip to log on without them being near a computer. When you log on using the tip, you log on under their name. So, for those willing to pay the price, third party access to the internet can be accomplished under someone else's name. At the same time Phil gets his credit for one hundred percent usage, so he gets a double payday."

"Dizz! This has got to be totally illegal. Why do you look for residents with no family or friend connections?"

"That's the creepy part. Since no one knows these people or cares what happens to them, Phil kinda prolongs their stay after they expire. I like to call it cryonics for the destitute."

"You mean you . . . "

"Yep! They are shrink-wrapped and quick frozen at death and are kept around anywhere between six and eighteen months, depending on the full occupancy numbers Phil has on file with the government. It does wonders for his revenue stream to have full occupancy with a hundred percent online participation. We really put together a pretty sophisticated system with the shrink wrap and quick freeze so that when we thaw them out they look and feel naturally dead with no freezer burn. If you want, I can take you down to the basement and show you the whole operation."

"No, no, no, no, that's okay," said Art nervously. "This is all making me nauseated, but now I understand what you were saying on the train about searching out mysteries using names we would forget and things in the basement I'd never dream of. Actually, I am more than a little horrified by the whole set up. It, well, it just doesn't seem right."

"Art, relax, it's really not a big deal. No one gets hurt, no one gets abused. Sure, we give the system a little beating, but it deserves it, don't you think? And besides, this little set up allows you to get the answers you're seeking."

Art squirmed in his seat, "Okay, Dizz, but I'm not going down to the basement and I'm going to pretend that you made this whole thing up."

"Hey, no problem—but you have to admit, it's a pretty clever scheme."

"Yeah, it's clever all right. How did you and Phil get hooked up together on this deal?"

"Phil used to date my mom, and when things were really tough in the early years, he let us live down in the basement. Pre-freezer, that is."

Phil came bouncing into the room with his infectious smile and winked at them, "I can't put my finger on it, but I think I got you two all set up and ready to go." He motioned for them to follow him down the hall.

The boys rolled their eyes to acknowledge the bad pun and followed Phil down another dark hall into a room with cubicles, keyboards and screens. Phil walked them past some of the older equipment. Art had never seen so much old computer equipment in one room. As they walked through, they passed a couple of residents sitting in front of computer screens playing online card games. They followed Phil over to a door in the back of the room. Phil unlocked the door and walked through. They followed Phil into a beautifully-appointed room filled with state-of-the-art equipment. He set them up in front of a screen and gave them each a small briefcase-type box, and opened the boxes so they could examine the contents. Inside each box were fifteen-to-twenty fingertip covers for the boys to use to sign on and off. Then Phil set up a timer that would go off about every forty-five minutes, reminding them to switch tips.

Dizz showed Art how to use the system and how to download any information that he wanted to study at a later time to a separate portable memory drive that was cleverly disguised as a ring Dizz wore on his right hand. This way they could capture more information and study it later without being detected online.

Phil chuckled as he watched Art grimace as he picked up a tip. Phil left the room, wishing the boys a good day of fishing.

Art placed his first tip on and logged in. He couldn't help but wonder if this person was currently breathing or frozen. *Whatever, just go with the flow.* After all, it did allow him to go look for information that he'd otherwise never be able to access. Art just stared at the screen for a while, trying to decide what mystery he would attempt to unravel first. He decided to start with information on the DHE.gov site. The home page was set up like a giant index. He visually scrolled through the site, looking for a place to start. When he came across "History of the Department," he thought this might be a good place to begin.

He was just starting to read about the founding of the department in 2010 when Dizz broke his concentration. "Hey, Art, I think I may be able to save you a lot of search time—at least in one area. Remember when I told you that the system shut down on me at Hawthorne when I started looking up information on the Board of Directors? That only piqued my curiosity, so I did a lot of TPA research on these folks. I have tons of information about Gene Taylor and his wife Virginia. You'll be amazed about Virginia—that lady is a genius in her own right."

As Dizz was speaking, Phil came bounding into the room, whispered something in Dizz's ear and handed him some keys. Dizz looked up at Phil, "No problem, we're gone." Then Dizz turned to Art. "Phil's got some high profile customers that want to do some TPA and they don't want to be seen by anyone. We need to log out and head out of here pronto. Bring your box of tips; we'll go to another access point and resume our searches."

Both boys logged off, and grabbed their box of tips and headed out the back door of the room. "Where are we going, Dizz?"

"We'll just head down to the other access point where we won't risk getting moved out by the paying customers."

"Did you say, 'down to another access point'?"

"Yep, don't get freaked out, Art, but we are heading down to the basement. No one will bother us there because, well, everyone's dead, and Phil doesn't want anyone else to know what all is down there, if you know what I mean."

"I can't believe the weird stuff you get me involved in."

"I choose to look at it as me helping you broaden your horizons."

"Yeah, whatever. Let's get going! I want to get some answers today."

They made their way down the narrow staircase. At the bottom of the stairs was a large metal door with a couple of deadbolts. Dizz pulled out the keys, unlocked the deadbolts and opened the door. As they walked into the room, he flipped on the light switch. To Art's amazement, it was a brightly lit, nicely-finished basement with a couple of small bedrooms, a computer room . . . and a huge walk-in freezer.

"Are they in there?" Art grimaced as he pointed over to the walk-in freezer.

"Yeah. We call them our *pop*-sicles."

"That's wrong. It's just wrong," said Art.

Dizz walked over to the freezer door and opened it just wide enough for Art to get a look inside from across the room.

"Come on, Art. Take a peek. You know you want to . . . it's no big deal." Art could not help but take a few steps forward to peek in the freezer. There they were, frozen bodies lying in orderly fashion on metal shelving in giant plastic shrink-wrap bags with an identifying tag on each bag.

"Now, that wasn't really that bad was it? They all died naturally and we are just prolonging the formal recognition of their death for a little while. It's no big deal; they don't even have any relatives or friends." Dizz shut the freezer door, looked at Art and said, "Okay, that's over with. Let's get to work."

The boys headed into the computer room, sat down at the screens, logged in with their tips and searched for the next four hours, only taking breaks to use the bathroom. During those four hours, they downloaded and saved large amounts of information to read and study offline.

Art spent most of his time skimming through the material on the DHE site. To his disappointment, he really didn't find anything that jumped out at him or directly answered any of his questions. He wanted to find some kind of link to his trustee, Jason Alexander, or to Mr. Taylor. Most of what he found was the standard government language, describing the history of the agency, their accomplishments, and their current goals and objectives. He found the information concerning the history and formation of the agency the most interesting. The stated reasons for its founding were somewhat similar in nature and tone to the philosophy espoused by Mr. Taylor regarding enhancement of the human race.

The most interesting information Art found was in old newspaper articles detailing the problems in controlling and regulating the technological explosion in the areas of genetics, pharmacology, and nanotechnology. It appeared that there was great confusion and disagreement regarding the application of existing law to these new areas of possible human enhancement.

No centralized agency or government-clearing house existed that could deal with these issues.

Apparently there had been great debate over the ethics of how far man should go in redesigning the human race and the possible dehumanization resulting from the process. It appeared that all involved wanted some kind of government oversight and structure for this new frontier, but there was deep philosophical division concerning the direction this new agency would take. Some wanted to go very slowly, asking and debating the ethical issues every step of the way. Then there were those who saw little reason for any restraint, totally focusing on the "betterment" of the health and welfare of the human race.

Dizz turned to Art and let him know that he had about three more minutes before they would have to logoff and take off to catch the train home. Just before they logged off, Art downloaded a series of articles which ran in the Boston Globe between 2007 and 2008 in which advocates and opponents from both sides debated the issues surrounding human enhancement.

They quickly gathered all of their stuff, thanked Phil for the free TPA, and headed out the back door for the train station. It was still bitterly cold and getting colder as the sun was beginning to set. It was going to be one of those clear, frigid, bone-chilling nights in the northeast.

Initially, neither Art nor Dizz were very talkative on the train ride home. Both were thinking about what they had found, and wondered if the mass of information they downloaded would provide them with any more clues to their past. Art broke the silence.

"Dizz, did you find any more information that may help you find the identity of your biological dad?"

"I didn't really see anything that would narrow my search, but I got a boatload of information to read through that may eventually lead me in the right direction, or at least narrow my search. How about you? Any luck?"

"I don't really know. At times I'm afraid my imagination may be taking me on some wild goose chase. I mean, I really don't know if the initials D.H.E. on Mr. Alexander's bag have anything to do with the Department of Human Enhancement. I'm just making assumptions because the Hawthorne system won't let me go there. I looked at some interesting stuff, and some of it seems to dovetail with what Mr. Taylor is doing, but I really don't know whether I'm headed in the right direction."

Dizz sat up. "Hey, that reminds me. I need to tell you what I found out about the Taylors from my prior research. We've got some time . . . want to hear about them?"

Art raised his eyebrows and shrugged. "Am I going to like what I hear?"

"I don't think it's bad or anything. It'll just give you a little background on where they came from and how they got to where they are now."

"Okay, what you got?"

"Okay, Virginia, formerly Virginia Holister, is from the small town of La Crescent, Minnesota. It appears that she grew up in a single-parent family where her mom worked night and day to keep the mortgage paid and food on the table. It kinda sounds like my mom. Anyway, Virginia was an intellectually-brilliant young girl and out of high school received a full academic scholarship close to home from the University of Wisconsin in Madison. There she didn't disappoint, getting involved with genetic research and the stem cell research that the University of Wisconsin pioneered in the early 2000s.

"Mr. Taylor also attended the University of Wisconsin during the same time period. Unlike Virginia, Mr. Taylor was from very well off upper middle-class family from the northern suburbs of Chicago. Mr. Taylor was a very good student, but in brainpower, he wasn't even in the same league as the brilliant Virginia.

"Now, this next part is kinda weird. Growing up and all the way through college, he went by his given name of Aaron, but for no apparent reason that I can find, a couple years out of college he legally changed his first name to Gene. Aaron had a double major in Pharmacology and Biochemistry and was engrossed in examining and redefining the basic concepts of heredity. During their last year at the University of Wisconsin, Aaron and Virginia met in a lab they had together, and apparently hit it off and dated a little between experiments. After graduation, they both ended up working for companies in the Boston area. Virginia continued with her genetic research and Aaron—now Gene—worked for the research division of a major pharmaceutical company. The information is a bit sketchy, but it appears that they continued dating and ended up getting married a few years out of college in 2010. It was not long after their marriage that the two of them quit their jobs to form TEI, Taylor Enhancements, Inc. Obviously, TEI has been wildly successful. A while ago Gene took control of running the corporation, with very little involvement anymore from Virginia."

"Wow, I would never have guessed that about Virginia. I thought she was just a submissive little corporate wife who followed her genius husband around. I wonder what happened that caused her to back off her career? Having kids, I guess."

"Maybe, but it's all kind of a mystery why she dissolved into the background. The corporation is privately owned, so there really isn't that much information available to the public."

Art looked at Dizz, smiled, pulled his wallet out of his pocket and produced the interactive business card Mr. Taylor had given him in Arizona. "When I was in Arizona with the Taylors, Mr. Taylor and I were talking about TEI and the business of human enhancements. I think he liked it that I was interested and he gave me one of his TEI interactive business cards."

"Let me take a look at that card." Dizz turned the card over a few times, examining both sides. "The only problem with this card is that once you insert it, it goes online and sends information about every page you have accessed."

"Yeah, but he gave me the card, so doesn't he expect me to access information?"

"Sure, I guess, but I would be very careful. Maybe we can have you access the information once and do a quick download so it doesn't appear you are going back to it several times to try to figure something out."

"Dizz, I think you're being super paranoid about this. I know these people. They gave me the card so I would look at the information. I don't think it's a big deal."

"Maybe, but I'd rather always error on the cautious side."

Living the Double Life

BY THE TIME THEY MADE all of their train connections and walked back to Hawthorne from the station it was about eight o'clock at night. Both boys were exhausted from the day and headed to their rooms.

Art walked into his room, lay down on his bed and stared at the ceiling. Did he really just give up a semi-date with Elisha for a weird day with frozen dead bodies at an old folks' home in Boston? He was starting to have little running arguments with himself about this quest he was on. Was it really worth it? Was it right of him to try to dig up information on the Taylors? After all, they had been extremely nice to him, treating him like one of the family. He was also feeling a little pressured now that he had fabricated the big lie about the weekend. He really had to come up with some kind of composition for Elisha or figure out an excuse to put off its completion.

At the same time his curiosity would not let him just blow it all off. He decided that he should at least take the time to look at the downloaded information to see if there were any clues that may give him an answer or point him in the right direction.

Art was so mentally and physically exhausted from the day that he fell asleep on top of his bed, fully clothed. He awoke the next morning still in a quandary about where he would go from here. He was smart enough to realize that to continue his quest would require a lot of effort. It would mean purposely living a double life around the Taylor family and everyone else except Dizz. While getting ready for his first class he mulled the situation over and over until he finally came to a mental compromise. He would continue his investigation for the next two weeks. If nothing of substance came to light he would shut the whole thing down, cover his tracks with Dizz and play out the partial charade with Elisha.

He left his room for his first class. Since he was likely to run into Elisha at lunch, he decided to be proactive by seeking her out to ask about the concert. He spent most of his class time that morning day dreaming and rehearsing his upcoming encounter with Elisha.

It was finally lunchtime and he felt prepared to talk with Elisha. He walked into the cafeteria and spotted her alone at the table where she always sat with her friends. He hurried over before the rest of the crew showed up for lunch.

"Hi, Elisha. How was the big concert?"

"Art! You would have loved it. That band is so tight, they sound better in person than they do on their recordings. I kept watching the guy on the keyboards and thinking I actually know someone who is so good, he could be sitting in that guy's seat."

Art was flattered and loved the thought of Elisha actually thinking about him at all, let alone picturing him as one of the star musicians in the band.

"Wow, that's nice of you to say, but those guys have been together for about ten years and they are really, really good."

"Don't be so modest, Art. You are an incredibly good musician, and I can't wait to hear the special piece you are putting together for me. How'd that go this weekend?"

As convincingly as he could, Art lied, "It went pretty well. Although I still have a lot of work to do on it before actually performing it for anybody."

"Oh, Art, couldn't you play just a little of what you have so far? It would be so exciting to hear it as you develop it."

"Oh, ah, that really kind of violates my own personal artistic rules."

Art melted as Elisha displayed a cute little pout, sticking out her bottom lip and looking at him with her sad eyes. He immediately folded under the intoxicating pressure. "Well, maybe I could make an exception, once I get a little further into it."

"That would be great, Art. I can't wait. What did you do this weekend? Did you stay around here and work on it or did you actually get out of here?"

Art had not anticipated that question and without much thought, found himself telling Elisha about getting up early and taking the train to Boston to spend the day at the Boston Public Library. He had never been to the Boston Public Library but he found himself going into detail about how he walked around in the library to find the most isolated spot in order to sequester himself to work on the composition and how he got so lost in working on it he lost track of time and almost missed the train back out of Boston.

As he spoke, he watched as Elisha listened intently, soaking up every detail about her song. By that time, the rest of the group started arriving and the conversation turned to the concert of the night before. Art saw this as his way of escape and politely excused himself to get some homework completed before his next class. On the way out of the cafeteria he happened to walk past Dizz sitting at a table by himself.

"Paying homage to the royalty, Art?"

Art gave Dizz a disgusted look. "Yeah, sure, Dizz. Actually, I was just covering. I'll talk with you about it later tonight in my room."

"Sure, Art, wouldn't want to blow your 'cool guy' cover."

"Knock it off, Dizz! I'll talk with you later."

Irritated, Art headed back to his room and skipped his afternoon classes. He spent the time reading through the series of articles that he had found in the *Boston Globe* featuring an ongoing debate between those who advocated there should be no restrictions placed on any research that had the potential of enhancing and improving mankind and those who, for moral, religious or ethical reasons, desired that each new technology be extensively scrutinized in order to assure that society would proceed in a way that would preserve humanness. Art thought that the articles clearly leaned in the favor of allowing any and all research that may enhance or improve the 'human experience'.

A good number of the experts quoted in the articles had, at sometime, participated or had been invited to provide input to the President's Council on Bioethics that was put together just after the turn of the century, back during the Bush administration, when discoveries in biotechnology were booming. The Bush administration clearly came down on the side of restraint, weighing the possible impact of the implementation of each new technology. With the new administration in 2009 stating that it would "restore science to its rightful place", those wanting to cast aside all restraint came into favor and were successful getting the government to fund the majority of their research.

Of great interest to Art was an article mentioning two up and coming young scientists in the field of human enhancement who were providing amazing breakthroughs in the areas of genetics research and pharmacogenetics. It appeared that the information from the Human Genome Project had allowed these two to leap to the top of their respective fields. Art was somewhat stunned to see their names in print—Virginia Holister and Aaron Taylor. This confirmed the information that Dizz had relayed to him earlier. The article included a few quotes from Mr. Taylor about how the driving force behind his work is the elimination of pain, suffering, and disease. Art thought to himself that Gene had certainly ventured way past the elimination of suffering and disease. Now he wanted to enhance appearance, personality, and athletic performance for the rich and famous.

There were no quotes from Virginia, just the mention of her amazing breakthroughs in the area of gene manipulation to eliminate disease and to select desirable traits in future generations.

Art was fascinated with the arguments from the other side of the issue. Most were promoted by a local Boston-area geneticist named Derrick Moss who had been involved with some early genetics work with Virginia and was at one time a participant on the President's Council of Bioethics.

Art was impressed by the thought-provoking issues raised by Moss. Issues like where would all of this technology take us as a human race? Would we be content with curing the sick, relieving suffering, and eradicating disease, or would we be more interested in improving our existence and literally engineering future generations? Who would define improvement? Who would control access to those improvements? Would only those who could afford the improvements have access to them? Would this create two distinct classes, or even races? Would this create another layer of discrimination? Who would decide what or who was good and desirable and what or who was bad or undesirable? Would these improvements be forced upon people for "the greater good"? Who would decide when these technologies should be used and when they were being abused?

Moss's statements in the articles consistently voiced his concern that the means and the ends were quickly becoming detached from each other. He said that initial advancements in technology had been properly used to accomplish the primary end of alleviating suffering and curing disease. Now he saw that the incredible advances in technology were allowing a shift away from the primary goal to a new goal—that of re-engineering society. Moss believed this could possibly result in the end of the human race as we now know it.

Some of the other information that Art had brought back with him made it clear that after 2009, those who had wanted the elimination of all restrictions on research, for all practical purposes, won out. That was about the same time that the Department of Human Enhancement was brought into existence, bringing all of the issues arising from genetics research, embryonic stem cell research, human cloning, nanotechnology, genetic engineering, pharmacogenetics, and the patents generated by these new technologies under one roof. From that point forward, Art found no mention of Moss or the dissenting point of view.

Reading through the information only aroused Art's curiosity. Was his presence at Hawthorne and his new-found inclusion in the Taylor "inner circle" just a coincidence? He had a nagging suspicion that the Taylors had some kind of connection with DHE, a connection that somehow included him and his past. Was Jason Alexander really from the DHE and not the bank? Art knew that he needed another trip to Boston to dig up more information on the Taylors, DHE, and maybe Mr. Moss. Maybe he'd even have time to look up some information about chimeras.

Art had been scouring through the information for the last seven hours without a break. He'd missed dinner, but he wasn't hungry. He decided to formulate a future strategy with Dizz. He bolted out of his room and down the hall to Dizz's door. He had to knock several times before Dizz finally opened the door, looking like he just woke up.

"What's up, Art?" said Dizz looking annoyed.

Art pushed the door open just wide enough to walk in and close the door behind him. "I read through most of the information from the weekend and I need to go back and do some more searching."

"Wow, Art, you are more fired up than I have ever seen you. What did you find out that's got you so eager to go back to Phil's place?"

"Nothing really that specific, but enough that I need to look for some more information to see if there is some kind of connection between the Taylors, DHE, Jason Alexander, and my own history, or lack thereof."

Art spent the next half hour sharing with Dizz in a general way what he had found. Dizz patiently listened to Art's disjointed presentation of the information, then agreed that he didn't hear anything that was earth shattering, but it was enough to give rise to questions that might lead somewhere. Dizz also agreed to try to set up another session at Phil's place this coming Saturday or Sunday.

Art then asked for some strategy for approaching Jason Alexander. "Dizz, what would you think if I were to contact my trustee through the school office like I always do? I'd ask him a few questions about my parents, possible relatives, and getting to see court records after my eighteenth birthday?"

Dizz thought about it for a little and then grinned deviously, "I think it may work. You could tell him that since you are a senior with open campus privileges, you'd like to come down to his office at the bank in Boston and meet with him. If he squirms, it might be a good indication that he really isn't with the bank."

"Great idea, Dizz. What do you think about accessing the information on Gene Taylor's business card?"

"I think its okay, but I wouldn't do both too close together. Hey, I just thought of something. Let's take the card when we go to Phil's and see what we can access on the stand-alone system without going online. We may not get much, but at least it will be undetected. Then you can access the rest of it here sometime later. It will be interesting to see if the Hawthorne system's built-in restrictions let you access the information online through the card. If it doesn't, it means that someone at Hawthorne has purposefully restricted your access to information about Gene Taylor and TEI."

It was getting late. Art left and went back to his room. His mind was racing. He wondered if he was actually getting close to information that would help him figure out the mysteries of his past. He had a couple more articles to read through, so he decided to forego his homework and continue to plow through the information.

He didn't find much else of interest except the mention of Virginia's employment at Massachusetts Cryogenic Centers, Inc. located in Newton, which specialized in sperm banking, assisted reproductive technology, and umbilical cord storage to preserve stem cells for future use in treating disease. It dawned on him that Dizz had mentioned that his donor sperm came from a sperm bank in Newton. He walked out of his room, jogged down the hall and banged on Dizz's door. The door cracked open and Dizz, somewhat annoyed asked, "What now, Art? Its really late, and some of us actually like to sleep."

"Dizz, what sperm bank did you, I mean your father or donor, whatever, come from? Was it from a sperm bank in Newton? Was it the Massachusetts Cryogenic Center?"

Dizz perked up. "Yeah, how would you know the name?"

"Virginia Taylor worked for MCC during the period of time that your mom got the sperm donation from there."

"So, where does that get me?"

"Well, I was thinking that I have a pretty decent relationship with Mrs. Taylor. Maybe I can get her to do me a favor and help you get to the background information on your donor."

Dizz rolled his eyes and cocked his head slightly to the left, looking a little peeved. "It's a nice thought, but she could get sued big time for breaching the confidentiality of a donor source."

"Oh, yeah, I hadn't thought about that. Sorry . . . really sorry I bothered you, goodnight, Dizz." Art turned and walked away, embarrassed that he hadn't thought it out better, but disappointed he could not help Dizz. Still, there had to be a way Virginia could help him access that information. Feeling depressed, he immediately climbed into bed upon entering his room.

During his free hour the next day, Art went to the office and put in his request to be contacted by his trustee, Jason Alexander. The office informed him that they would contact Mr. Alexander and have him get back to Art. Art really liked the idea of testing Mr. Alexander by suggesting he come to Boston to meet him at the bank office.

It didn't take to long for Mr. Alexander to return the call. The office paged Art and told him that the call would be forwarded to his cell phone. Art was a little nervous, but ready to test Mr. Alexander.

"Hello, is this Mr. Alexander?"

"Yes, Art, this is Mr. Alexander. Is everything all right at Hawthorne?"

"Yes, yes, things are fine, I just wanted to get a hold of you to set up a time to meet and discuss the terms of the trust when I turn eighteen in April."

"Oh, sure, we can do that. I had planned to come and visit you about a week after your eighteenth birthday. Your birthday falls during the Hawthorne spring break this year, and I assumed you will be hosted by one of the Hawthorne families and will be out of town that week. When we meet, I will explain all of the terms of the trust triggered by your birthday. I can try to answer any questions you may have then."

"Actually, Mr. Alexander, I was thinking that I would like to know what is coming at me, so I would like to meet sometime during the next couple of weeks. Since I am a senior this year, I have open campus privileges and I would like to take a little trip into Boston to meet with you at the bank. I only have one class on Fridays—music theory—which I don't need to attend. I thought I could catch the train in and meet you at your office."

"Well . . . Art, that would be fine, except that I'm scheduled to be in New York this Friday to meet with another one of our trust clients. If you really want to meet earlier, I'll try to find some time to come out the week after next to meet with you."

"Thanks, Mr. Alexander, but I'm really looking for a good reason to get off campus for a day and I think a trip to Boston would help my mental disposition. I've been feeling cooped up here and need a change of scenery."

There was a longer than normal pause in the conversation before Mr. Alexander replied. "I'm going to need to sit down with my assistant and see if there is a Friday in the next couple of weeks where I can squeeze you in for a meeting. My Fridays are usually pretty packed. I'll give you a call back in a few days and let you know if it will work out. Okay?"

"Okay. Thanks, Mr. Alexander. I'll be waiting for your call. Have a nice trip to New York."

"Pardon? Oh, oh, I will. Take care of yourself, Art. I'll get back with you. Goodbye."

"Goodbye, Mr. Alexander."

10

Gene's Quandary

ERIC HUNG UP THE PHONE and immediately placed an emergency call to Gene. The receptionist at TEI pulled Gene out of a new product meeting to take the call from Eric.

"Eric, this better be exceptionally important to pull me out of a scheduled meeting. What's up?"

"Gene, it's your project, Art. He just called and requested to set up a meeting with me at the bank office to go over the items in the trust that will be triggered by his eighteenth birthday."

"I hope you were adept at sidestepping his request."

"I think I did pretty well, but he was persistent. He said that he's been feeling cooped up and wants to make a trip into Boston to meet with me. I deflected all the dates he requested, telling him I had already scheduled out-of-office appointments for those days. He wants me to get back with him to see if I can meet with him sometime in the next couple of weeks. I'm also wondering if something has happened to bring about this request. You said you had people at Hawthorne keeping a close watch on him. I think I would give them a call and see if there is anything strange going on."

"Eric, for the time being, continue to stall. I don't want to go to the trouble of setting up a fake office unless I absolutely have to. It would take a lot of favors to pull it off and it would signal the board that things may not be going well with our project. Also, we need those fake trust documents, along with the death certificates for his parents. I can't believe we waited so long before we started working on all of this backfill stuff."

"Gotcha, Gene. I'll work on the documents and let you know if I hear from Art again. I think what I'll do is wait a week or so, then call him back and tell him I am totally booked up until after his birthday, but tell him I could try to get out to Hawthorne on my way to one of my other appointments."

"Sounds great, Eric. I'll get with my Hawthorne sources and see if they have noticed anything out of the ordinary with Art lately. I'll get back to you once I know anything."

"Thanks, Gene, we'll be talking."

As soon as Gene hung up he put in a call to Elisha's cell phone. "Hi, Elisha, honey. This is Dad—did I get you at a bad time?"

"Hi, Daddy. This is a good time. I just got out of class and I was taking a break before swim team practice. Is everything okay? You and Mom usually only call on the weekend."

"Everything is fine. I just had an unexpected break and I haven't talked with you for a while so I thought I would call to see how you're doing. Is everything going well for you?"

"Yeah, things are going great. I like my classes, my grades are good, swim team's good, and my social life has been really fun lately. We all went to a great concert last weekend in Boston."

"Sounds great, honey. Did Art go with you to the concert?"

"No, but Dad, you're not going to believe this. Art is writing a composition for me. Instead of going to the concert, he spent the day at the Boston Public Library working on it."

"So, he went to Boston and spent the day at the library working on a musical composition for you? Very impressive! Is Art doing okay? Is he fitting in with you and your friends?"

"Oh, yeah, he hangs out with us quite a bit. He's really a pretty nice guy."

"I'm glad to hear you're having a good winter session. I'm looking forward to spending time with you during spring break. I think we'll go down to the beach cottage in New Smyrna Beach."

"Sounds great, Dad! I love that place and all the memories of those monster sand castles and sand sculptures you used to make for us."

"Yeah, those were good times. We'll have to build one more for old time's sake. Well, honey, I've got to get back to a meeting. Keep up the good work at school."

"Bye, Daddy. See you at the beach."

Gene immediately placed a call to the Director of Security at Hawthorne. "Hello, Marcus, Gene Taylor."

"Hello, Mr. Taylor, what can I do for you?"

"I have a small favor to ask. I am doing a little checking into the background of one of our Hawthorne students who has shown some interest in my daughter, Elisha, and I am wondering if you can help me with some information?"

"Sure, no problem. Always happy to help you out, Mr. Taylor. What would you like me to do for you?"

"It's not much really, I just need you to send me the phone and internet records for Art Jenicks for the last month. Cell phone records, too, if you can. Oh, and also I would like a record of anytime he left and returned to campus."

"No problem. Since cell phones are issued to the students when they arrive, we have access to those records too. I'll have those for you this afternoon. Where would you like me to send the information?"

"Just send it to my email and I'll look through them tonight."

When Gene arrived home that evening he went into his study and opened the email from Marcus containing the information he requested. He started by searching the internet records, wading through the listings of mostly music and video sites. He then reviewed the section showing the attempted searches to Hawthorne restricted websites. Art had made several attempts to access the Department of Human Enhancements website. Noting the date of the searches, he pulled out the chronological data to see what other searches Art had made that day and found that Art had also entered searches for Boston Mercantile Bank & Trust and for Jason Alexander.

Art's outgoing cell phone records were sparse, but Gene did note a call to Boston Mercantile on the same date of his internet search. Next, Gene looked at the records of when Art had left and returned to Hawthorne. There was only one exit and one entry logged. Both were on the Sunday Elisha indicated that Art had gone to the Boston Public Library.

Marcus noted for Gene that there was an exit and later entry to Hawthorne by Edward Benson occurring at about the same time, which indicated that Art and Dizz had probably gone together that Sunday.

After reviewing the information from Marcus, Gene leaned back in his desk chair to contemplate the situation.

"Gene, are you okay?" questioned Virginia.

Gene was startled as Virginia's voice broke the silence. "You scared me for a second. No, I'm not okay. I have a gut feeling that something strange is going on with Art."

"Why, what happened?" Virginia leaned against the doorway, a note of concern in her tone.

"It appears that Art has been doing some digging into his past as well as a few other things."

"It's only natural that an orphan is going to try to dig into his past. What other things has he been digging into?"

"I had his internet records pulled. It showed that he tried to look up some information about the Department of Human Enhancement. I can't figure out what might have prompted Art to search for information about the D H E."

"That does seem a bit strange, but maybe it had to do with one of his school assignments."

"I seriously doubt that. It doesn't sound like something a music major would be required to look up."

"Is that it?" Virginia queried, obviously hoping to minimize what Gene had found out and put his mind at ease.

"No, there's more. I just can't believe how stupid I've been not to anticipate the possibility that a curious teenager would look up information on his own trustee. His phone records indicate that he called the trust department at Boston Mercantile, probably looking to talk to his trustee, Jason Alexander. I'm assuming he was told that no such person worked at the bank. Now, I'll probably have to set up a fake office and come up with a believable explanation for why Mr. Alexander's name is absent from the company directory. Making up the story will be the easy part. Setting up an office that looks legitimate will take some favors—favors that I really don't want to use."

"Don't you think you may be overreacting?"

"I wish! After that Art contacted Eric, or should I say Jason Alexander, through the school and requested a meeting with Eric at the bank to discuss the terms of his trust and what happens when he turns eighteen. He said he felt cooped up and needed to get off campus for a day and come to Boston."

"That doesn't sound like an unusual request."

"No, not unless you were just in Boston the weekend before. I called Elisha just to see how Art was doing and she said Art told her he went to the Boston Public Library last Sunday to work on a composition for her."

"That still doesn't sound too bad. What are you thinking?"

"Well, I've always been concerned about Art getting mixed up with Dizz in one of his little schemes. According to the Hawthorne entrance and exit records, it looks like Art and Dizz left and returned together that day, which means they spent a whole Sunday together off campus a few weeks back doing who knows what. I seriously doubt that Dizz and Art went to the Boston Public Library."

"Maybe you're jumping to conclusions. You don't know that Dizz is getting him involved in something bad, and you don't know that they actually went to Boston. You have to remember that they are just a couple of teenage boys exploring life."

"Are you kidding? This is Dizz we are talking about. That kid is always up to something bordering on the illegal. I really thought exposure to Hawthorne would inspire him to channel his intellect in the right direction. Instead, I think we have provided him with more tools to put in his little bag of tricks."

"You still see a lot of yourself in him, don't you?"

"I'm not sure how to take that."

"I don't mean it in a bad way. I just think you see his potential based on a similar set of gifts and talents that you possess."

"Well, I do think I've passed a lot of those traits on to him."

"Are you still feeling guilty about not responding to all of those donor inquiries?"

"No, no, I've never felt guilty, only responsible. That's why I pulled some strings to get him a full scholarship to Hawthorne. The kid has a lot of potential, if he could just get focused in the right direction."

"You mean like you did."

"I'm not quite sure how to take that statement either."

Virginia smiled slightly, shrugged her shoulders and slowly turned and walked out the door of Gene's study leaving him with a final sarcastic jab. "Take it the way it works best for you."

After Virginia left, Gene immediately placed a call to Eric and started peppering him with questions. "Eric, I have a few questions on the status of the Jenicks case. When will all the death certificates be fabricated and placed in the records?"

"They have been prepared but we have not gotten them into the public records yet. We're working on it."

"The sooner the better, Eric. How about Art's birth certificate?"

"We have it all prepared to show Art, but we haven't inserted it into the public records yet either."

"What about old newspaper stories of the explosion, with pictures of the house?"

"We had one of NSA's best document experts put a bunch of stuff together. It's pretty impressive, extremely believable, including some old newspaper clippings. He even told me he was going to insert the story and pictures into the *Boston Globe's* online archives."

"And how are you on the story? Are you prepared to walk through the file with Art and tell the story?"

"I'm almost ready. I'll keep rehearsing it. My presentation will be extremely believable and professional."

"Okay, this is big. There is no room for error. No room for even a hint of question. No room for any inconsistencies. Okay?"

"Okay, Gene, this will be perfect."

"Good, that's what I wanted to hear."

"Gene, why all of the questions. Do we have a problem?"

"Maybe, I don't want to talk about it on the phone. Why don't you drop by my office tomorrow afternoon so I can bring you up to speed and we can put together a plan of action.

11

Searching for Answers

ART WAS DISPLAYING what appeared to be all the signs of "senioritis"—skipping classes, failing to turn in assignments, daydreaming in class. This was a common occurrence for most of the seniors in their final semester, so when Art started displaying these behaviors, his teachers attributed it to the normal course of a senior's year.

It was Wednesday, and Art had daydreamed his way through yet another day at Hawthorne. Unlike the other seniors who were dreaming of graduation and a summer break, Art's daydreams were about finding answers to his past.

Finally, the last class of the day was over and Art hurried back to find Dizz to see if he was able to set up the TPA session with Phil. He found Dizz in his room listening to—what else—jazz from the previous century.

"I've been expecting you," Dizz said as he opened his door for Art. "You are no doubt wondering if I got things set up with Phil. The answer is yes, with conditions."

"Conditions? What do you mean by 'conditions'?"

"It's like this. Phil's got a pretty big TPA day booked for Saturday. He said we could come as long as we do all of our TPA down with the popsicles in the basement."

"That's not a condition. That's a curse, and you love it, don't you, Dizz."

"Yeah, I kinda do. Are you in?"

Art closed his eyes and with a disgusted look on his face reluctantly uttered, "Okay, okay, I'm in, but here's my condition: we do not talk about or go see the other people who will be down there with us."

"Deal. Come by my room around ten on Saturday morning. We'll take the train in and spend four or five hours there and come back Saturday night after we hit the best pizza joint in Boston."

For the rest of the week, Art felt like he was living in slow motion. Saturday finally arrived and Art and Dizz officially checked out of Hawthorne at about ten-fifteen in the morning and headed for the train station. The weather was much warmer for this trip, which made the final trek from the Roxbury train station to the Essex almost enjoyable.

Phil met them again at the back door and ushered them down to the basement. He hardly spoke to either of them, other than reiterating that everything that happens at the Essex is never shared with anyone, anywhere, for any reason. Phil abruptly left the boys and headed upstairs.

"He seemed a little cool. You think he is really okay with us being here?" questioned Art.

"Don't worry, Art. Phil is just a moody creature. He tends to get pretty stressed on busy days and his focus can be misinterpreted. He's fine with us being here. If not, he would have just said no when I asked him if we could come again. Hey, time is a wastin'. Let's get going. I have nothing to look for today, so I'll help you look for anything you want. What do you want me to find out for you?

Art smiled and pulled a handwritten list out of his pocket and handed it to Dizz. "Thanks, Dizz. That would be great. Could you try to find out any information you can about my parents' death, like obituaries, newspaper articles about the accident, death certificates? Basically anything you could find would be great."

"I'm impressed, Art. You've really thought about this."

"All I've done for the last week is think about this."

"What are you going to be looking for?"

"I'm going to see if I can find some more information on the DHE and a Mr. Moss. I also want to take a look at the TEI business card that I got from Mr. Taylor."

"You're really into that Moss guy. What's up with that?"

"I don't know exactly. The stuff written by this guy fascinates me and I have this hunch, or maybe you could call it a premonition, that somehow he may be the key to unlocking some of my past."

"Spooky. Okay then, what were your parent's names?"

"Henry P. and Sarah M. Jenicks. They lived in the Boston area, so searching old newspaper archives and government records will hopefully turn up something."

The boys went to work. Neither talked for a period of about two hours, until Dizz broke the silence.

"I can't find a thing, not a single thing. Nothing comes up anywhere. The newspapers, county records, state records, vital records, nothing. Nothing even comes up when I do a general search on the name Jenicks, except articles about you. And just out of curiosity, I did a search for your birth certificate. Zip, zero, nothing, man. You don't even exist! Wow, I can think of a number of things you can get away with if you weren't even born, like—"

Art interrupted Dizz midsentence, "This may seem like an exciting opportunity for you, but this is a disaster for me. I'm trying to find out who I am and where I came from and you tell me that I don't even exist."

"Sorry, Art. You exist man, you know . . . "

"I know, I know, you just like to beat the system and you think this provides some great opportunities to pull off another scam of some kind. Dizz, I'm not you, okay? I just want some answers."

Dizz forced a smile, indicating that he was sorry for his comment. "What else can I look for? Hey, have you searched for chimeras yet?"

"No, see what you can find. I'm still trying to find out more about the Taylors' ties to the DHE and what happened to Moss."

"Any major discoveries yet?"

"Well, I found out that Moss and the Taylors collaborated on some early projects in the quest to eliminate birth defects and genetic diseases, but then there seems to have been a definite break in the relationship when the Taylors shifted from eradicating birth defects and disease to the field of human enhancement. Moss was quoted as saying that he was extremely disappointed that the focus of their research had taken a new direction that did not match with his ethical and moral views. I'm really curious to look at the TEI Business card to check out the direction Mr. Taylor and Virginia have taken since parting ways with Moss."

"I'd like to see what ol' Gene is up to also. Let me know when you are going to look at the card. Remember that when we do it, we have to use a computer that is not connected to the internet. We can't risk TEI being able to track the access back to the computers here at the Essex. That would raise a huge red flag. Why would an old geezer in a flophouse have Gene's personal business card, you know what I mean?"

Art nodded his agreement and both boys returned back to their searching. With about half an hour left in their session,

Dizz interrupted Art's searching, "Hey Art, we're running out of time. Let's take a quick look at that business card. There's an old stand-alone computer in the other room that I can fire up."

The boys headed to the other room, started up the computer and inserted the business card into the reader. The information available from the card was limited to the basic corporate information about TEI found on their company website. As Dizz predicted, most of the categories on the card were empty shells that required connection to the internet. With a computer that was connected to the internet, insertion of the card would allow the card to access the internet to retrieve specific information off of the company website. Obviously, the card was used as a business tool, so that the areas accessed and the areas of the user's interest could be tracked, recorded, and stored in anticipation of future business meetings with the person to whom the card was given.

"I really don't think it's a big deal for me to use the card back at Hawthorne. After all, Mr. Taylor did give me the card with the intention that I would look at it."

"Yeah, it's probably not a problem. Anyway, grab the card. We need to get out of here or we won't have enough time for the best pizza on the planet."

Art grabbed the card and the two boys jogged up the stairs, let themselves out the back door, and headed down the alley on their way to Michelangelo's Pizzeria. On the way, Dizz broke the silence. "Hey, you must have found some interesting stuff. Are you okay?"

"Yeah, sure, I'm fine. I don't think I found anything amazing. I'm just trying to figure out if any of this fits together. I wish I could talk to that Moss guy. I bet I could get some good information from him."

"Maybe you can. Did you try to locate him?"

"He seems to have just disappeared from the public eye in late 2008. At least there is nothing in the papers or anything else about him after that date. The only mention of his whereabouts was in an article where he was being interviewed at his parents' farm just south of Walden Pond in Baker Bridge. But that was years ago and it was his parents' farm, not his."

"You know, Walden Pond is only four or five miles south of Hawthorne. It couldn't hurt to run down there sometime and see if you can dig around and come up with information about him."

"Okay, maybe I will. I guess I've got nothing to lose. Hey, did you find out anything about chimeras?

"Actually, I found quite a bit. I'll tell you all about it at Michelangelo's. Come on, we gotta get moving or we'll be late for the train."

The boys jogged the last few blocks to Michelangelo's Pizza. Not being in the best of shape, it was several minutes before they were breathing normally. Once Art sufficiently caught his breath, he anxiously asked Dizz what he found out about chimeras. Dizz loved that he had information that Art so badly wanted to hear.

"What's it worth to you to find out about chimeras, Art?"

"Oh, no, you're not going to lower yourself to extortion are you?"

"Come on, Art, you know I don't have a strong moral compass, so extortion is not a problem for me."

"All right, Dizz, you've had your fun. What did you find out?

"Not so fast. For all of this, the TPA, the information, the excellent company on train rides, the humor, the secrecy, the intrigue, you owe me dinner and a favor yet to be determined. Deal?"

Art took a deep breath and folded his arms. "I'm going to regret this. Deal."

"Great! No backing out on this."

"Deal. I said deal, okay?"

The waitress came over to their table and Dizz immediately ordered an extra large mushroom and sausage pizza for the two of them.

"Okay, while we're waiting for our pizza, here's the info. I downloaded a lot of it on my PACA so I wouldn't miss some of the details." Scrolling through information, Dizz finally said, "Okay, here it is. The actual word 'chimera' comes from Greek mythology. It was used to describe a creature that was part lion, part goat, and part serpent that terrorized some Greek city. It appears that right before the turn of the century, a professor in developmental biology applied for a patent with the U.S. Patent Office for a biotechnological contrivance that would combine two or more species that normally would not cross sexually. He found that injecting the embryonic stem cells of one or more species into the embryo of another species and then allowing the embryo to develop in the womb of the other species would create a hybrid creature. The new creature, called a chimera, would contain cells of each species. The type of creature would pretty much depend on the number of cells placed in the embryo. So, it seems that the new chimera could end up looking like one creature but have the organs and intelligence of another."

"You're embellishing this a bit, aren't you, Dizz?"

"Nope, I'm basically paraphrasing right from the article."

"That's pretty weird stuff. What else does it say?"

"It seems that the professor who applied for the patent did so because he found the possibility of creating such creatures morally offensive. He thought that if he controlled the patent, he could keep such creatures from being brought into existence at least for the length of the patent, which is twenty years. The article also says that the patent application cited biomedical uses like growing rejection-proof organs in animals like pigs, but that the technology could be used to breed soldiers who were impervious to heat, with armadillo-like skin."

"Wait, what did you just say?"

"The patent application cited bio . . . "

Art interrupted, "No, what did you say about skin?"

"Oh, it said that the technology could be used to breed or produce soldiers with armadillo-like skin."

"Now I see the connection. If you could breed a species with armadillo-like skin, they would not be affected by cactus needles, would they?"

"Probably not."

"But why would Mr. Taylor get so freaked out at Chris for bringing up chimeras? What did he not want me to hear and why did he not want me to hear it? What else does it say?"

"It seems the U.S. Patent Office kept turning the patent down until finally after about seven years, the patent office officially rejected the patent application. That was in 2005."

"So, does that mean it's legal or illegal to make or engineer these creatures?"

"I don't exactly know. It did say that there was a company out of Boston, Advanced Cell Innovations or ACI, that was putting human DNA into cow embryos to make and then patent human stem cells. ACI was also breeding designer pigs to produce rejection-proof, human-size kidneys, hearts, livers, and pancreases for transplant patients."

"Wait! The information I have said that Moss used to work with ACI. Moss, Mr. Taylor, and Virginia, collaborated on some projects at ACI that Moss said was responsible for waking him up to the potential harm genetic technology could bring about if not carefully controlled and monitored. Is there any thing else?"

"Yeah, it appears that this was one of the issues that got the Federal Government to step in to form the Department of Human Enhancement. Now all issues and anything dealing with the ability to patent or own such processes or creatures have to be approved by DHE.

"So, Dizz, what do you think? Do you believe Mr. Taylor or TEI have any connection or link with DHE?"

"My guess would be a giant, yes! Isn't that what Taylor's business is all about, enhancing or improving the human species? How could he not have some connection with DHE? TEI probably has classified contracts with DHE and DARPA."

"Darpa? What's darpa?"

"DARPA stands for the Defense Advanced Research Projects Agency. It's the research arm of the Pentagon. They take any technology out there, whether genetic, nano, robotic, or informational and develop it for national defense purposes. They're the guys, who among other things, figured out how to use robotics to connect a fighter pilot's brain to the controls of the plane so the pilot can directly control the plane with his brain.

"So, do you think Taylor and TEI are part of some kind of secret research arm for DARPA that may be doing genetic research for defense purposes?"

"I don't know, but it certainly seems possible knowing what we know. You have to admit, it's a great little conspiracy theory."

"This is all wild stuff. I just don't know if any of it actually fits together. I guess it's all possible. I mean, we could imagine and speculate all day, but it could all just be us creating fiction."

"I don't know, Art, I think there are an awful lot of pieces that fit together rather nicely. I really think something weird is going on with Mr. Taylor. If I were you, I would at least see what happens with the meeting requested with your trustee, and I would try to locate that Moss guy and talk with him."

A steaming hot pizza was delivered to their table and silence, except for an occasional moan, overtook the table as the boys inhaled slice after slice.

"Dizz, you were right. This is the best on the planet. Well worth the money."

The boys left for the train station stuffed to the max, almost to the point of being sick. Fortunately, they had about a half-hour's wait prior to boarding to let their digestion catch up with their gluttony before having to experience the motion of the train.

When the boys finally made it home to Hawthorne, they were both happy just to go to bed.

12

Boston Mercantile Bank & Trust

ART WAS IN HIS ROOM on a late Tuesday afternoon taking a little nap before dinner when he received a call from Mr. Alexander. Art, a bit stunned by the call, didn't immediately respond when he heard his trustee's voice.

"Hello, Art. Hello? Art, are you there?" questioned Mr. Alexander.

"Yeah, I'm here," replied Art, trying to wake up.

"Art, I am wondering if you can come into the bank and meet with me this coming Friday afternoon at two o'clock?"

"Ah, I . . . I'll just check my schedule. Yeah, Friday at two works great. Should I just go to the trust department at the bank?"

"No, we're separate from the main trust department. I am in the Private Trust Division, which is totally separate from the main trust department at the bank. The Private Trust Division is set up specifically to handle trusts for minors and, as such, has strict privacy standards in place. As a result, we are virtually invisible to the public and accessible only by appointment. Even our offices are not located at the main bank facility, and we have a totally separate unlisted phone number."

"How do you get your customers if no one can find you?"

"Good question. Anyone coming into the bank looking to set up a trust for a minor is referred to our office."

Eric provided Art with the address and private telephone number for the Private Trust Department. By the time the phone call was over, most of Art's doubts about Mr. Alexander actually working at the bank had dissipated. For the most part, Art bought the explanation, but lingering doubts prompted him to call the private trust department's phone number, just to make sure.

"Boston Mercantile Bank & Trust, Private Trust Division. May I help you?"

"Yes, this is Art Jenicks. I was just speaking with Mr. Alexander and had another question for him. Is he available?"

"I'm sorry; Mr. Alexander just went into a client meeting. Would you like me to have him return your call?"

"No, I'll just call back later. Thanks."

Art hung up, sufficiently satisfied that Jason Alexander did, in fact, work for the bank. He sat on his bed questioning all the assumptions he had made based on his belief that Jason Alexander was really not his bank trustee. Mr. Alexander certainly appeared to be legit. Art wondered if he and Dizz had let themselves get carried away with their little conspiracy theories. He had thought they were connecting the dots and putting things together. Now he was not sure of anything.

He left his room and walked down the hall to Dizz's room. He was glad to find Dizz in his room and willing to listen to the most recent turn of events. Dizz listened to Art's verbal replay of his conversation with Jason Alexander and his call back to the Private Trust Division office. Art rambled on about letting their imaginations get away from them and being the victims of their own little conspiracy theories.

Finally Dizz broke into the rambling, "Art! Art! Wait a minute! Slow down! What happened with Mr. Alexander doesn't prove anything or negate any of our speculations. It only gives us more information and time to see how things will play out. I have personally never heard of a private trust division inside a trust department at a bank. That doesn't mean they can't have one, it just sounds odd. It also doesn't even begin to nullify all of the other weird stuff that's going on-like the Hawthorne computers freezing up, the initials DHE on Mr. Alexander's brief case, Mr. Alexander being at the hospital when you were attacked by cactus, and Mr. Taylor freaking out when Chris mentioned chimeras. And don't forget my not being able to find anything about your parents or a birth certificate for you. All these things may have no connection, but you should at least play things out a little further before you just give up."

Art looked even more confused. He felt like he was being emotionally tossed back and forth between reality and fiction. After not saying anything for a couple of minutes, he finally broke his silence.

"Okay, I'll play this thing out and see what develops. I'm really at a loss. What do I do next?"

Before he could answer, Art's cell phone rang. The words TEI showed up on the touch screen.

Art, looking perplexed, answered the call. "Hello, this is Art."

"Hi, Art, Gene Taylor. Did I get you at a bad time?"

"Oh, no, this is a good time."

"Good, I just wanted to give you a call and invite you to spend spring break with us in Florida. I feel bad that you didn't get to enjoy much of the Arizona trip so I thought some time on the beach would be a good way to make it up to you."

"Make it up to me? You don't have to make anything up to me."

"Okay, but at least let us try to make a better impression on you this time. Can you come for spring break with the kids?"

"Uh... yeah, I don't know why not, that would be great!"

"It's settled then, we'll expect you to come. We're going down to New Smyrna Beach, Florida. I'll have Elisha and Chris give you more details as the date approaches."

"Thanks, Mr. Taylor. I really appreciate you inviting me down."

"No, no, it's our pleasure! We'll see you on the plane. I've got to go. Take care, and study hard. Good-bye."

"Bye."

Art looked blissfully stunned.

"What's up?"

"Dizz, you won't believe it. I just got invited to go to Florida with the Taylors for spring break."

"Art, doesn't that seem at all strange to you that they would ask you to go on spring break with them?"

"No, they're my friends and we got along really well at Christmas. It seems natural enough. Why? Do you think it's strange?"

"Yeah, I think it's a little odd for them to take such a liking to you all of a sudden. However, it may be all a part of letting things play out. Earlier you asked me what you should do. Do you still want to know, or are you lost dreaming about Elisha and you and moonlight walks on the beach?"

"C'mon Dizz, you know I'd rather daydream about Elisha, but go ahead. What would you do next?"

Dizz rolled his eyes and shook his head. "Okay, the first thing you need to do is to get some exercise to tone yourself up for spring break. I think a good way to do that would be through a cycling exercise program."

"Dizz, what should I really do?"

"I'm serious. I think you should start cycling two-to-three times a week, and one of your trips should take you down past Walden Pond to see if you can dig up any information on the whereabouts of Mr. Moss. The cycling program will be a great cover if anyone asks you why you were gone. Besides, you really do need to tone up for your swim trunk debut at the beach. The other thing you need to do is put together your list of questions for your visit with Mr. Alexander. I'll help you with that. You'll need to really pay close attention to see if there are any inconsistencies in his answers. Next, you need to access Mr. Taylor's business card to see if there is any information that is tied into any of the other information you have already dug up. Accessing the business card will also help you be prepared to skillfully ask Mr. Taylor questions when you're with him in Florida. Lastly, at least until I think of other stuff to do, I will do a little more research on Boston Mercantile Bank & Trust and the so called "Private Trust Division." If what Mr. Alexander told you was correct, I should be able to get a referral to the Private Trust Division from the trust department at the bank if I ask about setting up a trust for a minor."

"Dizz, you're amazing! How do you think of all of this stuff?"

"Well," Dizz now grinned deviously, "I am a genius, and besides, I can think clearly not having a gorgeous blonde girlfriend to fog up my thinking processes."

13
Letting Things Play Out

IT WAS ELEVEN O'CLOCK on Saturday morning and there was an incessant knocking on Art's dorm room door. Reluctantly, Art got out of bed and shuffled over to open the door. He was met by Dizz's smiling face looking back at him.

"Why are you up so early, Dizz. What's going on?"

"Time to go check out some bikes from the rec center."

"How about in two or three hours. I stayed up till four A.M. watching old movies with Elisha and her friends and I'm exhausted."

"Four A.M.! That means you have gotten seven hours of sleep. That's plenty. Besides, the sun's out and it's nice and warm. In three hours it will be getting too cold to bike, and you gotta get in beach shape. Being laughed at on the beach could emotionally scar you for life."

"Dizz, you're a total pain, but I'm awake now. I'll be with you in about ten minutes."

Art got dressed, grabbed a bottle of water and an energy bar and headed to the recreation equipment shed with Dizz to check out some biking equipment.

Art was a little nervous. The last time he had ridden a bike was in middle school. When they arrived to check out the equipment, the attendant barraged them with questions.

"Would you like to check out an off-road bike, touring bike, or racing bike?"

Dizz piped in, "Two touring bikes."

"You want smart bikes or dumb bikes?"

"What's the difference?"

"The smart bikes will track your speed, mileage, your respiration and heart rate, and record where you've been. When you get back we take the information and provide you with a print out to show how you responded to different parts of the course. We can also set you up with beginner through expert courses so you can compare your times and physical responses to the norm."

Dizz interrupted, "We definitely want dumb bikes. We don't want to get too discouraged our first time out. Maybe after a few treks we'll move to the smart bikes."

"Okay. I'm assuming then, you just want the basic helmet?"

"What's the difference?" Dizz asked.

"The smart helmet will, if you want, provide constant readouts of your location, speed, etc. It will also give you directions if you get lost."

"We'll just go with the dumb everything . . . but we would like to see your suggested beginner courses."

"No problem. I'll get your measurements, set up your equipment and you'll be ready to go in about ten minutes. In the meantime you can take a look over the five suggested beginner courses."

While they were waiting for their equipment, Dizz and Art looked over the trails for beginners. They were bike paths of varying lengths through and around Concord. Simultaneously, they pointed to the one that they knew went by the Conrock Ice Cream Store.

"Don't you think we should get some reward for working hard?" rationalized Dizz.

Art nodded and smiled his agreement.

The attendant rolled up with the bikes and equipment. "Here you go, guys. You'll need to have it all back by six P.M."

The boys mounted the bikes and took off through the Hawthorne gates. They took the beginner's course directly to Conrock. Overall, they probably spent more time at Conrock than biking. While at Conrock, Dizz told Art that he was going into Boston on Monday afternoon to see Phil and he would try to check out the Boston Mercantile Bank & Trust "Private Trust Department for Minors."

In total, they stayed out on the bikes about four hours. It was the perfect early spring day for ice cream and just goofing around on the bikes.

On the final stretch back to Hawthorne Dizz commented to Art that he should establish the habit of biking two-to-three times a week with a longer ride on the weekend. He also told Art to always choose the dumb bikes and helmets so there would be no GPS record of where he went. Dizz suspected that the dumb bikes and helmets also probably had an imbedded chip so they could be located if lost or stolen but probably were not designed or used for live tracking.

Art was impressed with Dizz's foresight, but he was more impressed that Dizz really cared about him and was willing to stick his neck out to help him in the quest for his identity.

As promised, when Dizz finished his classes on Monday afternoon, he headed out to visit Phil at the Essex. He wanted to use the old landlines at the Essex so that the calls he intended to make would show up originating from a retirement facility.

Upon arriving at the backdoor of the Essex, Phil opened the door, looking perplexed. "What in the world are you doing here on a Monday? Aren't you supposed to be out at Hawthorne with all the little rich kids?"

"Yeah, I just needed to make a phone call from the Essex for a friend to check something out. I won't be long. I gotta get right back. I kinda snuck out through my secret exit, so I don't want to be gone too long and raise any suspicion."

Phil gave Dizz a stern look. "This isn't something that will get me or the Essex into any kind of trouble is it?"

"Na, I just need to get some information from a local trust company about the types of trusts they manage and I need to do it as an eighty-year-old and not a kid living at Hawthorne."

"You love this sort of stuff. You just can't keep from pulling a scam, can you?"

"It hasn't hurt your wallet any has it?"

"Okay, okay, point taken. Get in and make your call and then disappear. I mean that in the nicest way possible."

"Thanks, Phil, really, thanks, this will mean a lot to a friend of mine. Hey, do you still have that old box of stuff that I left here when I moved to Hawthorne?"

"I think it's still in the basement. Why?"

"I think it's got that phone prank kit I bought a long time ago from that spy store that used to be down the street. It's got a phone voice changer attachment that you can adjust to make yourself sound like an old man."

"The box should be in that little room right behind the freezer room."

"Thanks Phil. By the way, how's the occupancy rate down there?"

"Currently there is no room in the inn, so cash flow is good."

Dizz skipped down the stairs through the freezer room and into the back storage room. He found the box and the phone prank kit. He took it into the basement office, found some new batteries for the kit, and hooked it up for a test. He was pleased; it still worked perfectly, giving him the raspy voice of an eighty-year-old. Taking a big breath, he called Boston Mercantile Bank & Trust. He worked his way through the automated responses until he got a live person in the trust department.

"Trust Department, how can we help you today?"

"Yes, yes, are you there?"

"Yes, sir, can I help you?"

"Well, I certainly hope so. My name is Vincent Purdue and I would like to speak to someone about setting up a trust for a minor."

"Mr. Purdue, I'll transfer you over to our Minors Trust Department and let you speak with someone in that department. They can answer any questions you may have regarding establishing a trust for a minor."

"Well, thank you young lady."

"Please hold while I transfer you."

Dizz took another big breath and thought to himself, *So far, so good*.

"Minors Trust Department, this is Jason Welch, how can I help you?"

"Yes, yes, this is Vincent Purdue and I'm interested in finding out about setting up a trust for a minor."

"I can help you with that, Mr. Purdue. Can you provide me with some background information concerning the reason for the trust, so I can steer you in the right direction?"

"Well, it's a sad, sad, circumstance young man, a sad circumstance. You see, the trust would be for my grandson, Ren

Nolte. His mother, my daughter, died during childbirth, so he has been living with his father, Mark Nolte. Ren is currently eight years old and his dad has been diagnosed with cancer and probably only has a couple of months to live."

"I'm really sorry to hear that Mr. Purdue."

"Thanks, it's a tough situation because I'm eighty-seven years old, living in a retirement home, if you could call it that, and I'm not able to take care of the boy. I wish I were. It breaks my heart. Anyway, his father has a very substantial life insurance policy of which Ren is the beneficiary. Currently, Mark has no will or trust set up to handle the whole situation. Can you guys put a trust together to handle something like that?"

"Oh, yes, Mr. Purdue, we put them in place everyday. We would need Mr. Nolte to set up an appointment with us as soon as possible to work out the details in order to get the trust put in place."

"Good, good. I have another question. What do you do there at the bank to protect a minor's privacy? You know, to keep him from financial predators. Do you have a special private trust department for minors?"

"We have all kinds of special protection in place to protect the identity and privacy of all our minor trust beneficiaries. It is standard operating procedure for all of our trusts and all of our trust beneficiaries. We have a division that handles trusts for minors, but we don't have any special or separate private trust department because all of our trusts are private."

"Sounds good. I must have you mixed up with one of the other banks I've talked to. This can get pretty confusing when you're my age. Do you have a trust officer in your minor's trust division named Jason Alexander? I was told to ask for Jason Alexander."

"No, Mr. Purdue, he must be with another bank. We have no Jason Alexander in our trust department, but we do have a number of other highly qualified people who can help you."

"Oh, well, I've been confused before. I'll pass this information on to my son-in-law and try to get him to set up an appointment with you."

"Thank you Mr. Purdue. Is there anything else I can help you with?"

"No, no, not unless you got some extra money laying around that you need to get rid of. Ha, ha!"

"No, sir, not today. Thanks again for considering our services."

Dizz hung up. He grabbed his stuff and ran up the stairs, said good-bye to Phil and headed across town to check out the office address for the Private Trust Division that Jason Alexander had given to Art during their phone call.

The building was in downtown Boston. He walked inside the lobby and checked the directory. The directory read "Private Trust Division (access by appointment only)." He took the elevator up to the fifth floor and found the suite number corresponding to the directory. The suite was just a door at the end of a long hallway of other small offices. There was no glass, so he could not look in, and the door was locked. He quickly put his ear up to the door to see if he could hear anything. There was nothing, just silence.

Suddenly, the door across the hall opened and an older woman started to walk out. Dizz quickly stood straight up, taking his head off the door. The woman gave him a suspicious look.

"Can I help you with something, young man?"

"I was just trying to see if anyone was in this office. I think this is where I'm supposed to meet my trust officer, but the door is locked and no one answers when I knock."

"I've worked here for the last two years and the last people I ever saw there was when the space belonged to TEI. They moved out about six months ago and that Private Trust Division sign went up about a week ago. We've been waiting for someone to move in, but we've never seen anyone there."

"Thanks. My trust officer is probably still at the main bank. I'll head over there."

"You're welcome."

Dizz turned and walked to the elevators without looking back. He left the building and made his way to the train station and back to Hawthorne.

Once back at Hawthorne, Dizz found Art in his room. He played the recording of the phone conversation he had with the bank, and told Art about the office and TEI. Art turned an ashen color as if he was in shock, then he spoke, "If Jason Alexander is not really my bank trustee, then who is he? Maybe he really is with DHE. If he is not my bank trustee then all of the arrangements that Mr. Taylor made with the bank to fly Mr. Alexander out to Arizona at Christmas was a big ruse. It's just hard to believe he's not my trustee; I've been meeting with him for years as if he was. Who have I really been meeting with, what is this all about, and why is TEI involved?"

"I don't know, Art, but I would get all your questions together for Mr. Alexander. I wouldn't question who he is to his face. Since you don't know who or what you are dealing with, that could be dangerous, but I'm willing to bet that you'll never have that meeting at the Private Trust Division."

Art did not sleep well that night. He kept waking up thinking about his upcoming meeting with Mr. Alexander. He needed to ask good questions but at the same time not tip Mr. Alexander off that he knew something was not right.

The next day he was exhausted and struggled to stay awake in class. After his final class of the day, Art ran into Elisha. She was all bubbly and excited to see him.

"Art, Art, I hear you are coming to the beach with us during spring break. You are just going to love it. It's my favorite place to go. I love the beach, fresh seafood, the warm sun, boogey boarding, and making sandcastles, its, its, just my favorite place. Are you excited?"

"Yeah," Art responded, trying to look and sound excited, "especially the way you describe it. It will be all new to me but it sounds really great."

"Just think, three weeks from today we'll be digging our toes down into that warm, white, Florida sand. And I think while we're there, someone turns eighteen. Well, gotta go, see you at the beach, birthday boy."

Art stopped and watched that beautiful creature walk away. He couldn't help thinking it would be great to spend time at the beach with Elisha, but the current information was making him nervous about being around the Taylors, especially Mr. Taylor. Art traversed the grounds back to his room where he took a good two-hour nap. After he awoke, he ate dinner and spent the rest of the night writing down possible questions to ask Mr. Alexander at their Friday meeting.

It was one o'clock on Wednesday, and Dizz was about to look like a prophet.

Art got a text message from the office and excused himself from Ancient Literature class. When he arrived at the office,

Headmaster Stevens and Mr. Alexander were there to meet him.

"Art, sorry to pull you out of class, but your trustee, Mr. Alexander, stopped in and requested to meet with you."

"Hi, Art." Mr. Alexander smiled. "Before I left the office this morning, my assistant told me that my afternoon appointment in Concord may have to cancel and since I already had your file updated for our Friday meeting, I brought it with me just in case it may be possible to meet. Is this going to work for you?"

Art looked at Headmaster Stevens, and then back at Mr. Alexander, "Yeah sure, the only thing I'll have to cancel is my reservation at the rec center for my cycling exercise."

Headmaster Stevens jumped in, "I'll give them a call and tell them you won't be needing the reservation today. The board room is not being used, so why don't the two of you meet in there so you can have more privacy."

The Headmaster escorted Art and Mr. Alexander down the hall and let them into the boardroom.

"You don't seem that excited to see me, Art. Is everything okay?"

"Yeah, I'm fine. I was just looking forward to a trip into Boston."

"Well, this will give you the opportunity to go to Boston and do something much more exciting than meeting with your trustee. You can still go, just do something else."

"Good idea, maybe I'll do that."

"Art, I was going to wait until after you turned eighteen to go over things with you, but when you requested an earlier meeting, I went back and reviewed the terms of the trust. The trust provides that certain items in the trust be shared with you on or near your eighteenth birthday. I think we're close enough to your birthday to satisfy the terms of the trust."

Art nodded in agreement.

"What I'd like to do first is walk through the non-monetary terms of the trust triggered by you turning eighteen and then review the monetary provisions. If you have any questions while we are going through any of this, feel free to interrupt me, okay?

"First, the trust provides that we provide you with more detailed information regarding your parent's death. The terms of the trust state, 'In the event both grantors of this trust become deceased through accidental death prior to beneficiary's age five, the trustee shall withhold any and all information concerning the accident or accidents, which in the trustee's discretion may be deemed detrimental to the mental health of the beneficiary. In the event the trustee withholds information from the beneficiary under the circumstances set forth in the preceding sentence, said information shall be disclosed to the beneficiary at such time the beneficiary turns eighteen years of age'.

"This is known in our business as a minor's mental health protection clause. Up to this point in time we have only informed you that your parents died in a natural gas explosion. We have withheld from you the details available to us through the NTSB and newspaper accounts. I will try to summarize the information that we have and provide you with the file containing the NTSB investigation report, photos, and newspaper articles."

"What's the NTSB?"

"The National Transportation Safety Board."

"Why were they involved in this?"

"They had the jurisdiction at that time over accidents resulting from natural gas explosions."

"Oh, okay, what happened?"

"The records indicate that you were about eleven months old at the time of the accident. Your parents had just purchased a home in a new subdivision south of Boston. The utilities to the subdivision were installed in what they call a joint trench."

"Joint trench?"

"Yes, that's where the gas, electric, telephone, and water lines are all installed in one common ditch, or trench, to save money. Anyway, according to the NTSB's final determination of what happened, all the utilities were installed and in place but the electrical was not working correctly. The electric utility company came back in and dug up their line at the problem point, made their repair and reburied the electrical line in the common trench. Your parents were the first to move into the subdivision and were already living in their new house at the time the repair was made. According to the report, the electrical company nicked the gas line in the trench at the time of their repair. When there is a natural gas leak, it flows to the lowest level, so the natural gas followed the trench line back to your parent's home and eventually filled the basement of your parent's new house.

"On the day of the explosion, your parents got up, got ready for work, packed your diaper bag for the daycare center and left the house. When they arrived at the daycare center, they discovered that they had left all of your bottles for the day back in the refrigerator. They left you at the center and drove back to the house. That's where we don't know exactly what happened. It appears both of your parents went back inside the house and did something to trigger a spark that blew-up not only their house, but also destroyed the houses on either side. By the time the rescue units arrived, there was virtually nothing left. It took the fire department over five hours to get the fire under control.

"As I mentioned earlier, I have a folder for you with copies of your parent's death certificates, the NTSB report, newspaper articles, and the photos taken by the NTSB and the newspapers. If after reading through them you have any questions, I will do my best to try to find answers for you."

"What about other relations?"

"Good question. The total absence of an extended family was one of the stated reasons your parents came in to set up the trust with our bank. As far as we can determine, your mother, Sarah Jenicks, had no living relatives at the time of her death. Her maiden name was Sarah Wilson. Her mother was a single mom who died of a drug overdose when your mother was three or four years old. From that point on, your mother went from foster home to foster home until she enrolled in college. She was very bright and very needy and received a full scholarship to Penn State.

"Your father, Henry Jenicks, was also an orphan who was adopted at age four by a couple in their fifties who were both only children and unable to have children. They both passed away when your father was in college.

"Your parents met at Penn State and married right after graduation. Both of your parents were accountants and got jobs in Boston at a small boutique accounting firm. After working a couple of years, they decided to start a family. They came to Boston Mercantile Bank & Trust when your mother was pregnant with you. They wanted to put a will and contingent trust for minors in place in the event something happened to them.

"They were very well off financially at the time of your birth. Your father had inherited a sizeable sum of money from your grandparent's estate. Both of your parents also had large life insurance policies and their estates were awarded quite a generous sum in the wrongful death actions brought against the electric utility company. These assets have been invested and managed by the trust department and have grown considerably over the last seventeen or so years. The result of the above is that by most people's standards, you are a very wealthy young man, which brings us to the monetary provisions of the trust."

"Before you go on, did my parents leave any personal items behind like pictures, or, I don't know, ah, jewelry?"

"The explosion and fire destroyed everything. We do have a few photos in the file at the trust department that I will copy for you. I believe they are from high school and college yearbooks."

"Thanks, I really would like to see what they looked like."

"No problem, Art. I'll get them sent out to you. Now, concerning the monetary provisions of the trust . . . .your parents really wanted you to go to college so the trust instructs the trustee to pay all tuition, books, room and board, and reasonable and necessary expenses for as long as you are attending college and are progressing toward a degree. In addition, if you attend college, the trust provides or allows you to purchase a vehicle of your choice between your high school graduation and the commencement of your freshman year. The terms of the trust are not so generous if you choose not to attend college. It seems that your parents wanted to provide some negative incentive as well as positive. Anyway, if you are not enrolled in college and progressing toward a degree, the trust limits the trust's provision to health care costs. Regardless of whether or not you attend college, you are to receive fifty percent of the trust corpus at age twenty-five and the balance of the trust at age thirty. So, if you don't go to college, you'll need to have a good paying job until at least age twenty-five."

Art sat expressionless, listening to the terms of the trust. He really could care less about the terms of the trust; he only cared about figuring out who he was and where he came from. The information supplied by Mr. Alexander was of little help.

"Do you have any questions? Art?"

Art awoke from his daydream. "Yeah, I mean, no, I don't have any questions right now. Maybe I will later."

"Well, if you do, make sure you give me a call. Do you have any firm college plans?"

"Nothing definite, yet. I've been accepted to eight of the ten schools where I applied. I haven't heard back form USC and Berkley yet, which is okay, because I just haven't figured out what college would be the best fit yet anyway."

"I'm sure you'll figure it out. If your decision was going to be based on the financial cost, that is one care that need not enter into the decision."

"Were my parents killed instantly?"

"We believe so—no one could have survived from a blast of that magnitude. I'm sure they never knew what hit them."

Mr. Alexander stood and shook Art's hand. "Well, Art, that's pretty much all the information I have for you at this time. Please let me know if you have any questions and also inform me as soon as you make your decision on the college you will attend so we can set up some kind of payment schedule."

"Sure, I'll get back to you."

Art walked slowly back to his dorm room. He was numb from the conversation. The meeting had caught him completely off guard. He had not been prepared, and he was overwhelmed by all of the information about his parent's tragic deaths. Once he got back to his room, he lay down on his bed, depressed and hopeless, and fell asleep.

After the meeting with Art was over Eric stayed behind in the boardroom and put in a call to Gene.

"Gene, Eric here. What did you think?"

Gene had pulled some strings to link into the Hawthorne Security System for a live feed of the meeting from the boardroom.

"Eric, I even believed you were the trustee from the bank. Great job!"

"How did you think that Art responded? Do you think he was convinced?"

"Eric, he appeared stunned, overwhelmed and depressed. If he didn't believe what he was hearing, I think he would have been alert, engaged and probably a little belligerent. I think he bought the whole story to the point of giving up hope of ever finding any living relatives. He appeared genuinely depressed and even grieving the loss."

"Good, I'm relieved. I was so nervous about playing my part well that I couldn't really tell how he was responding. I will need to get back to him with the file of information I promised. We still need to get those computer generated composite photos of his parents that resemble Art. Other than that, the file seems complete."

"Great job, Eric. Great job! Let me know of any future contact with Art."

"Will do."

Art was awakened by the sound of non-stop knocking on his door and a loud voice repeating, "Art, are you in there?" He recognized Dizz's voice and slowly got up to open the door, then walked back and fell lifeless on his bed.

"What's wrong with you? You look horrible!"

"All I can say, Dizz, is that you are a prophet."

"What are you talking about?"

"You know when you said that you bet that Mr. Alexander would show up unannounced and that I should have my questions ready? Well, he showed up and I didn't have my questions ready."

"I knew he wouldn't meet you at that office! There's nothing there. Did you ask him anything?"

"Sure, I asked him a few things."

"What did you ask him?"

"Well, I asked him if I had any other living relatives anywhere."

"Oh, let me guess, the answer was no!"

"And I asked what the NTSB was."

"And what is the NTSB?"

"It stands for the National Transportation Safety Board."

"Why would you ask that?"

"Supposedly the NTSB investigated the gas explosion that blew up my parent's house."

"And where were you at the time?"

"I was at the daycare."

"How convenient. Art, there was nothing in the papers, and no death certificates in the county records."

"I know. I don't get it. He's going to give me a file with all the documentation and news stories. Maybe your search was faulty."

"I guess it's possible, but I'm pretty sure I did a thorough search. Let me know when you get that information. I'd like to look at it and then go do another search to see what I can find."

"I'll let you know when I get the file."

"Did you ask him anything else?"

"Not really, but he said if I had any questions to give him a call. I feel like I really blew it. I just couldn't think. It all seemed to make sense."

"Don't be so hard on yourself. Even if you did have lots of questions he would have only told you what he wanted you to hear."

"I don't know, Dizz, what he told me really did make sense."

"Something's not right, Art. This whole thing doesn't smell right. You really need to follow through with trying to find that Moss guy to see if he knows anything that can help you find the truth."

"I'm on schedule to take a bike ride down to Baker Bridge this Saturday to see what I can dig up. And I plan on accessing Mr. Taylor's business card tomorrow night."

"I need to get back and study for a test, but make sure you come and get me when you access the card. I'm very curious to see what's on that card and to see if the Hawthorne System let's you get to the online information.

14

The Tei Process

THE NEXT EVENING, Art sent a text to Dizz. *My room @ nine. Business card.*

I'll be there, was Dizz's response.

At around nine o'clock Dizz showed up at Art's room to view the information on Mr. Taylor's business card. Both Art and Dizz were anxious to find out more about Gene Taylor and TEI. They knew the information would be presented in more of a marketing format, but they were hopeful that something on the card, or the information accessed through the card, would in some way give them additional insight into what was really going on.

They spent the next two hours reading through the information and watching the multimedia downloads which were mostly little promos by Mr. Taylor, pitching the TEI process of Identify-Enhance-Monitor-Adjust, "IEMA," and the constant repetition of the TEI slogan, "We Bring Out the Best in You."

It appeared to Art and Dizz that the company had two major divisions, the consumer division and the government division. The consumer division was divided into three main areas: adult enhancement, pre-birth planning, and corporate and team consulting.

The stated goal of adult enhancement was to provide the general public with mood and personality enhancement control through specially formulated supplements and pharmaceuticals individually tailored to the client's needs, as determined by an extensive questionnaire and individual counseling sessions. The questionnaire was designed to "Identify" the client's natural gifting and preferences. The counseling was designed to help the customer decide on his or her preferred self or "best version". In the second stage of the process "Enhance," TEI designs specially formulated supplements and pharmaceuticals for the client, based on specifications agreed upon by the client. The client is then closely observed during the "Monitor" stage so that changes can be made if needed in order to provide the desired results. The last stage of the TEI process, "Adjust" is the TEI lifetime guarantee to provide needed adjustments as life circumstances dictate.

The pre-birth planning division was essentially a service to design children. The TEI process for pre-birth planning included a full inventory of the genetic possibilities provided by the birth parents. From the genetic possibilities, the parents are then assisted in selecting or emphasizing the traits or features that they desire in their child. These traits or features included, the child's sex, complexion and skin tone, hair color, eye color, height, body style, and also what TEI called "bents" to enhance a child's intelligence and or gifting in the areas of math, science, music, language and athleticism.

The pre-birth planning also included the disease/defect-free promise that guarantees that no genetically transmitted defects or diseases will be passed down from the parents. The material emphasized that every child brought into this world should be a wanted child and that pre-birth planning was a logical and thoughtful approach to bring about achievement of that goal.

Dizz and Art were both shocked when they saw the fees associated with the services. They were sure that only the elite and super rich would be able to access these services. It dawned on them at about the same time that the kids they went to school with were the children of the wealthy and elite and were the brightest and smartest.

It also answered how average-looking people like Gene and Virginia could have such beautiful children. Everything was making sense—except for Art and Dizz being at this school with such an elite group. Were they the charity cases?

As Art and Dizz dug deeper into the information they found very little to describe the actual work of the TEI Government Division. The one link that they did find that mentioned DHE immediately froze the computer. When this happened, all Dizz could say was, "See! See! I knew it! I knew! I knew it!" They were able to find some biographical information that indicated that Mr. Taylor served on two of the "Restructured President's Counsel for Bioethics & Human Enhancement Boards" and had participated in several government contracts with the DHE. They also found some interesting little clips of Mr. Taylor speaking about his philosophy regarding enhancements.

In these clips, Mr. Taylor argued that controlling one's biofunctions is no different than the building of a house for the purpose of controlling one's external living environment. He said enhancements were a way to control one's biological environment, which in turn results in desired outcomes. He also described the TEI process as a way to discover and leverage the natural talents that are present in each of us.

Regarding the ethical use of the TEI process, he stated very little other than that he believed the TEI process, when applied to adults, should always be strictly consensual unless absolutely necessary for societal control and stability. He said, for example, that TEI's experimentation with certain modifications to treat sexual predators would allow them to assimilate back into society without the fear that they would return to their former predatory, violent, illegal behavior.

In regard to designing children, Gene believed that the IEMA process in no way violates any rights of the child because embryos are incapable of consent. He further stated that parents are naturally suited to make decisions about their future children. Who besides the parents would always have the best interest of the child in mind?

Both Art and Dizz were surprised that there was not more information about the history of the company and Virginia's role in the early years. It was as if Gene had purposely fashioned all of the information to make it look like he was the sole brains and genius behind TEI.

When they had exhausted the information capable of being accessed on the card, Dizz turned to Art and said, "Well, Art, not a lot of big surprises other than the revelation that we are going to school with a bunch of designer babies."

"You don't know that for sure, Dizz."

"Oh, come on, Art! Take a look around. Everyone here, other than us, is smart, beautiful, and athletic. We're just smart. And think about how all the parents treat Gene like a god at school functions. Have you ever noticed how ugly some of those parents are compared to their kids?"

"You could still be good looking if your parents are ugly. A lot of people lose their good looks as they age . . . and Mr. Taylor is the chairman of the board for Hawthorne and so it would be natural for all the parents to kiss up to Gene for the sake of their kid's future at Hawthorne."

"Whatever, Art. I think we are going to school with the new genetically-enhanced elite master race and Gene is the new Hitler."

"That's a pretty harsh comparison. Gene hasn't killed thousands of Jews by experimenting on them."

"Yeah, that's true, he's only gone through thousands of embryos who can't consent and whose parents didn't mind discarding them in search of their 'perfect child'."

"It's not the same!"

"Whether it's the same or not, this type of stuff will create a huge social and economic gap between the "haves" and the "have-nots." The stupid, ugly and poor are destined to become servants of the new elite with no chance of ever bettering themselves. So much for the American Dream of becoming anything we want through effort and hard work."

"Dizz, I think you're getting way too carried away."

15

Baker Bridge

SATURDAY MORNING ARRIVED BRIGHT, warm, and clear. It was an early April day that had spring fever written all over it and Art couldn't wait to get out on a bike and ride down to Baker Bridge, regardless of what he might find in the way of information.

He dressed, grabbed a quick breakfast at the cafeteria, and headed down to the Recreation Office to check out his bike. As Dizz had prompted him, he made sure to check out one of the "dumb bikes" and "dumb helmets" that did not have tracking capability. He mounted the bike and took off out of the Hawthorne grounds, going south on Monument by Minute Man Park.

Dizz told Art not to take his PACA or cell phone due to the GPS tracking capability. He had given Art handwritten directions to take Monument to Monument Square, then go left as though he were going to the Concord Commuter Rail Station, except to take a left at Walden Street prior to getting to the Rail Station. Art had always struggled with directions and getting lost. Today was no exception as he started day dreaming and rode right past Walden Street and the rail station. He regained his senses as he rode up to the front gates of Concord Academy.

He remembered taking the Hawthorne shuttle over there one time to watch a soccer game when he was a freshman. He thought that Dizz had said something about Concord Academy on the directions, so he pulled Dizz's scribbled directions out of his back pocket. There was a little note in a circle to the side of the directions that read "if you end up at Concord Academy, you went too far, turn around and go back to Walden and go right." Art was amazed on how well Dizz knew him and how he looked out for him. It made him feel guilty about his abandoning Dizz for the "beautiful people."

Jumping back on his bike, Art headed back to Walden Street and turned south until he came to the Walden Pond bike path. After an exceptionally cold winter, the path was bustling with families releasing their pent-up demand for sunshine, exercise, and fresh air. He enjoyed seeing children pedaling in little rows behind their dads. He so wished he could have followed his dad somewhere in the same way. He so wished he could have been with his dad doing anything. Living without a dad had left a persistent ache with no cure. He was hopeful that finding out the truth would eliminate some of the pain of not knowing his parents.

As he rode south past Walden Pond, the bike traffic cleared out, and he rode on in solitude, accompanied only by his thoughts. What would he say if he actually found Moss? How would he go about asking the things that he really wanted to know? If he did find Moss and told him his story and his suspicions, would Moss think he was some whacked out kid living in a dream world of made-up conspiracies?

Art was now coasting into Baker Bridge as Walden Street turned into Concord road. He slowed down and started looking over the few houses scattered here and there to determine which one looked like its inhabitants might be friendly and helpful if a stranger were to stop in and ask questions. He spotted a little café down the street, so he peddled until he was in front of a sign that read "Café Diem." Customers were sitting outside under blue and yellow flowered umbrellas at small wooden tables on a deck adjoining the café, drinking coffee, and engaging in conversation. He rode his bike up to a small bike rack just outside the front door.

The café appeared to be fairly new construction of large white pine logs topped with a green metal roof. The deck wrapped around three-fourths of the structure. The architecture looked oddly out of place for the area, but Art thought it was a refreshing change to the northeast colonial look.

Art opened the front door and walked into the café. He was instantly greeted by the aroma of roasted coffee beans and fresh-baked goods. The café was spacious, clean, and very comfortable, providing patrons the choice of sitting at tables, easy chairs, couches or rocking chairs. At the far end of the café was a massive stone fireplace surrounded by leather couches and easy chairs. It looked like a great place to be on a chilly northeast winter day.

To Art's left were the counter and the baking display case. Art thought that this was perfect—grab a latte, a scone, and talk with the locals to see if there were any Mosses still around town.

He bent over to peer into the baking case and started perusing all of the choices when he heard a perky voice with a hint of raspiness coming from behind the counter. "They're all good. You really can't go wrong."

Art looked up into the smiling face of a young lady in her late teens or early twenties. She had sparkling green eyes and brown hair sprinkled with highlights and pulled into a ponytail. She wore a blue apron with yellow lettering spelling out

Café Diem. Above the Café Diem logo was a heart-shaped name tag bearing the name "Marie." Her smile was infectious, and Art could not resist smiling back at her.

"Okay, so they're all good, but what's your favorite?"

"I guess my favorite is the white chocolate raspberry scone."

"Sounds fairly exotic for a scone."

"We also have blackberry, blueberry and chocolate chip scones and fantastic cinnamon rolls as well."

"No, no. I'll go with your favorite and a medium latte."

"Great choice. I'll have the latte ready in a minute or two."

"Hey, Marie, do you live here in Baker Bridge?"

"No, I live in Concord, I just work down here."

"I live in Concord, too. My name is Art. I'm in my senior year at Hawthorne."

Marie stopped in her tracks and gave Art a wide-eyed look. "Wow, I never thought I would see a Thorny here at Café Diem."

"A what?" Art replied quickly.

"Oh, oh, I'm sorry. I can't believe I said that out loud."

"No, that's okay, what did you call me?"

"Sorry, a Thorny. Comes from the 'thorne' in Hawthorne and . . . well . . . " She hesitated and looked at him uncertainly, like she'd already said too much.

"Go on, I won't be insulted."

"It's kind of code for 'look but don't touch'. You know, thorns? If you touch one, it's painful. Hawthorne is kind of a world to itself and any time the locals have gotten involved with anybody or anything at Hawthorne, it didn't turn out very well."

"Oh, I see, very interesting. Knowing that I am a dangerous thorny, will you still serve me at this café?"

Marie laughed. "Oh, sure, as long as you keep your barbs to yourself."

"I promise. Oh, uh, Marie, I have another question. I am working on a paper for one of my classes, and I have been trying to find a guy by the name of Derrick Moss to interview. I know his parents used to live in Baker Bridge. Ever heard of him or the Mosses?"

"Heard of him? I work for him. Around here we call him Professor. He and Mr. Barger own Café Diem."

Art, stunned, was speechless for a couple seconds.

"Hey, are you okay?"

"Yeah, sorry, oh, uh, you called him the professor?"

"Yeah, that's his nickname around here. The guy's brilliant and he always figures out everything and then explains it in exciting ways. Plus, he does all the baking here and almost all of the fruit we use for baking comes from the organic farm he owns over on the Sudbury."

"Do you think there is any way I can get a chance to talk to him?"

"Oh, I'm sure he'll talk with you. He'll talk to anyone. He's almost done with his morning baking. I'll go back and tell him that you would like to meet him and talk with him. He'll love it. Every day after baking, he comes out and goes from table to table just to chat. That's what he loves to do. I'll send him out to your table when he's done."

Art gave Marie a big smile as she handed him his latte and scone. "I'll just be right outside on the deck. Thanks a lot, Marie."

"No problem, I mean, you're welcome, but I really didn't do anything."

Art took his scone and his latte and headed for the outside deck. He placed himself by an outside window on the deck so that he could see Marie at the front counter. He bit into his scone and thought he had gone to epicurean heaven. The flavors of white chocolate and raspberry exploded in his mouth. He had never experienced home cooking, but he thought to himself that this is what it should be like. While he waited, he sipped his latte, and nervously tried to think of all the questions he would ask Mr. Moss. He decided to maintain his little deception about an interview until he heard something that would lead him to believe that Mr. Moss may have information that could possibly unlock the mysteries of his past.

Art nervously nibbled on his scone and sipped the latte. He couldn't believe that he was actually going to get to speak with Mr. Moss. He kept looking back through the glass waiting to get a glimpse of Mr. Moss coming his way. Then he saw a slender older man a little over six-feet tall wearing a blue and yellow apron head across the room toward the door leading to the deck. The patrons at tables along the way stopped him several times. Art saw him smiling, shaking hands, talking briefly, and then pointing to the deck and waving goodbyes. When he finally came out on the deck, several people at different tables called out their greetings to which the Professor smiled and gave a friendly wave. He turned and headed over to Art's table. As he approached, Art instinctively stood up and extended his hand to introduce himself. He clasped Mr. Moss's hand and politely said, "Mr. Moss, thanks so much for taking time to speak with me."

"My pleasure, young man. Mr. Moss sounds so formal. Everyone around here calls me Professor. Why don't you have a seat and we'll relax and talk a little."

Before sitting down, the Professor looked down at his flour covered apron. "I always forget that I'm wearing this." He took the apron off, hung it on the back of his chair and sat down. "Marie tells me your name is Art, and that you are from Hawthorne Academy."

"Yes sir, my name is Art Jenicks, and I'm a senior at Hawthorne Academy. I was—"

The Professor interrupted, "Art? Art Jenicks?"

"Yes, and—"

The Professor interrupted again, "Not to be too personal but are you Art Jenicks, the concert pianist?"

"Well yes, yes I am, have you heard of me?" Art noticed that the Professor was now staring at him intensely in a dead, unwavering stare. The Professor's hazel grey eyes felt almost piercing, and his graying eyebrows were furrowed in intensity.

The Professor broke his stare like he was coming out of a hypnotic trance, straightened up, and smiled at Art. "Yes, yes, I have heard of you. Almost anyone interested in the arts in the Boston area is familiar with your exceptional talent. Marie said you wanted to interview me for some paper you're writing. I'll be happy to try to answer any of your questions, but I can't give you any of my scone recipes."

They both laughed. The humor made Art feel a little more comfortable.

"I don't know how to bake so I think your recipe's are safe," said Art, "but, yes, I am writing a paper for an independent study class. The paper has to be about some social issue that affected government policy in the United States during the first decade of the second millennium."

"Interesting, and on what issue have you chosen to write your paper?"

"I haven't come up with the exact issue yet, but I am interested in the history and social issues surrounding the formation of the Department of Human Enhancement."

The Professor placed his hand on his chin as if to help him think. "Mmm, that's a very broad topic indeed, with historical events dating back over a hundred years leading to its formation. And how does an interview with me, help you? What are you looking for, Art?"

"In some of my research I came across some articles in the *Boston Globe* where a Derrick Moss seemed to be the main spokesman calling for scientists and the government to proceed slowly and carefully with human enhancements. Are you that Derrick Moss?"

"Guilty as researched. Now a question for you. How did you go about finding me here?"

"Finding you was just luck. In one of the articles in the *Globe*, it mentioned that you were interviewed at your parent's farm in Baker Bridge. So, I decided to ride down here from Concord and ask around to see if there was any one by the name of Moss still living around here and the first place that I stopped to ask was here at Café Diem."

"Do you believe in luck, Art?"

Art shrugged his shoulders. "I guess so."

"I'm not a big believer in it myself. I think there may be some purpose in our meeting other than just a simple interview for your independent study paper. But I've been wrong before. We'll see what unfolds. Okay, I'm ready for questions, fire away."

"Thank you so much, Mr. Moss, I mean Professor." Art reached into his backpack and pulled out a miniature handheld computer in order to take notes.

"Oh, Art," said the Professor pointing back to the door to the outside deck. "Did you happen to see the sign over there where you came in?" Art looked in the direction where the

Professor was pointing and saw a sign over the door that read "Computer & Internet Free Zone".

"We made that rule to encourage face-to-face conversation between human beings versus pseudo-interaction in the world of virtual reality. So if it's okay with you, let's just have a conversation."

Art sheepishly put his computer back into his backpack. "Sorry, I didn't see the sign, I'll just start asking you questions if that's okay."

"Sure, I'm ready."

"I am curious about the statement you made earlier about more than a hundred years of history leading up to the formation of the DHE. Can you explain a little more about that?"

"Sure, let me see if I can fill you in on a little history. In the first decade of the 1900s a biologist by the name of Davenport established the National Center for Eugenics Research and Policy. Davenport had been inspired by a man named Francis Galton who was considered a Victorian genius and who also happened to be the cousin of Charles Darwin. Galton lived in the mid-1800s and was bothered by the growth in the population of what he called 'undesirables'. He believed that the wrong kinds of people were having too many children. Like his cousin, Charles Darwin, he believed that man was just another animal, and similar to the purposeful breeding of animals, the evolution of the human race could be controlled for the greater good. Galton called this purposeful breeding of humans 'eugenics,' which comes from the Greek word meaning 'well born'."

Art piped in with a question. "Who decided the definition of 'the greater good'?"

"Exactly, Art, exactly. It appears that the greater good is always decided by those with the greater power. Anyway,

Davenport wanted to direct human evolution by preventing the unfit from propagating. He and another man named Laughlin created a Eugenics Office and developed the American Compulsory Sterilization Policy which was placed into law in Indiana and California. It basically let scientists use surgical methods to eradicate those deemed to be unfit. Doctors, in the name of the greater good, performed sterilization operations on healthy individuals without their consent. Laughlin also helped the U.S. Congress put an immigration act into place that kept so-called inferior humans from southern and eastern Europe from entering the United States."

"Wow, they thought there were whole areas in Europe with inferior humans? Didn't anyone object?"

"If there were objections, there is little evidence of it. In fact, people like Winston Churchill, Theodore Roosevelt and George Bernard Shaw endorsed the goals of eugenic cleansing. Even churches supported the early eugenics movement in the United States. The quest to purify the human race made its way all the way to the U.S. Supreme Court where the famous Justice, Oliver Wendell Holmes, penned the decision in Buck v. Bell that upheld a Virginia law authorizing the forced sterilization of the 'feeble minded'."

"Feeble minded—couldn't that mean just about anything you wanted it to mean?"

"Yes, I think it could and did. Justice Holmes wrapped his decision in the 'greater good' language stating, 'It is better for all the world if society can prevent those who are manifestly unfit from continuing their kind.' Holmes actually wrote in the opinion in regard to several generations of one family that had been sterilized that 'three generations of imbeciles are enough'."

"I've never heard about any of this before."

"You haven't heard of it because the Nazi's took eugenics and quickly ran with it to its logical conclusion, which was hideously gruesome. After that, it was political suicide to be associated with eugenics in any way, shape or form. The amazing thing was that the defense counsel for the Nazi leadership at the Nuremburg war criminal trials argued over and over that the German leadership had done nothing that had not already been done in the United States. In fact, Hitler modeled Germany's sterilization policies on California's 1909 sterilization law."

"When did eugenics start making its comeback?"

"The Genome Project and advances in science began to open up all kinds of possibilities in regard to controlling and directing human genetics. The results of research originally designed and intended to find cures for diseases quickly and easily opened up amazing opportunities for the age-old desires of human improvement and social control. The dirty word 'eugenics' quickly did an etymological makeover and presented itself anew as the new genetics of the biotech age."

"Professor, what was the extent of your involvement in all of this? Weren't you behind much of this genetic research?"

"Oh, yes, I am very proud of all of the work I was able to do in this field."

"So, are you saying that genetic research is or has been for good?"

"Good? Hmmm... 'good' is a loaded word that's usually used to judge or evaluate the merit of something. Genetic research and science is supposed to be neutral. Well, it's really not. I think that for genetic research or science to be 'good' it must have at its heart a moral purpose."

"So, when you were involved in the research, what was the moral purpose you were trying to achieve?"

"I, and many others like me, some of the best and brightest all over the globe, got into genetic research because we honestly saw it as a way to help others. We were young idealists striving after what Francis Bacon called 'the relief of man's estate'. Our involvement in biomedical genetics was driven by a 'good' moral purpose. We viewed the relief from pain, disease, and the hope of a healthy life as a primary good worth working to bring about."

"That makes sense, but I picked up from some of the articles that you wrote years ago that you thought things were getting out of control. Why? What did you see happening?"

The professor furrowed his brow and looked away briefly before meeting Art's gaze. "The dream of a healthy life, left to itself with no restraint, can easily become perverted and corrupt to the point of being evil. The whole issue stems from the evolving definition of health. Because of the new opportunities and powers that became available through biotechnology, nanotechnology, and pharmaceuticals, 'health' was redefined as overcoming the natural constraints of our bodies and living free of necessity and fear. Health no longer meant living disease free, it meant living indefinitely, pain and disease free, with good looks, talent, vitality, athleticism, high intelligence, and with all of our needs and even whims satisfied. Health, as then redefined, has become the 'primary good' to be achieved at all costs. So when the 'primary good' conflicts with equality, protection of the weak, human rights, and even self government, guess what wins out?"

"Health?" said Art in a questioning tone.

"Right, and if health and overcoming nature becomes the highest human good, where do you think that places science?"

Art looked at the Professor and shrugged.

"Science became the instrument of the fulfillment of the highest good and as such became untouchable, above being questioned. If science spoke, it was deemed the highest truth and off limits to religious and personal views, moral premises, tradition and even the policy makers. Anything then that got in the way of science or inhibited scientific freedom became an enemy, a roadblock to providing what the public so desperately wanted—the new health. Art, is this making any sense to you?"

Art nodded. "I think so. I think you're saying our greed for health has blinded us from being able to see or determine what is good or what is bad."

"Yes, yes, our greed for the expanded definition of health has silenced all other voices of wisdom and we are slowly becoming unable to distinguish between good purposes, and evil and immoral purposes."

"Professor, are you saying that science is evil or immoral?"

"Not at all, science can and has done great good. We just cannot separate science from moral wisdom and moral judgment. We cannot let science be its own moral authority."

"I'm assuming that not many of your colleagues agreed with you."

"There were a few, but most of them liked the power, money, and potential of unrestrained research, and many believed that science should be considered the ultimate truth with no moral judgments attached."

"So, how did that impact you?"

"I was immediately labeled as the enemy and branded with names and labels like anti-science, anti-cure, and religious nut."

"Were you religious? Were you biased by your religious beliefs?"

"The funny thing is that at the time, I was agnostic. Religion really meant nothing to me."

"You said 'at the time', so are you religious now?"

"I wouldn't characterize myself as religious, but I do believe there is a God."

"Professor, you have been talking in broad general philosophical terms. What is your personal story? How were you involved in genetic research and what happened to you?"

"This could take a while, are you sure you have that sort of time, Art?"

"I've got a couple more hours before I need to bike back."

"You biked down here? Impressive. How about a little lunch first before I have to disgorge my tale of woe?"

"Sure, Professor, sounds good to me."

"I'll go back to the kitchen and have Marie put together some sandwiches. Do you like turkey?"

"Sure. I'm not picky; anything you have will be fine."

"I'll go put in our order and be right out."

Art waited anxiously at the table. He was excited and nervous at the same time. Excited that he actually found Moss and had the opportunity to talk to him, and nervous about what he may or may not find out.

How would he get around to asking the real questions he wanted answered?

16

Trading Stories

MOSS WALKED QUICKLY to the kitchen, leaving Art at the table outside on the deck. He walked by the counter and asked Marie to put together a couple of turkey sandwiches for him and Art.

"Hey, Professor, I hope it was okay that I had you meet with that kid from Hawthorne."

"No problem, Marie, it just seems very odd that he came to Café Diem."

"I thought the same thing. It's strange to have a Thorny down here."

The Professor, still looking perplexed, said, "It could be more than strange." Looking around, he said, "Do you know if Barger has come in yet?"

"I think he is unloading some kitchen supplies in the back storeroom."

The Professor hurriedly made his way through the kitchen to the back storeroom where he found Barger stacking some large sacks of baking flour.

Barger stopped stacking flour sacks and looked at Moss. "By the look on your face you must have just seen a ghost, cause you're white as sheet. Are you okay? Why don't you sit down for a minute?"

Moss took the suggestion, sat down on a stack of flour sacks and ran his fingers through his graying hair, "I think I'm okay,

I'm just kind of in a state of shock and my mind is racing all over the place. Barger, you are not going to believe who I have been talking to for the last half hour." He paused and shook his head as if to wake up. "I have been talking to Art Jenicks."

"Who?"

"Art Jenicks, one of the boys from the Jenicks project."

"No, are you sure?"

"Not totally, but that's who he said he was."

"What's he doing here?"

"He said he came down here from Hawthorne Academy looking to interview me for a school paper he is writing about the social issues surrounding the formation of the DHE."

"Sounds a little fishy to me . . . do you think he is telling the truth?"

"I don't know, but I kind of doubt he's down here to get research for his school paper."

"What do you think is going on, Derrick?"

"I'm not sure, but I really don't think DHE or anyone else would actually send him here to talk with me," he hesitated for a moment, " . . . unless it's really not him and they are trying to set me up."

"I don't know, Derrick, if they really wanted you, they wouldn't need to set you up. They would just take you out and make it look like an accident."

"Yeah, I guess you're right, but why don't you look around and see if you notice if any of our other customers are acting suspicious or like government agents."

"Okay, I'll take a look around. Has he asked you anything yet that raises any red flags?"

"Well, right before I came back here he asked me to tell him my personal story about how I was involved in genetic research."

"This could get interesting. If it's really him, I wonder how much he knows about himself? Derrick, I got an idea, why don't you ask him to tell you his story first. That may give you an idea about how much he knows."

"Good idea, Barger, you always come through with a plan or scheme that makes sense."

"I hope that was a compliment."

"It was," Moss said, smiling.

"Also, Derrick, you need to just come out and ask him if he really came down here to talk with you for the paper he is writing. He may just be willing to tell you what he is really up to. Hey, do you think I could meet him?" Barger said looking excitingly curious.

"Sure, I'd like for you to meet him. I'll go back out there and when Marie is finished making our turkey sandwiches you can bring them out to our table and stay a while."

"I just thought of something else, Derrick—didn't you show me an article about him in the *Boston Arts* magazine a few months back? I think it had a small picture of him in the article. If we could find the magazine we could at least determine if it's really him."

"Great idea. Why don't you have Marie see if she can find the article? I'm going to head back out there and see what happens."

"Good luck, Derrick. I don't think we've had this much excitement since the time we tried to sneak out of the country back in 2013."

"Don't remind me. That's the kind of excitement I think I can do without!"

The Professor left Barger in the back storeroom and made his way to the outside deck where Art was sitting. "Sorry that took a bit, I had some Café matters to attend to. Marie is making our sandwiches and will have them sent right out."

Moss sat back down at the table beside Art and leaned forward, almost as though he was getting ready to tell Art a secret. "Art, I've been thinking about your request to hear my story. One of the reasons my business partner and I opened this place was to have a venue, or create an environment, where people could get together away from outside interruptions to just talk, share their lives and dialogue. So far, I feel like you have had to listen to a monologue. So, I'll make you a deal, you tell me your story first and then I'll tell you mine. That way we both get to know each other a little better. Okay?"

Art, wide-eyed, stared at Moss. He swallowed hard and replied, "Okay, but there's really not much for me to tell. I'm not that old and not that much has happened in my life that's interesting."

"I doubt that, but no matter, tell me about your life so far."

Art agreed and began with the story he had been told by his trustee about the gas explosion that killed his parents. He had just got started when Barger came over to their table carrying a large serving tray loaded with sandwiches and drinks.

"Art, sorry to interrupt you when you were just getting started but I want to introduce you to my good friend and business partner, Will Barger. Both Will and I were biotech scientists in our prior lives."

Art stood politely and shook Barger's hand. "Art, is it okay for Will to sit with us a while and listen to your story?"

"Uh, yeah, sure, if he's prepared to be bored."

"Well, what you have told me so far is certainly not boring." Moss turned to Will and said, "Art was just explaining how, when he was a baby, both of his parents were killed in a natural gas explosion."

"I'm so sorry to hear that, Art." said Barger.

Moss turned to Art, "Go ahead with your story, Art. Tell us about your adoptive family, growing up, and where you lived and went to school before coming to Hawthorne."

"Well, I really didn't grow up with a family. I wish I did." Art went on to explain to them about his parents' background and about not having any living relatives. He told them about growing up in institutions, monitored only by a trustee from Boston Mercantile Bank & Trust.

Moss interrupted, "Art, that sounds strangely out of the ordinary. Didn't you ever have foster parents?"

"I guess I did when I was very little, but I really don't remember much about them. It seems like they were changing all the time. The foster parent program ended when I started going to boarding schools. I then went from boarding school during the school year to camp and music programs in the summer, then back to boarding school. That's been my life for as long as I remember."

Barger looked puzzled and asked Art about his trustee from the bank. "Art, with all of the changes in your life, I hope the bank at least kept you with the same trustee."

"Yes, they did. That's one thing that has been constant, even though I really wouldn't characterize my trustee as being very personable. Still, he has always made sure that I was taken care of and had everything I needed."

Barger continued, "Tell me a little about your trustee. What's his name, what does he look like, how old is he, what's he like to do?"

The questions from Barger were odd, but Art answered them anyway. "He's kind of short and stocky, bald headed with big tufts of hair on each side of his head. He has a big nose with dark beady eyes. He talks with a hint of a New York accent and my guess is that he is in his late forties. I really don't know what he likes or dislikes—all of our meetings are very business-like. He checks on my grades and asks me a ton of questions about my health and once a year he sets up a complete physical. Oh, and his name is Jason Alexander."

Moss squinted and furrowed his eyebrows like he was trying to think of something. "The description and name sounds familiar, but why?" asked Moss.

"Derrick," Barger piped in, "you're probably just thinking about that old sitcom 'Seinfeld'. You know, George, on the show, his real name was Jason Alexander."

"Oh, yeah, and remember that guy we used to work with who looked and sounded like him. What was his name?"

"All I can remember is that his first name was Eric, but we used to call him George. That was horrible of us," said Barger. "But don't forget that he called you Kramer."

Both Moss and Barger chuckled like they really didn't think it was that bad.

'What happened to him, Will?"

"I think he ended up taking a government position with the DHE."

"Oh, yeah, now I remember."

While Barger and Moss talked, Art took the opportunity to inhale a good part of his sandwich. Barger and Moss couldn't help but notice how hungry he was.

"Why don't you finish your sandwich, Art," said Moss "and I'll try to get started on the question you asked me earlier."

Moss proceeded to tell Art about his childhood growing up on his parent's farm right there in Baker Bridge. His parent's farm, which backed up to the Sudbury River, had been in the Moss family for five generations. He was an only child who had always been very idealistic, and looking back, very spoiled. His parents made sure that he had every opportunity to succeed in life. He was fortunate to be gifted in math and the sciences and ended up getting a scholarship to MIT where he majored in a relatively new field at the time, Biological Engineering.

"I was on a mission to help the world with the diagnosis, treatment, and eventual elimination of disease. I loved my time at MIT. If there were a time in my life I could choose to live over, that would be the time I would choose. It was intellectually stimulating and challenging. A time of great discovery for me, both personally and scientifically, and a time where I made some great friends, right Barger?"

"Right, Moss."

"Will and I actually roomed together our last two years there, harassed the same professors and even chased the same girls . . . remember that beautiful Joni Jansen? Anyway, now fate or destiny has brought us back together as café owners. We would have never thought that would happen."

"Okay, Art, it looks like you have fully demolished that sandwich. Would you like another?"

"No, no, I've had plenty. I'll have to tell Marie that the sandwich was great."

"Art, why don't you take it from here and tell us about your life at Hawthorne? You know, things like what you like to do there, what your friends are like, your favorite classes, whether you have a girlfriend."

Art, looking perplexed at the request, responded, "Do you really want to hear this stuff?"

Both Barger and Moss together answered, "Yes!"

"Okay then, I am a senior at Hawthorne majoring in music performance. My primary interest is in music and music compositions. Up until this last semester, I had really only one friend at Hawthorne named Dizzy. Neither Dizz nor I really fit the typical Hawthorne image or have the social standing to really fit in there."

Barger interrupted, "You said up until this last semester—what happened?"

Art went on, "I think I just got lucky. You see, every year over winter break, I kind of get adopted by a Hawthorne family for the holidays. This year I got to spend the holidays with the Taylors."

"And who are the Taylors?" asked Barger.

"Gene Taylor is the Chairman of the Board at Hawthorne and the founder and President of T.E.I. Professor, you must be familiar with the Taylors?"

"Oh, yes, I've known Virginia and Gene dating back to when I was first out of MIT. But, go ahead with your story."

"I went with the Taylors to their resort home in Scottsdale, Arizona. Both of their children, Chris and Elisha, go to Hawthorne and are pretty much considered the social elite. So, I got to know them over the holidays and got along with them pretty well. Now I have been included in their circle of friends."

Barger then asked, "What about this Dizzy person, are you still friends with him?"

"Yeah, but it's been difficult. He is really not included in on anything I do with the Taylor group."

Moss asked, "Do you have a girlfriend?"

"Well, no, not really."

"I picked up a little hesitation, so you must have your eye on someone. Am I right?"

"Yes, I do kind of like Elisha Taylor, but I know she's way out of my league."

"I see. Any college plans yet?"

"I've narrowed my choices down to about ten schools but I'm going to have to make my mind up pretty soon. Right now, I'm leaning toward either going to Princeton or USC if I get in, but I may put college on hold for a year and do something with my music. I don't know yet, the music thing has not yet fully developed."

"Sounds like you have some good options to choose from."

"Yeah," said Art in a dead-pan tone.

"You don't sound that excited," said Barger.

"Well, right now there's a lot of pressure to try to figure out the right thing to do."

About that time, the three of them noticed Marie over by the door sticking her hand out and motioning Barger to come inside.

Barger stood up and nodded to Art. "It's been nice to meet you Art, but it looks like duty calls. Good luck with your decision and good luck talking to the Professor!"

A moment later, Marie came out with glasses of iced tea for their table. While she chatted with Art, Moss saw Barger walk through the café, out the front door, and around the café far enough to re-enter the deck area so that Art's back was to him. When he got close enough, he stopped just long enough to point to the *Boston Arts* magazine and nod his head "yes" and walk away. Moss now knew he was talking to the real Art Jenicks.

After Marie moved on to another table, the Professor scooted his chair in, leaned over the table and made direct eye contact with Art. In a lowered voice, he asked, "Art, before I go on and share more of my story, I need to know something from you. Did you really come down here to interview me for a school paper, or is there something else going on here?"

Art immediately broke eye contact with Moss and looked down at the table. He stared down at the table a couple more seconds and then looked back up at Moss. "No, this is not about a school paper I have to write. Professor, I'm really sorry and apologize for the deception. I'm afraid if I tell you why I really wanted to talk with you, you'll think I'm some crazy, paranoid kid."

"Why don't you give me a try? You seem pretty sane to me."

Art took a deep breath and blew it out through his mouth very slowly. "Here goes. I've always struggled with the fact that I have no living relatives anywhere. It just doesn't seem right. I feel like I came out of nowhere. No history, no past, and no connection with a family. I feel disconnected, lonely, odd, and left out. I had pretty much just learned to live with it until strange little things started popping up."

"Strange little things? Like what?"

"Well, my trustee showed up in Arizona over the winter break. He had a briefcase with the initials D.H.E. on the side instead of J.M.A. for his name, Jason M. Alexander. I thought it was strange. Then, I had an accident while hiking in Arizona, and I'm pretty sure I saw my trustee at the hospital talking to Mr. Taylor when I arrived at the emergency room. Then, when I got back from the Arizona trip with the Taylors, I tried to do some online research into my past but couldn't get very far. I found out that my searches were being blocked by the Hawthorne intranet system. I can't tell you how, but I was able to do some anonymous searching at an access point off the Hawthorne campus."

"And, did you find what you were looking for?"

"Not really. Everything I found out just raised more questions, like the bank having never heard of my trustee, Jason Alexander."

"That would be very unsettling, Art. What were you looking to find out from me?"

"I was hoping that maybe you would have some information about the DHE and or the Taylors or something else that would help me figure out who I am or where I come from. So, I guess I'm fishing for information. I know this must sound like some far fetched conspiracy theory stuff, but I just need to find out if it is my own crazy paranoia or if there is really something more going on."

The Professor sat back in his chair and ran both hands through his hair until his hands clasped behind his head, uncertainty and excitement trembling through him. After taking a large breath and slowly exhaling, he broke the silence. "Art, I don't think you are crazy to want to know who you are and where you come from. Even though you haven't directly said so, I gather that somehow you believe that there may be information about the DHE and/or the Taylors that will somehow connect you with your past."

"Yes, I guess that's what I am saying," said Art.

Moss leaned back on his chair, looked up at the sky, and closed his eyes. Eventually, he opened his eyes, leaned forward, and in hushed tones, began to open up the mysteries that Art longed to understand.

"You know from your research that I know or did know the Taylors and that I worked with them on several fascinating projects. I also have knowledge about the formation of the DHE and the work the Taylors were involved in with the DHE. Some of the things I know about the DHE is information I obtained when I had top government security clearance; it is information that I swore under penalty of law not to divulge. At the moment, I am extremely torn by your request. I am struggling with what I should or should not tell you, not only for the sake of my own conscience, but also for both of our safety. I know this may all sound very strange to you, but before I tell you anymore, I need to think about if I should tell you, what I should tell you, where I should tell you, and how to make sure that our safety is not compromised."

Art exploded like his favorite team had just scored the winning goal. He jumped up out of his seat and blurted out, "Then I'm not crazy, there's really something to all of this!"

"Art, Art, sit down, you're attracting way too much attention."

Everyone on the deck had turned around to look at him. Art waved awkwardly and slowly sat back down.

"Sorry, Professor, I didn't mean to attract so much attention. I'm just excited that I haven't been imagining all these connections."

"Art, why don't you and I walk back into the kitchen and talk a few more minutes before you have to ride back to Hawthorne?"

"Sure, sounds good."

Art and the Professor walked back into the café and made their way into the kitchen. Once there, the Professor motioned to Art to follow him back into the storage room where they sat down on the flour sacks that Barger had unloaded earlier.

"Art, I know you're excited about the possibilities of what I just told you, but going forward from here is serious business and extremely dangerous. Does anyone else know that you came down here today looking for me?"

"Yes, but only one person, Dizz, the guy I told you about earlier. He's the guy who helped me to do some research away from Hawthorne. In fact, I think he is in Boston today doing some research into my birth records for me."

"Anyone else?"

"No, nobody. I even made sure that I rode down here on one of the bikes that couldn't be tracked by a GPS system."

"Very good. That was very prudent of you. Now, this may seem like a strange question but do you know if you have any imbedded chips on your body anywhere? They usually insert them somewhere on your left wrist."

"Not that I know of."

"Do you mind if we check?"

"No, I guess not."

"Stay right here, I'll be right back."

The Professor left Art in the storage room and came back with Barger about five minutes later. Barger was carrying a wallet-sized box that was held together in the middle with duct tape. It was obviously a homemade contraption with a small switch on one end and a row of different colored lights on the other end. The Professor informed Art that the device would detect the presence of a chip. It would also detect whether it was working correctly. He told Art that both he and Will bore within them implanted chips and turned on the device to demonstrate its detection capabilities. A glowing amber light indicated the presence of a chip, they explained, and a glowing red light indicated an active non-defective chip. He explained to Art that they were implanted with the chips for security purposes years ago, but that the government had required both of them to keep the chip embedded for reasons he would explain later.

They ran the device up and down Art's arms and legs and, to Art's surprise, found that a chip had been inserted in his right arm. However, to the surprise of all, the red light indicator failed to light up. The chip was defective.

The Professor chuckled and turned to Art, "They implanted the chip in you, but if doesn't work . . . very fortunate, very fortunate indeed. Okay, Art, it's getting late and I know you need to bike back to Hawthorne, so, let's figure out when we can meet again and discuss the ground rules of our meetings."

"Okay, sure," said Art, "I am free again tomorrow. Can we meet then?"

Moss and Barger looked at each other and shrugged their shoulders in a "why not" gesture. "I think we could swing it for tomorrow," said Moss. "We have a meeting here at the café in the morning that ends around ten. Anytime after that would work fine."

"Great, I'll bike down and try to get here around ten-thirty."

"Okay, Art," said the Professor, "now for the ground rules. I can see that you are very eager and excited to hear what I know, but I urge you to be patient and extremely cautious. There will be plenty of time for me to tell you what I know, so I do not want you compromising the confidentiality of our meetings just because you're impatient.

"You will always need to err on the side of caution. If anyone questions your going off by yourself on a bike ride, don't come down here. When you do come down, you cannot bring any device that is capable of communication or tracking like a cell phone, PACA or any device with GPS capability and that includes your little computer."

"I purposefully left my cell phone and PACA back at Hawthorne."

"Good. You must tell no one that you are coming and you will always need a credible explanation to defend your absence from Hawthorne. So far, I think you have done a pretty good job of keeping your trip down here a secret. I am also concerned about your friend Dizz knowing too much."

"Professor," interrupted Art, "without Dizz's help, I would not have been able to get here. He fully understands the secrecy necessary because he arranged for me to obtain access to information off campus and he is the one who insisted that I ride down here alone on a bike with no GPS capability and without my PACA. Believe me, if anyone found out about all of this, he would have a good chance of going to jail because of the way we procured our info."

Moss looked puzzled, then gave in. "I don't fully know why, but I am going to trust that it is safe for him to know about our meeting. I don't want to scare you, but if the fact that we meet gets out and DHE or the Taylors find out, jail time will be the least of your worries."

Wide-eyed, Art asked, "What does that mean?"

"I can't tell you right now, but suffice it to say, if we continue to meet, we are putting ourselves into very dangerous territory. Art, I want you to understand the seriousness of our continuing to meet. Do you agree to my precautionary ground rules?"

Art, looking and feeling somewhat stunned by what was being said, nodded his head. "Yes, sir, I agree."

"Good," said the Professor. "Now, get on out of here so you can get back before it gets dark."

Moss and Barger let Art out the employee's entrance. Art jumped on his bike and began pedaling back to Hawthorne.

After Art left, Moss and Barger remained in the storage room sitting on the flour sacks. Barger was shaking his head in a questioning manner, "What just happened here, Moss? Do you know what you have begun with this kid? There is no turning back now. Pandora's Box is now wide open!"

"I'm not sure what else I could have done other than just flat out lie. I honestly don't think he knows who he is, and I don't think it's a set-up or trap."

"I don't think it's a trap either, Moss. I believe the kid, but you are literally putting your life in the hands of a naïve, inexperienced, seventeen-year-old kid. One small slip-up and its over, and he is definitely not the person you want trying to conceal things, when Gene Taylor has all of the tools at his disposal. I don't get it. You have gone to great pains to become self-sufficient and fade into the background. Why jeopardize all of this now?"

Moss bent over, elbows on his thighs and chin in his hands, looking at the floor. "Well, Will, there was a time in my life when I believed in something and was willing to speak out and take risks for what I believed in. Then, the reality of the consequences of my boldness caught up with me and I couldn't handle it. I liked my position, my status, and my salary with all the benefits. However, most of all, I valued my personal safety. When it became very clear that I risked my personal safety by continuing to voice my concern and objections, I was cowardly and more than willing to disappear."

Will forcefully interjected, "You had no choice, Derrick. You know you would have become a statistic, one more of those many mysterious accidents—you wouldn't be here talking to me today."

Moss slowly looked up at Will, "I know you're right. I really don't think I would be here today, but I am, and for the past couple of years I've had this feeling that something was coming my way that would allow me to make one last stand for humanity. I think this might be it."

"This, meaning Art?" said Will.

"Yes, Art." said Derrick. "I don't know exactly where this will go, but Art and his brothers are living, breathing, examples of where the "positive eugenics" movements will take us and I don't think it's too late to get this story out and let the natural sense of right and wrong rise up in people's hearts to put a stop to this madness."

"I see your idealistic nature rising up again, Derrick. What do you intend to do with Art? Tell him he's a well-designed genetic marvel and then have him condemn the results of his own existence to the world?"

"In a way, yes," said Moss. "Even though he is a brilliant musician, a part of his humanity has been stolen from him. He longs to belong, he longs for family, for connection. We both know that Art was purposefully designed by Gene as the teaser to eventually sway public opinion. After all, how could anyone conclude that a brilliant young musician, using his artistic brilliance to provide the world with goodness and beauty was bad? Once swayed, the public would be ready to swallow the utopian hogwash of designing all new life for a purpose that will bring happiness and fulfillment. It then becomes only a few more easy steps to designer soldiers, transhumans performing undesirable labor, an elite ruling class, peace, prosperity, utopia. And don't forget, the promise of a disease and defect free life stretching two to three times the current life span."

"So, Derrick, you're going forward with this whole thing, betting that Art, instead of being the poster child of positive eugenics, will be a modern day Paul Revere sounding the warning of the coming loss of humanity."

"I guess the answer is yes. I know it's a long shot with lots of risk, but it may be our last best chance to awaken the public. Will, I am asking you to come along on this venture with me. I desperately need your support, your brains, your street savvy and your questioning nature. I know this is asking a lot and I would completely understand if you said no."

Will stretched and cracked his back, clasping his hands behind his head. He pressed his lips together and released a big questioning, "Hmmm, I'm going to have to think about this, Derrick. I'll let you know tomorrow after we talk with Art again."

"Fair enough," said Derrick, "But if you are not going to do this, the sooner you get out and the less you know, the better it will be for you."

17

Revelations

EVEN THOUGH IT WAS an incredible spring evening, Art hardly noticed the beauty of the sun lowering itself over Walden Pond as he rode back to Concord. He arrived at the recreation center just ten minutes before closing, and realized that he couldn't remember most of the ride back. His mind had been deep in thought, contemplating and imagining the various things the professor might reveal about his identity.

Upon returning his equipment, he asked to reserve the same bike and helmet for the next day. The attendant chuckled at the request and told Art it wouldn't be a problem because no one except him ever wanted the tech-deficient equipment.

Art went straight to his dorm room to avoid Elisha and her friends and did not come out the rest of the evening. He awoke early the next day excited, anticipating answers to the questions about his past. He went straight to the recreation center without stopping for breakfast, figuring he would save his appetite for the fresh scones and tasty sandwiches at Café Diem.

Art was becoming a regular at the rec center's checkout shed. Upon his arrival, an attendant who had helped Art before asked him if he wanted the same old bad equipment. Art replied that he liked the old equipment better because he didn't feel the constant pressure of having to better his time or log more miles. The attendant responded that he'd better get going because it looked like the beautiful morning was going to change that afternoon. The forecast called for high winds and rain to move through the area later that day. Art's face revealed that he was unaware of the weather change, so the attendant handed him a tightly folded rain poncho to stick in his backpack.

As Art rode away, he overheard the attendant comment to his co-worker that it seemed strange for a "music-geek" to spend so much time cycling.

Art just smiled to himself, and allowed his adrenaline to propel him over the approximate five-mile trip in less than fifteen minutes. He arrived at Café Diem at about ten-fifteen, just as Moss and Barger were saying their good-byes to their meeting attendees out on the side deck. He parked his bike, staying out of sight around the front of the café until only Moss and Barger were left on the deck. As he walked over to Moss and Barger, he noticed the closed sign on the front door of the Café. He had hoped they would be open for lunch.

Barger and Moss turned as Art walked toward them. "Hang on, Art," said Moss, "Barger and I'll grab our bikes and be right with you. We are going to head back to the homestead to ensure some privacy."

A few minutes later, Moss and Barger appeared on a couple of fat-tired beach bikes and Moss motioned for Art to follow them. They peddled away, going north on Old Concord road and then left on Fairhaven, heading west for about a quarter of a mile where the road emptied into a long, gravel driveway. On each side of the driveway were a couple of acres of fruit trees, just starting to blossom. At the end of the long driveway was a classic white, two-story, eighteenth-century farmhouse with three chimneys, one on each end of the house and one in the middle.

Art followed Moss and Barger as they took a smaller side road that went around the right side of the house. Behind the house were several small barns, a couple of small chicken coops and a larger fenced-in area where three goats and one milk cow were grazing. They stowed their bikes at a small storage shed west of the house. When Art got off his bike, he immediately noticed that all of the west facing walls and roof surfaces were photosynthetic. Looking to the west about a hundred yards out, he could see the Sudbury River and a small rustic cabin over near the bank of the river.

Art turned to Moss and said, "This is a beautiful farm you have, Professor. You must be extremely proud to own this place."

The Professor, looking forward, back, and all around said, "I am extremely grateful and blessed to own this place. This land has sustained me and provided for my needs, physically and emotionally, for the last eighteen years. I feel a real connection with this land. It has taught me much and given me purpose when I thought I had none."

"Professor," asked Art, "what is that small building out by the river?"

Moss and Barger both chuckled, "That currently serves as Barger's little bachelor pad and is the remaining evidence of my Thoreau experiment," said the Professor.

"Your what?" asked Art.

"You've certainly heard of *Walden* or *Life in the Woods* by Henry David Thoreau?"

"No, I guess I haven't," said Art.

"Good gracious! I can't believe Hawthorne would ignore one of the greatest pieces of American literature, and it was written right here at Walden Pond," exclaimed Barger.

"Art," interrupted the Professor, "Walden was an account of Thoreau's life in the woods, not far from here on Walden Pond.

He went out and built a small cabin in order to isolate himself from the society of the day in an attempt to gain understanding and to achieve his goals of simplicity and self-reliance.

"After I lost my job, lost my voice, and was ostracized, all I had left was this place. My parents left it to me. Until this calamity hit me, I had used this place infrequently as my country getaway. When I moved in here, I was defeated, depressed and fed-up with the world. All I wanted to do was to hide and be left alone. I had amassed a sufficient bank account and still had a sizable inheritance from my parent's estate. So, I decided to stock up on food and supplies that would last me a year, sequester myself, and contemplate where I would go from there. I decided I would take a page from Thoreau and build a small, primitive cabin to live in for the year, and so there stands my personal monument to isolation and contemplation."

"You really stayed in that cabin for a year with no outside contact?" Art said, in a tone of disbelief.

"Actually, Art, I stretched it out to about sixteen months."

Still in a tone of disbelief, Art asked, "What did you do all alone for that long?"

"I contemplated my life, what I believed to be true, read a lot, including *Walden* and the Bible, neither of which I had ever read before, wrote down my thoughts, planned how to become self-sufficient and self-sustaining with as little reliance on the outside world as possible. What you see around you is the result of my reading and planning. I grow all my own food and I create, or I should say, harvest my own energy. I have excellent water resources and no need for electronic media."

"Wow!" said Art, "then what caused you to open Café Diem?"

"Barger here tracked me down again about six years ago and challenged me with a quote from Thoreau asking me if I was going to waste the rest of my time leading a life of quiet desperation and go to my grave with the song still in me. He gently reminded me that no man is an island. Café Diem was his brain child and he convinced me that the world needed safe places dedicated to restoring the art of conversation.

"Enough about me, Art, I'll grab our lunches and drinks and let's the three of us walk out to the riverside by the cabin. We'll hopefully start unlocking some mysteries for you."

Barger, Moss, and Art walked out just past the little cabin where Barger had built a circular stone patio between the cabin and the Sudbury. The patio was equipped with a round table, a large umbrella, and four chairs. The Sudbury River adjoining Moss's property was more like a small lake with the river widening out to about a half mile across.

The three of them sat down at the table under an umbrella and unpacked the box lunches Barger had brought with him from Café Diem.

Moss, with a sense of urgency on his face, turned to Art. "Let's get going and get you out of here and back to Hawthorne before the weather front moves into the area. My achy joints tell me its coming our way, and I have quite a bit of ground I would like to cover before you leave. I want to make sure to tell you the most important information first, because you never know when and if we'll get to meet again. I think the thing you want to know about the most is your family. Am I right?"

"Absolutely!" said Art.

"Art, what I'm going to tell you will be shocking to hear. I apologize in advance for dumping all of this on you at one time."

"It's okay, Professor," said Art, "I have imagined so many things that it will be a relief to hear the real story."

The Professor took a deep breath and exhaled, "I hope so! Okay, here we go. Your parents' last name was not Jenicks. Actually, I don't know their real names. The information on them is sealed and probably only available to someone with the highest government security clearance. Supposedly, they lived out west somewhere back in the 1980s. They were unable to have children naturally."

Art broke in, "The 1980s? Did you really say the 1980s?"

"Yes, the 1980s. This will hopefully make sense in a minute or two. Anyway, they went to a fertility clinic somewhere out west and were involved in what was called 'Assisted Reproductive Technology,' known as ART."

"ART?" Art questioned, astonished.

"Yes, ART," repeated the Professor.

"The procedure they were using at the time was called 'In Vitro Fertilization,' commonly known as IVF. Without going into immense detail, the treatment involved a doctor who would harvest the mother's eggs, fertilize them with the father's sperm and place a few fertilized eggs into the mother's uterus, hoping to get a healthy baby. Because the procedure was inconvenient and expensive, the standard practice at the time was to create as many as twenty embryos, placing a few in the uterus, and freezing the rest as kind of an insurance policy, for later use. If unsuccessful on the first go 'round, the couple would unthaw the embryos and try again."

"Anyway," continued the Professor, "your parents were successful in the process and were able to have children who were born to them somewhere back in the mid-1980s. They also had ten frozen embryos left over. You were one that they did not use and until the late nineties, they paid a storage fee at the clinic to keep you and the rest of the embryos properly frozen."

"So, Professor, are you telling me that somewhere out there I probably have brothers and sisters in their mid-forties?"

"Well, yes, I guess that is probably true," said the Professor.

Art shook his head in disbelief. "So, if I found them I would probably be the age of some of their children?"

"Yes, that would likely be the case." The Professor then continued, "Art, your parents were actually killed in a terrible accident. The information that I had access to said they were both killed instantaneously in a head-on collision with a large semi-truck sometime in 1997. The frozen embryos, including you, were considered property of their estate. The executor of your parents' estate had no legitimate use for them after your parent's death and so the estate, needing to raise money to support the other children, sold the embryos to the clinic where Virginia Taylor ended up working. At that time, unused embryos were the center of a heated debate about the ethics of using or destroying them for embryonic stem cell research. As a result, the frozen embryos, including you, were kept frozen until they were later transferred or possibly sold to the U.S. Government to be used in a top-secret project.

The project was unimaginatively named 'the Jenicks Project' by Gene Taylor. Jenicks was short, of course, for eugenics."

Art, attempting to process the shocking information he just heard, froze, lost in his thoughts, staring out at the twinkling reflections coming off the Sudbury.

"Art," The Professor, almost yelling, tried to snap Art out of his trance. "Art, is this all making sense to you? Are you okay?"

Art jerked to attention as if he was coming out of a dream. "Yeah, I think I'm hearing you say that I've been part of some government experiment that happens to be named after my last name. I mean, my last name comes from the name of the project, which has something to do with eugenics. Am I the project?"

"Yes, Art," said the Professor as gently as possible. "You and three other brothers that came from the frozen embryos are the project."

Art, now anxious, agitated, and angry, exploded, "I don't think I like this. Who said they could use me as a guinea pig? I'm not just a bunch of cells in a test tube! I'm a real person! This has got to be a violation of some kind of rights or law out there!"

The Professor, seeing Art's intense agitation, tried to calm him down by talking in a softer, more affirming tone, "I'm sorry, Art. I agree with you. No one should have the right to use you or anyone else as an experiment without their consent."

The next few minutes they sat in silence staring out at the Sudbury. Finally, Art broke the silence, "Professor, do you think there would be any way to track down any of my family?"

"I won't say it's impossible, but it is highly improbable," replied the Professor.

"You would have to find somebody with the proper security clearance who would be willing to take quite a risk," said Barger.

"I see," said Art. "Brothers. You said I have brothers from the frozen embryos. Where are my brothers?"

"Yes, you have brothers, but . . . "

"But what?" Art asked excitedly.

"Well," said the Professor, "I don't know for sure if they still exist and I don't know where they would be now. You see, Art, they were the part of a project that, to my knowledge, has never been exposed to the public in any way."

"This is sounding creepy," said Art. "What did they do to them?"

"They were genetically manipulated to produce beings specifically designed to perform certain functions," said the professor.

"Beings!" exclaimed Art. "I don't like the sound of 'beings'. What is that supposed to mean?"

The Professor leaned back, glanced over at Barger, and then back at Art. "Art, I said 'beings' because one of them is not totally human. You see, in an attempt to design a prototype elite soldier who could withstand extreme weather and terrain conditions, and live on very little water, they basically created a—"

Art blurted out, "A chimera. They created a chimera."

The Professor looked at Art with a puzzled look, "Yes, a chimera. How did you know that?"

"When I was with the Taylors in Arizona, Mr. Taylor got really upset at his son, Chris, for bringing up chimeras when we were out on a hike in the desert. Chris was talking about chimeras with armadillo-like skin that could better withstand the harsh environment of the desert. I was puzzled as to why Mr. Taylor was so upset, so I did a little research on chimeras. Now it makes sense why Mr. Taylor preferred that I didn't hear about them."

"Art," said the Professor, "I, of course, do not know the current status of the project or your brothers. The original project called for the genetic engineering of three others besides you. Their project names were Hugh, designed for long-term space flights, Kapos, designed to be a laborer, and Stratos, designed to be the ultimate soldier. I have never seen any of them—only you. When Gene Taylor first briefed me on the project, I refused to be a part of it and was then summarily dismissed from working on any further government projects. I was also blackballed in the industry. After my dismissal, others, like Barger here, also objected to what was going on and their careers also ended abruptly."

Art sat emotionally numb, staring out at the river. He had realized his dream of finding out more about his past and his family, but the information was a devastating and disturbing nightmare. He still didn't have the ability to contact any of his family, and the information concerning what was done to him created a burning anger inside that he had never before experienced.

"I feel like I just hit you in the head with a shovel," apologized the Professor. "I'm sorry, Art. All of this has got to come as quite a shock."

"It's nothing you should be sorry for. I had to know. I needed to know, and I asked you to tell me. But, it's nothing like I had imagined. I just feel like I made all the correct turns and still came to a dead end."

"It's not a dead end, Art," said the Professor, "It's the information you needed to know to become who you really are."

"I don't know who or what that is," replied Art.

"You will. Just give it time," said the Professor. "Art, I hate to do this right now, but I need to switch gears with you so we can get you out of here and back home before the storm hits. Like it or not, you are now in possession of information that makes you a threat to D.H.E. and to Gene Taylor's plans. It is critical for you, and us, that all of this remain a secret. I have more to share with you about the Taylors and DHE but we need to have you vary the manner that you come to see us so that no one gets suspicious of your absences."

"Okay," said Art. "What do you want me to do?"

"Barger's got the plan," said the Professor. "I'll let him explain it to you."

Barger jumped in, "Our goal is to have your meetings with us be invisible. In order to do that, it is necessary that it appear that you never leave Hawthorne. I don't know a lot about Hawthorne's security, but I imagine they have a good system to track students when they come and go from the school. Do you know how that works?"

"Not completely," said Art, "but I know someone who will. All I know is that there are cameras everywhere, we have Hawthorne-issued cell phones and we have a student card that we are supposed to swipe when we leave. It also works as a key to our rooms and opens the pedestrian gates to Hawthorne."

"Can I see the card?" asked Barger.

"Sure," said Art.

Art stood up, pulled the card out of his pocket, and handed it to Barger. Barger examined it, turning it over in his hands several times and then, looked up at Art and Moss. "No matter if you swipe the card or not, it is automatically read when you leave and enter the Hawthorne property. The swiping is merely a formality, probably used as an indicator to determine your compliance with the rules. The problem is that you need the card to open the door to your dorm room. Your goal will be to come and go from Hawthorne without your card so you won't be detected."

"How am I going to do that?" asked Art.

"I am not sure, Art," said Barger, "but, most security systems aren't one hundred percent effective. There's got to be a way. We'll just have to figure it out."

"I know someone who may be able to help us," said Art. "It's Dizz. You know—the guy I told you about who arranged my remote access searches. He knows the Hawthorne computer and security system inside and out. He would be my only hope, because I don't have a clue about this stuff."

Barger looked at Moss and shrugged his shoulders. "Are you absolutely sure he is completely trustworthy?" asked Barger.

"He has been so far," said Art. "Like I told you, he's already stuck his neck out for me, big-time. If the authorities ever found out how we did the remote access research, I'm sure he would go to jail. So, he's got a lot to lose if any of this is ever found out."

Barger looked over at Moss again and Moss gave a small nod of approval. "Okay, Art," said Barger. "You and Dizz work on how to come and go from Hawthorne undetected."

"Now, let's discuss your means of transportation," said Barger. "We think it would be best if you quit using the Hawthorne bikes for your transportation down here. It makes it too easy to track your usage and time away from Hawthorne."

Moss leaned over the table and placed a large roll of bills in front of Art. "Here's enough money to buy a basic bike at Nathan's Bike Haven in Concord, plus, enough to rent a small storage space to store the bike for three months. This way, when you sneak out of Hawthorne, you can walk to the storage space and still have a way to get down here in a decent amount of time without walking the whole way."

"I can get money to do that," said Art. "You don't have to give me money."

"Art," said the Professor, "If you used your money, your trustee might question your use of such a large sum."

"I'll figure out how to pay you back then," said Art.

"Don't give it a second thought, Art," said the Professor, "It's not a big deal."

"Okay now, Art. We've got to get you out of here and back to Hawthorne. That bank of clouds to the northeast is really starting to look nasty. Remember, above all else, the cardinal rule to follow in all of this is, if you think that coming down here will raise any questions or seem peculiar to anyone in any way, don't come. You are welcome anytime, night or day, whenever you can get here. You'll probably want to stop by Café Diem first, if it's during business hours. Any questions?"

Art shook his head.

"Then, get going and go fast!" said the Professor.

The three of them got up and jogged back over to the small shed where they had parked the bikes. The Professor and Barger both shook Art's hand and gave him a big hug before Art got on his bike. As Art peddled away, the Professor yelled out, "Art, remember you are not alone in this!"

Moss and Barger watched as Art's bike sped down the lane through the middle of the apple orchards and out of sight.

"You think he'll be okay?" said Barger.

"I don't know. I hope so," said the Professor. "We just dropped an emotional bomb on his hopes for a family. It's a scary thing when you leave a person in a state of hopelessness. I am concerned that he may feel that he has nothing to live for, or that he has no purpose other than being someone's experiment."

"Do you think we should catch up with him and ride along with him until he gets to the south side of Concord?" asked Barger.

"Too dangerous," said Moss. "If he saw someone he knew, they would ask who we are."

the awakening

• • •

The wind was starting to pick up, and for most of the ride home, Art found himself riding headlong into the gusts. He peddled as hard as he could from Baker Bridge to the center of Concord. He started feeling drops of rain on his face in the increasingly colder and colder wind. During his ride, he had been thinking about being the object of an experiment. What had been done to him? What specific outcome were they looking for in him? Did they think they were successful so far? What would they do if he decided to be a construction worker? Did he even have that choice available? Was the outcome of his life inevitably based on how he was engineered? Would he ever get to meet his brothers? Would he really want to? Were they human? Was he human? Would he have been better off not knowing what he found out today?

As Art was just coming into sight of Hawthorne, giant drops of icy water began hitting his face and splatting hard on his helmet. He peddled hard and pulled in under the building overhang just as a torrential downpour let loose.

"Wow, kid!" said the waiting attendant. "Thirty seconds later and we'd have had to send a boat out for you."

Art smiled and managed to muster up, "Yeah, timing is everything."

Art waited for the squall to pass and then walked back to his dorm room where he collapsed on his bed, depressed, dejected, and emotionally and physically exhausted.

He awoke to a loud rapping sound at his door. He got up, shuffled his way across his room in the darkness, and opened the door. There was Dizz peering at him with his trademark sly smile.

"Hey, Art, did I wake you out of your beauty sleep? It's only seven-thirty."

"Oh, I fell asleep on the bed and was hoping to wake up in a different world!" lamented Art. "What's up?"

"Wow, sounds like you're in a funk." said Dizz. "I just got back from Phil's and stopped by to fill you in on additional information I dug up."

"Information, yeah, that's all I need, a little more information." Art retorted in a sarcastic tone.

"What is up with you, Art? I thought you were just dying to dig up more information."

"Oh, I've dug up a whole graveyard of information the last two days that I'll tell you about," said Art. "But, you go first."

"Okay, Art, but you are downright depressing. Like I said, I went to Phil's and took another run at finding newspaper stories about the gas explosion, death certificates and your birth certificate. It was amazing. They all showed up this time, when before, the search came up completely empty. So, it made me think."

"I think I can save you a lot of time," interrupted Art, "my real parents died in a car accident in the late-1990s. I was conceived—actually, 'came into being,' in the late 1980s and was frozen until they needed some embryos to experiment on. The newspaper stories, death certificates, and birth certificates are all fakes."

"Whoa, whoa, whoa, slow down! Where did all of this information come from? Did you actually find that Moss guy?"

"Yep, and I found out I'm a real freak."

"Hey, stop it, Art! What did that Moss guy tell you?"

Art spent the next two-and-a-half hours telling Dizz the whole story about Café Diem, Marie, finding Moss and Barger, his return trip today, and the story of his family and what Art called the "Jenicks Brothers' Freak Show."

Dizz took it all in, asking question after question, pumping Art for every detail. He also kept reassuring Art that he was not a freak, and that even if he was, so were all the designer babies at Hawthorne.

Art ended by telling Dizz about the cash for the bike and storage unit and Moss and Barger's insistence that he only come back if he could do it without appearing to leave Hawthorne.

Dizz's face became uncharacteristically serious. "Art," said Dizz, "this must be extremely dangerous. These people obviously know what, and who, they're dealing with and are going to great lengths to keep your movements undetectable. This must really be top-secret stuff. It sounds like they're putting their own necks on the line. Why would they do that?"

"I don't know. Maybe they'd like to beat the system," said Art. "They believe that what Taylor did was wrong. When they spoke up and objected, they lost their jobs, lost their careers, and probably had their lives threatened."

"Okay, but I wonder why they are willing to put themselves at risk again."

"I don't think they actually planned to. I think the opportunity just presented itself when I showed up. They still believe that what is going on is wrong."

"I know how to do it!" said Dizz.

"You know how to do what?" asked Art.

"I know how to get you off of Hawthorne grounds without being detected, and I already have a storage unit in Concord where I keep my scooter."

"You've never told me anything about having a scooter," replied Art.

"I always have a back-up plan, just in case," said Dizz.

"Okay, Dizz, how do I get off the property without being noticed?"

"When I hacked into the Hawthorne System a few years back, I retrieved maps and diagrams of the whole property which included all the surveillance camera locations and schematics of all the electrical, plumbing and sewage. I wanted to have the ability to come and go as I pleased without anyone knowing, so I thoroughly studied all the plans until I found a way. It's not the most pleasant way you could leave Hawthorne, but it works."

"Meaning you've actually come and gone without anyone knowing?" said Art.

"Yeah, a few times, but, like I said, it's not pleasant."

"What do you mean, 'not pleasant'?"

"The way in and out is through the sewer system," said Dizz, "but, it's really not that terrible. I will help you get through it when the time comes. You have one more weekend before you head off to Florida and your spring break. When are you going to try to see Moss again?"

"I haven't thought much about it. I guess, next Saturday, if I can pull it off," said Art.

"Do you think he would mind putting you up for the night if I got you out of here Friday night? It's best if you leave here under cover of darkness," explained Dizz.

"The Professor did say that I could come anytime it was safe, and that I could come night or day," said Art.

"Great!" said Dizz, "here's how we will do this. At your Friday afternoon get-together with Elisha and her friends, you'll need to come up with some excuse for not being around that next day."

"Got any ideas?" asked Art.

"I don't know—maybe you could get sick, feel like puking."

"That's atrocious," said Art.

"Come up with your own excuse then, but make it good. Anyway, I will come by your room around seven o'clock. It'll just be getting dark about then. We will go over to the locker rooms at the gym like we are going over to work out. The locker rooms are the one place on campus where there are no surveillance cameras due to privacy concerns. In the back of the locker room, near the showers, there is a metal panel on the wall about three-feet by three-feet. It can be unscrewed and taken off the wall. The panel allows access to the plumbing behind the shower room and to the sewer systems, which allows undetected exit and entrance to Hawthorne. We will get in through the panel and I will get you through all of the plumbing to the sewer access. You'll have to go through another metal panel access and climb down a built-in ten foot metal ladder to get you down to the sewer."

"Um, how disgusting is it in the sewer?" grimaced Art.

"It's actually not that bad. That branch of the Hawthorne sewer is just gray water—you know, used water from the showers, laundry, and kitchen. No urine or excrement. Anyway, the sewer is like a square concrete tunnel about five-feet high and three-to-four feet wide. You will take it until you come to another metal ladder built into the concrete wall. You will climb out a large, round, manhole in a wooded area just west of the Hawthorne property. About ten yards straight in front of you, as your head is coming out of the sewer manhole, is a hiking path. You will take the hiking path through the wooded area until it comes out where Estabrook Road dead ends. When you come out on Estabrook Road, there will be a couple of houses. Try not to be seen, it will only cause suspicion."

Art was starting to feel overwhelmed with all of the instructions. "How will I remember all of this and find my way back?" asked Art.

"We'll go over this several times before you go on Friday and I will make a little map for you. It sounds more complicated than it really is. It's very easy. Okay, then, where was I?" said Dizz. "Oh, yeah, you'll take Estabrook Road down to Liberty Street. Go left on Liberty Street. Liberty Street will take you to Lowell Road. Go left on Lowell Road. Lowell Road will take you all the way to downtown Concord, but before you get downtown, on the right you will see People's Storage. That's where I have the scooter stored."

"Dizz, I don't know how to operate a scooter. What am I going to do?" asked Art.

"Art! You are pathetically helpless. Okay, I will go with you to get the scooter and show you how to ride it. After that you are on your own."

Art, now looking relieved, said, "Thanks Dizz, I know I'm helpless, but I couldn't do any of this without you."

"All right, all right, I'll get you out of here, but you're going to have to get back here on your own. In the meantime, resume your normal schedule this week with the beautiful people. I'll get back with you on Wednesday or Thursday to go over your exit strategy again."

18

Escape to Baker Bridge

ART TOOK DIZZ'S ADVICE and resumed his regular routine of study, classes, and touching base with Elisha and Chris about the upcoming plans for the spring break trip to Florida.

Friday arrived too quickly for Art. He was nervous and very anxious about sneaking off the Hawthorne grounds. As promised, Dizz arrived at Art's room around seven and rapped on the door. Art opened the door, staring at Dizz with a wide-eyed, fearful look.

"Art, you need to relax. Things are going to work out fine," reassured Dizz. "Are you all packed? Where's your backpack?"

Art, without speaking, turned and picked up his backpack, holding it out to show Dizz.

"Good," said Dizz. "Did you come up with a good excuse for Elisha?"

"I didn't have to. They decided it was girl's sleepover night and I didn't qualify."

"Perfect," said Dizz. "Let's go."

The boys headed over to the men's locker room at the gym. As Dizz had hoped, the gym and the weight room were empty. They headed into the back end of the locker room. Dizz walked through the adjacent locker room and the bathrooms to make absolutely sure no one was there.

"Okay, Art," said Dizz, upon returning. "No one is here. Let's move quickly and get out of here. I need you to stand by the end of the lockers where you have a view of the door so you can let me know if anyone comes in. I will get the panel open." Art, still feeling scared, nodded and walked to the end of the row of lockers to act as the lookout.

Dizz quickly lowered the screen that allowed the panel to slide open. He then turned to Art and in a whispered yell said, "Let's go! Now!"

Art turned and ran down the row of lockers toward the opening. Dizz grabbed Art's backpack from him and then helped him into the passage. They both heard voices as a couple of students entered the locker room. Dizz started to slide the panel closed, but it was too noisy. He motioned to Art to stand as close as he could to the passage wall panel so as not to be seen through the opening. They stood motionless, waiting and hoping that whoever it was would not choose this group of lockers. Art caught a glimpse of two boys walking by the end of the row and on to another part of the locker room. Dizz gave Art a thumbs-up sign and then placed his finger over his lips to indicate they should stay quiet. They waited there in silence until they heard the showers turn on. The sound of the running water gave Dizz enough background noise to slide the panel and secure it back into place.

Dizz turned on his flashlight, pulled his student I.D. card out of his pocket, and wedged it between the wall and one of the pipes running up the wall. He then held out his hand and grabbed Art's I.D. and placed it in the same spot. Dizz then motioned Art to follow him down the narrow passage between the locker room plumbing pipes.

Just as Dizz had described it, at the end of the plumbing access passage, metal rungs protruded from the concrete wall, creating a ladder descending through an opening in the floor.

The boys climbed down the ladder to the wet floor below. They were now in the sewer and would walk the sewer passage until they came to another set of metal ladder rungs in the sewer wall that would take them to the wood outside the northwest corner of the Hawthorne grounds.

Art was relieved to see the next set of rungs; he had cringed with every step he took down the sewer passage. The boys climbed up the ladder, and then Dizz slid the manhole cover to one side, allowing them to climb out into the welcome fresh air.

As Art climbed out, he looked back and saw the large wrought iron fence marking the boundaries of Hawthorne Academy and the lights of Hawthorne shining through the twilight.

Dizz, noticing Art staring back at Hawthorne, commented in a hushed tone, "Makes you feel free, knowing that you're out of that medium security prison and they can't track your every move."

Art gave an affirmative nod and the two of them took off down on the trail through the woods. It did not take long until they came to the dead end of Estabrook Road. Dizz stopped in the heavily-wooded area to make sure they would not be seen coming out of the wood from the direction of Hawthorne. When he felt all was clear, he motioned for Art to follow, and then took off running from their wooded covering to the street. The boys hit the street and kept on running for another hundred yards before they slowed down to a walk, gulping in the night air. Dizz looked around at the randomly dispersed houses. There was no movement, and no indication that anyone had seen them.

They made their way through northern Concord, down to People's Storage. During their walk, Dizz—obviously nervous about Art's return the next day—went over and over the plan for Art's return to Hawthorne. Art was to be back at the plumbing access panel inside Hawthorne between seven-thirty and eight-thirty P.M. He would wait in the access passage by the panel until he heard Dizz knock on the panel three times, at which time he would respond with three knocks. This would be the signal for Dizz to slide open the panel.

Upon reaching People's Storage, Dizz pulled out his key and opened his six-foot by six-foot storage unit. He carefully rolled out a jet-black scooter with the word "Rebel" painted in bright red on both sides.

"This is my baby, Art," said Dizz. "I expect you to treat her with the utmost respect."

"Sure," said Art nervously, "but like I told you, I've never ridden a scooter."

"No problem, Art. After you get it started, it's like riding a bike, except you don't have to peddle. Come over here. I'll show you how to start it." He inserted the key, turned it to the ON position, and hit the starter button. It immediately started purring quietly, like a satisfied cat.

Dizz turned the scooter off and made Art first start it and then drive it up and down the driveway of the storage unit. The apprehensive look on Art's face slowly melted into a look of self-satisfaction as he found riding the scooter not only easy, but enjoyable. Dizz, seeing the change come over Art, began laughing and shaking his head.

"What?" asked Art.

"You had me worried there for a little bit, but I think you're going to be all right. Just don't get too attached to my baby. Oh, I almost forgot," Dizz walked back into the storage unit and brought out a black helmet with a mirrored face shield and a black jumpsuit. "Here, Art, put these on."

Art put on the black jumpsuit, along with the helmet.

"Wow, Mr. Bad. Mr. Hell-on-Wheels. Now put your shield down and you'll also be the Man of Mystery!"

Art pulled the shield down, which allowed him to be completely unrecognizable.

"Now, get out of here!" said Dizz. "I'll see you tomorrow."

Art mounted the scooter and sped away. Art loved the way riding the scooter made him feel free and in control. He buzzed through Concord and down to Café Diem in no time, wishing the ride were longer. He rode the scooter around to the back door of Café Diem. It was ten 'til eight and he was hoping someone was still there. There was a light in the back, near the storage room. He knocked on the back door and waited. An outside light turned on and he saw the small light from the peephole eclipsed as someone inside checked him out. The light returned to the peephole as the door slowly opened, revealing Marie's smiling face.

"Hi there, Thorny," Marie said with a little wink. "What's with the man in black get-up?"

"Oh, uh, none of this stuff is mine. I borrowed the scooter, and the outfit came along with it," replied Art sheepishly.

"Well, it does give you an air of mystery. You don't look bad in black."

Art smiled and blushed. It was nice getting a compliment from a cute girl.

"I have standing instructions that if you show up to send you to the Professor's house," said Marie. "I assume you know the way?"

"Yes, I know the way," said Art. He stood motionless, staring at Marie with a smile on his face. Marie smiled back and waited as an awkward silence grew. Marie finally broke the silence, "Well . . . don't you think you should get going?'

Art, now sensing the awkwardness of the moment, broke off his stare and said, "Yeah, sure, I should be on my way. Thanks."

Marie grinned, "You're welcome, Art. Be careful. I hope to see you again sometime."

Art smiled, nodded, put his helmet on, mounted the scooter and headed over to the Professor's house.

Moss heard the sound of the scooter and headed out his front door to see a man in all black riding up the driveway. It was a strange sight and he braced himself for possible trouble. He was quite surprised and relieved when Art's face was revealed as the black helmet was peeled off his head.

"I thought I only gave you enough money for a bike you could peddle," said the Professor, looking perplexed and a bit worried.

"I didn't need one," reassured Art. "Dizz already had his scooter sitting in a storage unit in Concord. I brought all your money back," said Art as he reached inside his pocket to pull out the cash.

"I'm not concerned about the money. I'm concerned about who may know about this," said Moss. "But, before we get into that conversation, why don't you pull that scooter around back so it is out of sight. Then, we'll go inside and hear all about how you snuck away from Hawthorne."

Art drove the scooter around to the back and stowed it, along with helmet and black jumpsuit in one of the small barns.

He walked over to the house with the Professor and left his shoes outside, explaining that part of his escape had involved traipsing through the sewer.

Once inside, Art explained how Dizz had helped him get off the Hawthorne grounds without being detected. He also told the Professor that he hoped it would be okay if he were a houseguest for the night.

Hearing the details of Art's escape from the Hawthorne grounds slowly transformed Moss's concern into relief. He told Art that he could stay as long as he needed and that he was surprised but happy to see him back so soon.

The Professor put a kettle on the stove to warm some water for tea and brought out a plate of unsold scones from Café Diem. Art was pleased to see the delicious scones he had been craving since his last trip to Café Diem.

"Professor," said Art, "where did you learn to make such delicious scones? It seems like a strange talent for a genetic scientist to possess. Did your mother teach you to bake?"

"No, actually, my mom, bless her soul, was one of the worst cooks I have ever been around. I learned how to make scones from Virginia Taylor's mother."

"How did that happen?" asked Art with a tone of disbelief.

"I had been working on a small summer project with Aaron, now Gene, and Virginia in Boston. This was when they were still dating, before they were married. Virginia had been trying all summer to set me up with a friend of hers. I had resisted because I secretly had a thing for Virginia. She put together a long weekend trip in late September, back to her hometown in Minnesota for Applefest. I finally broke down and said yes, figuring I would get to be close to Virginia and see where she grew up. So, Gene, Virginia, her friend, I think her name was Ellen, and I flew into a little airport in LaCrosse, Wisconsin, which was right across the Mississippi River from LaCrescent, Virginia's hometown. It was quite the weekend—lots of tension and awkward moments."

"So, I take it you and Ellen didn't hit it off?" questioned Art.

"Actually, Ellen and I got along fine. The awkwardness was from tension between Gene, Virginia, and Virginia's mother."

"What happened?" asked Art intrigued.

"Gene had never met Virginia's mother before and LaCrescent, the Applefest, and the local people—including Virginia's mother—were not up to Gene's elitist standards. He thought LaCrescent was a dumpy little hick town, that Applefest was a joke, and that the locals were uneducated, lower class people with limited vocabularies and drinking problems. He had come from an extremely wealthy family who lived in the upper echelon of the Chicago elite. Well, Virginia's mom saw right through him. She saw him for the spoiled snob that he was, trying to exploit the brains and talents of her daughter. When the two of them got together, it was like vinegar and baking soda. So, for most of the weekend, Gene stayed in his hotel room across the river in LaCrosse, refusing to participate in any of the weekend activities."

"How did you learn how to make scones out of all of this?"

"Ellen and I ended up spending a lot of time with Virginia and her mom. By profession, Virginia's mom was baker for a little co-op bakery and I ended up helping her bake apple pies for Applefest. While we were there, she baked some scones for us one morning and I was instantly hooked, so I asked for the recipe."

"Was Applefest really that bad?" asked Art.

"Oh no, it was delightful. It's just a small town, Midwest celebration of the local apple harvest, complete with a parade, a queen, carnival rides, pies, candied apples, and probably more drinking than should take place."

"Why did Gene hate it so much?" asked Art.

"I don't think he really hated Applefest or LaCrescent. He hated Virginia's mom for challenging his control over Virginia. He wanted her undivided loyalty. He wanted her in a position of desiring to please him so much that she would do anything he wanted. Virginia's mom, simple and unsophisticated as she was, exposed him for whom and what he was, so he tried to discredit and belittle everything about Virginia's mom and her community."

"Why didn't Virginia listen to her mom?"

"Good question, Art. Virginia is a giver by nature. She is extremely brilliant and, at the same time, emotionally needy. Raised solely by her mom, she grew up wanting and needing the love and affirmation of a strong man. Gene saw her talent and was intuitive enough to know that he could exploit it by being the strong man she needed. Virginia was willing to offer up all she had—her brains, her research abilities, her family, her past, her self will, and even her personhood—in order to be affirmed and loved by what she thought was a man who loved her. I am convinced that Gene has never really loved her for who she is. He is in love with the power she gives him, not only professionally, but personally, through his control over her life."

Moss sighed, then continued, "Gene is a user, a skilled, masterful manipulator, a borderline sociopath, an egomaniac.

He has used and will use any and all around him to accomplish his goals. This includes his wife and probably his children. Unfortunately, Virginia was so desperate to please her strong man, that she was even willing to cut her mom out of her life. She became his puppet. She was subject to Gene's every whim."

The kettle on the stove started to hiss, which turned into a full-blown whistle. Moss walked over and poured two cups of tea, placed them on a tray along with the scones, and suggested that they go sit on some comfortable chairs in the study. Art followed him through the dining room and down the hall to a cozy study with leather chairs. On the outside wall of the study was a fireplace that still glowed with the hot coals from an earlier fire. The Professor sat the tray down on the coffee table and threw a couple more logs into the fireplace.

"Find a comfortable chair and help yourself to some tea and scones," he invited.

Art wasted no time accepting the invitation as he grabbed a scone and began munching. "So, where's Barger?" Art said between bites, looking around.

"He lives out in the Thoreau cabin, but tonight he's staying in Concord. I expect he'll come knocking in the morning when he spots your scooter," Moss chuckled, then furrowed his brow, "Art, I have been concerned about you since the last time we talked. Do you have any questions or concerns you want to talk about?"

Art, still chewing on his scone, nodded and took a drink from his tea. "It really bothers me to think about myself as an experiment. Do you know what they did to me?"

"I don't know exactly what they did, but I was told that they were going to limit your genetic engineering to the enhancement of musical abilities and hand-eye coordination. From your obvious ability to compose and perform on the keyboards, I assume that they stayed with that plan. Art, have you ever tried to play table tennis, badminton, or tennis?"

"No," said Art.

"You might want to give it a try. I believe you might be really good at it," said Moss.

"Based on what they did to me, do you think I really have a choice about who I am?"

The Professor got up out of his chair, grabbed a poker, and stabbed the logs on the fire until a bright yellow flame emerged from the logs. "That's an excellent question, Art. If you believe Gene Taylor, each of us is just the sum of our parts. Taylor is a reductionist, believing we are just biological creatures who—thanks to technology—can be custom built and modified. He does not believe in human nature. He believes we are merely a product of our genes, as dictated by evolution, and now he thinks he has the tools to control evolution. What do you think, Art? Do you believe you have a choice about who you are?"

"I don't know . . . I used to feel like I did. But now I'm not sure."

The Professor sat down in the leather chair directly across from Art and stared intensely into Art's eyes. "Art, even if someone can pull a file out on you, tell you your genetic make up, your biological and physical history and even know how you were genetically engineered, they cannot describe who you really are, neither can they control your future. You are a person, with feelings, emotions, passions, and a soul. Your genes may have been tweaked, but you are not a computer, where all you get is what has been programmed."

Art's eyes misted up as he nodded in affirmation to what the Professor was saying. Once he regained his composure, he asked the Professor what he thought they expected him to be, to do.

"Well, they—or I probably should say Gene—since Gene believes that all the traits you or anyone possesses are merely a result of biological and chemical processes, then he expects you to be what he programmed and designed—a musical genius, a wonder, an amazing talent."

"So, Professor, do you think there is some ultimate purpose they are looking for me to fulfill?"

"Once again, you have to define who 'they' are," said Moss. "There is the government, and then there's Gene. I don't think the two are in sync as to the exact outcome they are seeking.

"You see, Gene has been very skilled at manipulating the government, convincing them that there is an impending genetic 'arms race'. He scared them to death about what his competitors in nanotechnology were likely to do, convincing them that they needed one centralized agency to oversee and control anything and everything that involved human enhancement or trans-human genetics.

"Gene wants to be known as the 'Father of Positive Genetics,' a new world order in which people are genetically programmed for the greater good. To him that means no disease, no sickness, no infirm—or what he calls deformed humans. What's more, he wouldn't have any money 'wasted' on those who do not contribute to society in an acceptable way. He paints a picture of a world where everyone is happy doing what he or she is programmed to do, from laborers to the intelligent elite class who would govern and control a society with no social unrest." Moss paused. "Gene sees all of this being accomplished through genetic modifications, pharmacology, limited nanotechnology, and education—or more appropriately called brain washing."

"So what do you think Gene is looking for from me?" asked Art.

"Gene never talked to me about this, but knowing Gene, my guess is that he wants to use you and your talents as a showcase to the public, to help convince the world of the common good that can come to society through the use of positive genetics. He wants the public to see that you are not a monster, but on the contrary, an incredibly talented human being who brings joy and happiness to the world through music. The possibility of having happier, healthier, incredibly talented children will open the door to people thinking differently about genetic manipulation. What people will not know is how far Gene really wants to go with human engineering. These changes to our looks, our memories, metabolism, personalities, thinking and abilities, will challenge our whole social structure and what it means to be human."

"What if I don't cooperate?" asked Art.

"I think it would be a major blow to his overall plans. I think Gene is working very hard right now to insure your cooperation. Not through physical force, but by manipulating people and situations to make it very difficult for you to choose anything counter to his will and his plan."

"I'm not sure I understand what you mean," said Art.

"Gene is known for manipulating situations and people in order to create an emotional and psychological indebtedness in order to get what he wants."

"Now I really don't understand what you mean."

"Let's take your situation," said Moss. "I imagine he is in the process of arranging an emotional haven that will entice you to totally buy into positive genetics and have no problem being his 'poster child'. He will figure out your needs and what you want most in life. Then he'll arrange the circumstances to meet your needs, and take the credit for being your gracious benefactor. After that, if you ever cross him, he will remind you of everything he's done for you."

"And how do you think he's doing this?" asked Art, sensing he already knew the answer.

"Judging by what you've already told me, I think he's starting by giving you a sense of family, and the experience of being popular," said the Professor.

"So, you're saying that my friendship with the Taylor family has been arranged to set me up?" asked Art.

"Yes, Art, as nice a young man as you are, I don't think Gene Taylor actually cares for your well-being other than how it impacts his well being. Now, I will say that Virginia is not a manipulator and would not purposefully appear to be your friend in order to manipulate your life. I don't know about his children, Chris and Elisha, but, I suspect they are, to a great extent, controlled by their father."

The more the Professor explained his suspicions, the more the overwhelming feeling of disappointment engulfed Art. The Taylors were the closest thing to a family that Art had experienced during his lifetime, but now he was being told it was all a giant charade.

"Art, I can't help thinking that all I do is give you bad news," said Moss.

"I, I guess I really don't want to believe what you're telling me, but I know it's probably true. It's just that . . . holiday break with the Taylors and being friends with Chris and Elisha has made me feel special as a person other than for my musical talent. I want a family. I want to belong. For a while, I thought that was possible. Now, I feel like I am spinning in the middle of a blender. I'm not sure what to think. I'm supposed to go to Florida with the Taylors next weekend. This is going to be incredibly awkward and uncomfortable, knowing what I know. I mean, what am I supposed to do with all this?"

Art and the Professor stared at each other in silence. Then Moss scooted forward in his chair and took a sip of his tea, and attempted to answer Art's question. "Art, I can't begin to imagine how disappointing and confusing all of this is to you. I guess the most important thing is that you be careful in your dealings with Gene Taylor. He is a very calculated, sinister, devious, and insidious user who will stop at nothing to accomplish his agenda."

"So, what do I do when I'm in Florida with this monster that you've just described?" asked Art.

"If I were you, I would appear to soak in everything he says, like a sponge. Act as if you are enamored with his views. Fall all over yourself in gratitude for anything and everything he has done and will do for you. Give the impression that you are falling in line with his plans. Do not challenge him. Do not contradict him. Come off as a green, naïve, eighteen-year-old whose only interest is music."

"Then what's the point of you telling me all of this?" asked Art.

"Because you asked, because you deserve to know the truth about yourself, and because you need to know who and what you're dealing with," replied Moss in a firm tone. "Art, you would have found out about a lot of this eventually, but under different circumstances."

"Different circumstances?" inquired Art.

"Yes, different circumstances. Gene will not give you any information until you are deeply indebted to him, both emotionally and in regard to your career. Having the truth in advance puts you in the driver's seat. You will be the one who knowingly decides how you live your life, what you will be involved in, and what it will cost you."

"Cost me, what cost? What do you mean?"

"No matter what you do from here on, it will cost you. If you don't go along with Gene and his plans, it will probably cost you fame, fortune, and personal comfort. If you go along with Gene's plans, it may cost millions their humanity. Whether you like it or not, sometime in the future, you may be in the position to help expose and possibly help stop the dehumanization of the human race. I'm sure this sounds crazy to you, but I am convinced that what Gene is planning with genetic engineering is a watershed issue for the human race."

A look of fear and shock crept over Art's face. Art's shock slowly gave way to denial and then, anger. This was too fantastic to be real. How could he be put in the position of 'saving the human race'? This was absurd. It was insane. It was crazy. Why him? He did not ask for any of this. His anger erupted into a verbal explosion.

"I didn't ask to be frozen! I didn't ask to be chosen for an experiment and then genetically modified! I didn't choose to be musically talented! I didn't choose to be put in a position to stop genetic dehumanization! I didn't volunteer for any of this and I don't have to do anything! This is not right! This is not fair!"

"You're absolutely correct, Art," said Moss. "It's not right and it's not fair, but, it is where you find yourself. If you do nothing with your newfound knowledge, millions may grow up to find themselves in the same condition, manipulated and modified without their consent. The choice of what you do will be totally yours. However, how do you know that your destiny is not to be one who stands against the wrong being done to humanity? How do you know that you were not born at this time and for this purpose?"

"Well, Professor, if what you told me is true, I wasn't designed to save the world, but to be an artist. Don't you think you got the wrong guy?"

"You'll have to decide that for yourself, Art. I certainly don't have the ability to force you to agree with me let alone take any action."

It was starting to get late, and Moss said that they should get some sleep and talk more in the morning. He showed Art to the stairs up to the guest room. Art politely thanked the professor for letting him stay the night and apologized for his angry outbursts. Moss assured him that there was nothing to apologize for, and that it was only natural that all of this would be extremely upsetting.

Art lay down in the bed and stared at the ceiling. He was overwhelmed by the desire to run . . . just to get away, to be someone else, somewhere else. How could this be happening to him? How could this be his life? Everything was out of his control.

Art awoke the next morning to wonderful smells wafting up from the kitchen. He got dressed and headed downstairs where he found the Professor making bacon, eggs, and pancakes. Art smiled broadly as he inhaled the aroma of a home-cooked breakfast. Moss smiled back at Art and pointed toward the cupboard with his spatula, "The dishes are on that cupboard right behind you and the silverware is in the drawer below the dishes. Set three places—Barger should be getting back from his overnight in Concord and he loves breakfast."

"So if he has the cabin here, why was he in Concord last night?"

"He was away making some arrangements for Café Diem. He stayed the night with his daughter in Concord."

"He's got a daughter in Concord? Does he see her very often?" asked Art.

"Well, almost everyday," said the Professor. "You see, Marie is his daughter."

"I didn't know that," said Art.

"Hardly anyone does. Barger and his wife were divorced when Marie was only two. His wife remarried and Marie was officially adopted by her stepfather so she has a different last name," said Moss.

"Didn't he try to stop it and get custody?"

"No," said the Professor. "The attempt would have been a waste of time. Barger was black-balled from the industry about the same time I was. I escaped by becoming a hermit . . . Barger chose alcohol, which was the reason for the divorce. Barger was a full-blown alcoholic when the adoption went through and he believed Marie was better off with a stable family so he willingly but reluctantly relinquished his parental rights."

The Professor set a large, steamy plate of pancakes on the table along with miniature pitchers of melted butter and maple syrup. "Dig in," he invited.

Art wasted no time piling a stack of pancakes onto his plate, slathering them with butter and immersing them in syrup. Moss smiled as he watched Art thoroughly demolish the stack.

Art, his mouth full, muttered a muffled, "What happened to him? He seems fine now."

"I assume you mean Barger?" asked the Professor.

Art, with his mouth still full and syrup now dripping off his chin, nodded affirmatively.

"After a couple of failed treatment center experiences and running through all his money, he ended up in a residential AA program through the Salvation Army. With their help, he was able to get his mind, body, and spirit working together in harmony. He's been dry, or alcohol free, for about seventeen years now."

Art and Moss heard the squeak of the back door opening. Barger walked into the kitchen, saw Art and the pancakes, and smiled.

"You always seem to have perfect timing when it comes to food," said the Professor.

All three of them dug into the breakfast feast while Art and Moss filled Barger in on Art's escape from Hawthorne.

After the last strip of bacon had disappeared, the Professor invited Art to take a hike with him, hoping he could discuss a few more items with Art. Barger volunteered to stay behind to clean up.

It was a bright and sunny, but chilly, spring day. The Professor threw Art a hooded sweatshirt and jacket. It was about thirty-six degrees when they started out and they could see their breath each time they exhaled.

"We'll take my back trail through the woods over to Walden Pond," said the Professor. "The trail starts out by the Thoreau Cabin."

They started out at a brisk pace to try to keep warm. They picked up the trail by the cabin and headed north along the

Sudbury for about one hundred yards, before turning northeast and heading into Walden Woods toward Walden Pond.

"You know, Art," said the Professor, "it seems like I'm always apologizing to you. I'm sorry if I put any undue pressure on you last night. After you went to bed, I got to thinking about the irony of the whole situation. If I were to force you to be or do something against your will, I would be guilty of practicing the same thing I'm fighting against."

"I'm not sure I understand," said Art.

"If I don't think its right for the human race to be manipulated and forced to be changed without their consent, how could I justify forcing you to do something against your will?" explained the Professor.

"Oh, now I see what you're saying," said Art. "No apology necessary. I really don't feel like you would force me to do anything. I feel like you have a strong opinion about what I should do, so I feel pressured, but not forced."

The Professor slowed his pace almost to a stop and turned to look at Art. "To be honest with you, Art, I want you to feel pressured. Not by me, but by your own conscience, your sense of right and wrong."

Art did not reply but merely nodded that he understood. The two walked on without speaking, the only sounds being the crunch of broken sticks under their feet and the sound of the breeze high in the fir trees. Art, becoming uncomfortable by the quiet, broke the awkward silence. "Professor, tell me more about your relationship with Gene and Virginia. Did you spend very much time with them?"

"Actually, I spent quite a lot of time with them," said the Professor. "Art, follow me over here a ways, I want to show you a few things."

The Professor meandered through the woods until he came to an opening with a small slough. He walked over to the edge of a pool of water and bent over, peering into the water, his hands on his knees. "Take a look, Art," said Moss, now peering intensely into the pool. "What do you see?"

Art bent over the pool with the professor and gazed into the pool. "It looks like worms coming up out of the bottom of the pool," said Art, slightly disgusted.

"I guess it does, doesn't it," said the Professor, "but they are actually water lily pods rising to the surface. And look right over there," said the Professor, pointing about ten yards away from the slough, "what does that look like?"

"Uh, well, it kind of looks like a giant lobster claw coming out of the ground," said Art.

"You have a great imagination," chuckled the Professor. "That's actually a skunk cabbage just barely appearing above the ground. That reddish claw will unfold into very large, green leaves in a couple of weeks." The Professor stopped and inhaled deeply. "I love the earthy smell of spring." He continued to meander through the white pine and oak trees, looking for the early signs of spring in Walden Woods. He stopped along the way, pointing out wildflowers that had just emerged and bloomed and picked a few morel mushrooms that he stowed away in a small plastic bag he brought with him.

Art loved the nature hike, but he was more interested in finding out more about the Professor's history with the Taylors.

"Professor," pressed Art, "other than work, what kinds of things did you do with Gene and Virginia Taylor?"

"For a while, we did about everything together," said the Professor.

"We worked long hours together and then, after work, we would usually get dinner together and hang out at Virginia's apartment," said the Professor. "We're almost there. Walden Pond is just on the other side of those railroad tracks, just ahead."

They walked up and over the tracks to the water's edge where they picked up the trail that went around the pond. There was a slight breeze and the morning sun glittered off the slightly choppy surface of the pond.

"So, you must have got along with them really well."

"When I look back on it now, the early days with Gene and Virginia were wonderful days," said the Professor. "I got along with both of them extremely well in the beginning. Then as time went on, I discovered that I was very different from Gene, but Virginia and I were very much alike in many ways."

"What did you discover was so different about you and Gene?"

The Professor laughed and shook his head. "I think we disagreed on just about everything. I was a Patriot fan, he was a Bears fan, I liked John Mayer, and he liked Dave Matthews. I liked dogs, and he liked cats. At first I thought he was just being competitive, but the more time I spent with him the more I realized that we really had a different view of the world."

"What do you mean, a different view of the world?" asked Art.

"I realized that I believed in a divine or supernatural dimension to reality," said the Professor. "Gene had an almost violent reaction to anything or anybody remotely related to faith or God. He defined himself as a student of objectivism. He believed that since there was no God, and no real moral authority, man's highest purpose was his own happiness. So, true, ultimate freedom was the ability to define oneself. He looked at self-sacrifice and altruism as a personality flaw, a betrayal of a person's highest value of his or her own well-being. He believed that there really wasn't any true altruism or self-sacrifice in the world, that it was only a trade-off for something else the person really wanted. I argued that a society that was ultimately based on selfishness could not be a healthy or just society. It would be doomed to fail."

Moss paused a moment, then continued, "Art, I really think his view of the world is what has allowed him to exercise control over his victims. He sees them as weak and inferior, so he has no guilt or remorse about his abuses. If you believe there is nothing greater than yourself, it not only affects your view of purpose, it also affects your view of time, power, love—everything."

"I can see how being totally selfish can't be good for a relationship, but I don't quite understand what you mean about it having an effect on time, power, and whatever else you mentioned," said Art.

"How can I explain this in a way that makes sense?"

As they continued walking, Art noticed a clump of runners dressed in purple running gear coming around the pond on the trail ahead of them.

"Oh, great. We need to disappear quickly," said Art. "That bouncing glob of purple coming our way is the Hawthorne track team. They must be out on their Saturday training run!"

The Professor and Art quickly turned their backs to the oncoming runners. "Put your hood on and follow me," said the Professor. Moss, with the agility of a twenty-year-old, bobbed and weaved his way up a small incline into the wooded area by the pond until there were enough trees between them and the trail that they would be difficult to see. Panting and out of breath, they sat with their backs to the trail, leaning against a couple of large white pines.

"Chris Taylor is running with that group," Art managed to gasp in a panting, heavy, whisper.

"Don't worry, I don't think we were seen," said the Professor. "I feel pretty negligent bringing you to a place where we could be seen. I got carried away with taking a hike to look for early signs of spring. I just forgot that one of those signs is the start of the track season." They both laughed under their breath and the Professor pulled a couple of water bottles out of the inside pockets of his coat and handed one to Art. They guzzled the water as they waited for the track team to clear the area before moving on.

"I think the smart thing would be to head back to the cabin and finish our conversation there," said the Professor.

They took off, walking at a steady pace, but still meandering back and forth through the woods looking for signs of new life. On the way back, Moss pointed out blue-flowering Hepatica, the fuzzy tops of ferns emerging from the forest floor, and some multicolored Colt's Foot.

"During my Thoreau experience, I was inspired by Thoreau's attention to the details of nature," said the Professor. "I spent a lot of time just wandering in the woods that year, looking for the subtle changes in the seasons. I think it has helped me appreciate the delicate balance of life on this earth."

By the time they reached the Thoreau Cabin, he had pointed out turtles on a log sunning themselves, squirrels, rabbits, a Marsh hawk, and a group of Canadian geese, heading north. Art realized that he had never taken notice of so much wildlife in his life.

The temperature had risen to the low fifties, but with clear skies and no wind, the sunshine made it feel much warmer. They went over by the river's edge and sat down in two large wooden Adirondack chairs that they turned to face the sun.

"Okay, Professor," said Art, "You were telling me something about how Gene Taylor's view of the world effects his perception of time and a couple other things."

"Power and love," said the Professor.

"What?" asked Art.

"Time, power, and love," responded the Professor.

"Yeah, what do you mean by that?" asked Art.

"Well, let's start with time," said the Professor.

"If there is no creator of time, no divine plan to things, then time becomes purposeless. Essentially, without a creator of time, time would simply be the neutral passing of events. Events would unfold because they happen to have happened. If you believe as Gene does, that there is nothing greater than he is, time is merely a tool to accomplish his selfish desires. Time, like everything else in his life, is to the extent possible, to be manipulated for his highest good."

"Based on what I've seen, and what you've told me, Professor, it looks like he's done a fairly good job of controlling time," said Art.

"Yes, so far he has certainly manipulated outcomes in his favor, but he is not in control of time and the final outcome is not his to decide," replied the Professor.

"I am assuming by that statement that your view of time is quite different than Mr. Taylor's?" asked Art.

"Oh, quite different," said the Professor. "I believe that time is anything but the neutral passing of events. I believe time is an agent of divine providence."

"Divine providence?" questioned Art. "What do you mean by divine providence?"

"If time is created," said Moss, "time is a tool in the Creator's hand to bring about his ultimate purpose. The author of time can weave into each of our lives all kinds of twists, turns, and surprises. He can frustrate and nullify our plans and expectations or he can put them into effect in ways we would never have guessed. I believe that our time here is providentially planned, but most of the time we are unaware of that design."

"I'm guessing then, you believe that we have all been placed here for a specific purpose. And I'm also guessing that Mr. Taylor believes that he is the only one that can decide the purpose for his existence and, I assume, my existence," said Art.

"Yes, Art," said the professor, "there is far too much complexity of design everywhere you look to believe this all happened without design or purpose, but I believe you are totally wrong to think that Gene has decided the purpose of your existence."

"Wait, wait a minute!" exclaimed Art. "This sounds a bit inconsistent. If our time here is 'designed' by some author or creator of time, why does he let Gene Taylor do the things he does?"

"That's a fair, logical question," said the Professor. "We are not robots without a will of our own. We are free moral agents. As such, I believe we are free to make our own choices, but that's where some irony comes in."

"Irony?" questioned Art.

"Irony is where there is an apparent discrepancy or incongruity between what we expect or believe is happening and what actually happens," said the professor. "We see what Gene is doing as evil, but the author of time, through what I like to call providential irony, works it all together to bring about good."

"So, does that make what Gene is doing essentially good?" asked Art.

"No, no, absolutely not," said the Professor. "The author of time takes Gene's evil actions and uses them or works things together to bring about ultimate good."

"I think I see what you are saying, but, it seems a bit fantastic," said Art. "What about Mr. Taylor's perception of power?"

"Power... let's see," the Professor said, rubbing his unshaven, stubby, chin. "Art, you seem to believe that Gene Taylor has power over the ultimate purpose of your existence. I think that Gene probably believes he does too, but Gene is mistaken. He does not have the ultimate power of a creator God. He may move, shape, and tweak things already created, but he really is not in ultimate control. I believe that through the positive eugenics movement, Gene wants to shape life in a way to serve him and his vision.

"Since Gene believes that there is nothing greater than himself, he believes ultimate power is possible, but he does not, nor will he ever, possess ultimate power. You've probably heard the old saying 'absolute power corrupts absolutely'. Well, I think the possibility of that kind of power has already corrupted Gene to the point of him having no problem crossing any moral boundary that gets in his way."

"He may not possess ultimate power," countered Art, "but it appears that he has more than sufficient power to do about anything he wants, and that probably involves shutting both of us up."

"The key thing you just said was that he 'appears' to have sufficient power, but, the one with ultimate power may interfere at anytime to strip him of his power and shut him down," replied the Professor.

"I assume you are referring to this creator or god as the one having the ultimate power?" questioned Art.

"Yes, Art," said the Professor. "I do believe that God has the ultimate power. And the interesting thing is that he has a way of giving true power to those we would least expect."

"Like?" questioned Art.

"Like, a young boy too small to put on armor who was able to kill a giant, a young Jewish girl chosen by a mighty king to be his queen who ultimately saved her whole race, grossly outnumbered armies, a baby boy king born in a stable," responded the Professor.

"I assume you are referring to stories from the Bible," said Art. "You got any examples in recent history?"

The Professor leaned back in his chair, closed his eyes and wrinkled his forehead. "Hmmm," said the Professor, "I can think of a couple from my lifetime. Ever heard of Agnes Bojaxhiu?"

"Ah, no," said Art.

"Well," said the Professor, "you probably have. She is better known as Mother Teresa. She was a tiny little woman, barely five-feet tall, but they say she had the longest arms in the world. She was just a little woman with no apparent power, reaching out to the poor, sick, and dying in India, but she literally changed the world's view toward the poor and under privileged. How about Lazlo Tokes, ever hear of him?"

"No," said Art again, shaking his head.

"Lazlo was a Bishop of the Romanian Reformed Church back in the late 1980s when Romania was under a ruthless communist regime. Not considering his own safety, he spoke out against human rights abuses. He was ordered by the government to stop preaching. When he refused, they cut off his ability to buy food and attempted to evict him from his church. He refused to leave and his parishioners surrounded his church to protect him. When ordered to disperse, they refused and then thousands more came and joined the protest. The protest grew and turned into a revolt of the people that ended up overthrowing the totalitarian government of Romania. This was done with no guns and no organized army, all because a bishop stood up and said, 'No'!"

"And you attribute what happened in these cases to God?"

"Yes, Art, I do. So did those people," said the Professor. "They had no other explanation for the irony of power working through them."

"That leaves love," said Art, "and I think I can already see how Taylor's view of the world affects his perception of love."

"How so?" asked the Professor.

"Well," said Art, appreciating that the Professor would listen to his analysis, "if you believe that self-sacrifice and altruism are personality flaws and that your highest purpose is your own happiness, your definition of love is love of yourself or self-fulfillment."

"I think you got the picture," said the Professor. "Like I mentioned before, Gene is a user and Virginia is a giver."

The sun scooted under a bank of clouds and the wind picked up, making it feel like the temperature instantly dropped twenty degrees. They both felt the chill and decided to head back over to the house to grab some lunch. After lunch, they headed for the study. The Professor started a fire as Art perused through his collection of antique books lining the large built-in bookcases.

"Let me know if you see anything that you'd like to borrow," said the Professor.

"Maybe I'll borrow a couple after finals," said Art.

The two sat down in the leather chairs facing the fireplace. The Professor sank back into his chair and exhaled, then addressed Art with a tone of completion. "Art, I've tried to provide you with the answers you were looking for and hopefully with additional information to allow you to assess your current situation and decide how you will handle yourself going forward. Is there anything else you would like to know from me?"

Art thought for a few minutes and then responded, "I know you and Mr. Taylor disagree on many things, but it sounds like Gene and Virginia were pretty good friends of yours at one time. What happened to cause you and Gene Taylor to face off against each other as enemies?"

"Enemies?" responded the Professor. "That's a strong word, but I guess in truth, that is what we are. It wasn't one specific thing. It was a series of things that, over time, culminated in both of us clearly knowing where the other stood on vital issues and what action each of us would take to defend and enforce each of our positions."

"What type of things?" questioned Art. "Give me your perspective."

"I came to the conclusion that advances in genetics, nanotechnology, and pharmacology, if pursued without some kind of reasonable restraint, would eventually pose a grave threat to humanity as we now know it. When I raised objections, Gene immediately accused me of taking the 'Amish approach' to genetic technology. All I was really after was a way to make use of the creative advancements in the fields, and at the same time acknowledge our humanity and the potential destructive capability of our newly-found knowledge. Gene strongly advocated that science should be able to pursue knowledge, free from any ethical or moral judgments or restraint. Gene painted my concerns as anti-science, anti-progress, and anti-cure, which he knew was not true. He basically betrayed our friendship and distorted everything I was saying so that he could proceed with his agenda with no questions asked."

"You sound pretty hurt," Art said softly.

"I was hurt, and I was bitter and angry for a long, long time. His actions took away my life's passion, my livelihood, my identity. It has taken me a good deal of time to get over my resentment and anger and forgive him."

"Are you sure you are over it?" asked Art. "It still seems like you want to take him down."

"I can see how it might look that way," replied the Professor. "I no longer have any desire to hurt Gene, but I would like to help put a stop to where Gene's brand of genetic manipulation is taking us."

"Where do you see it taking us?" asked Art.

"Left unchecked, I foresee a society divided between those who are genetically and economically rich and those genetically and economically poor. I think you can already see this happening at Hawthorne. East coast elites have taken the step with Gene Taylor to genetically insure the success, power, control, and the status of their children. This is what wealth allows. It only follows that the poor have-nots should be genetically tweaked to be happy with their lot in life in exchange for a disease-free, fulfilled life. I worry how all of this will affect the institutions that are extremely important to maintain social stability. Take the concept of democracy. It will no longer be a given that all men are created equal.

"I feel like we are on the verge of dehumanization, but it is being sold as super-humanization. Our lust for enhancement has distorted our view of humanity. This new potential for immortality has overloaded our desires and blinded us to the immorality of the actions we have taken.

"Art, are you familiar with the story of the fall of man in the Garden of Eden?"

"You mean the story of the serpent and eating the forbidden fruit?" responded Art.

"Yes," said the professor. "I see our biotech lust as the same temptation brought on by the enticement of the serpent. We desire to be gods. We want to overcome God's control. We want God to be irrelevant. The possibilities in genetics have created desires in us where none previously existed. It has created a desire for more and more of the forbidden fruit. I'm sorry . . . I kind of got on my soap box again, didn't I?"

"Your soap box?" asked Art, with a confused look on his face.

"It's an old saying that means I got carried away making a speech," said the Professor.

"That's okay," said Art. "I have one more question. How do you feel about Virginia after all this has happened to you?"

The Professor took a deep breath, pursed his lips, and exhaled slowly. "I was always much closer to Virginia," said the Professor. "And, as I mentioned earlier I was very taken by her at one time. When I realized that she was only interested in Gene, I had hopes that she would be able to have some kind of positive affect on Gene. However, deep down I knew that her need for a strong man in her life would not allow her to oppose him in any meaningful way. Her helping me, or sticking up for my views or for me in any way, would have been seen as a huge betrayal. Knowing that, I had no real expectation that Virginia could or would do anything. So, overall, I'm really okay with Virginia."

Art gave the Professor a nod and an understanding smile and he smiled back.

"Art," said the Professor. "I'm probably just getting old, but I'm in need of a nap. Feel free to look through the library, grab a snack, or even take a nap yourself. Once Barger gets back from Café Diem later this afternoon, we want to talk with you about an escape option if you get in trouble and need to disappear."

The Professor got up and walked down the hallway, leaving Art alone in the study. Art pulled a book of Thoreau Quotes out of the bookshelf, sat down in the large leather chair, read a few, and fell asleep.

He awoke to see Barger and the Professor sitting across from him, sipping tea.

"Wake up, sleepy head," said Barger. "Did you have a good nap?"

"Yes, I really did. This is a great napping chair," said Art.

Barger chuckled, smiled, and then his expression immediately turned serious. "I'm sure you know this by now, but our meetings have placed all of us in serious danger. There may come a time when the situation requires us to disappear. Even before you arrived on the scene, I had been working on a plan for the Professor, Marie, and I to vanish without a trace. I have arranged to broaden our plan to include you and your friend Dizzy if necessary. I am not going to tell you the details of the plan for security reasons, but I want you to know that if you need to run, you have a place to come."

Art murmured a polite thank you. Hearing Barger talk about disappearing frightened him. He knew in the back of his mind that what he was doing was dangerous, but Barger talking about running and vanishing without leaving a trace made the danger somehow more real.

"If you have to run, just show up either here or at Café Diem and we'll take it from there," said Barger. "Whatever you do, don't ever try to contact us by any electronic device, or ever mention our names to anyone. Are we clear on that?"

"Yes, yes, quite clear," said Art.

"You must make sure you are not followed. With that in mind, I want you and Dizz to have a pre-planned escape procedure and route. I like the way you got down here this weekend. If you could duplicate that exit it would be fantastic. Speaking of that exit, when are you supposed to be back at Hawthorne?"

"Between seven-thirty and eight o'clock," said Art.

"Well then, we need to get you out of here. It's already 6:45."

That being said, the Professor, Barger, and Art all stood up and made their way through the house to the backdoor. The men walked Art out to the shed where the scooter was stored. Art slipped into the all black jumpsuit, thanked the professor and Barger, put on the all black helmet, and rode away toward Concord.

The Professor and Barger stood together and watched Art ride down the driveway.

Still watching, Barger asked, "So, what do you think?"

"I think we are doing the right thing," replied Moss.

"I meant, what do you think about Art?"

"I think he's finally going to be able to figure out who he really is," said the Professor.

Barger asked again, "No, I mean, do you think he understands the change he is capable of bringing about?"

"I don't know . . . only God knows," replied Moss.

"You could say that about anything," quipped Barger.

"Yes, and I would always be right," the Professor quipped back.

Barger looked at the Professor and shook his head in semi-disgust. "Let's go inside and I'll tell you about how our escape plan is coming together."

Once inside, Barger informed the Professor that he had lined up all of the final details with the buyer for Café Diem and the Professor's homestead.

"Moss, this is certainly not a typical real estate deal. Are you sure you can trust this guy?" said Barger, sounding unsure that the buyer would make good on all of his promises.

"I'm absolutely sure, Barger. I have known the buyer for over thirty years. Ever since my parents died, he has been making me offers for this place. He's extremely wealthy and has connections all over the world. What we're asking of him is a relatively simple matter for a man like him."

"I just feel like giving him a signed quit claim deed to hold in advance before we get what we need from him is foolish," said Barger.

"We can't risk having a trust company or attorneys hold them. We would have to provide too many details. Someone would end up talking. Don't worry, Barger, we can trust this man. He will do what he promises. Now, tell me how everything is shaping up."

"Okay, here's the list of consideration coming from the buyer:

1. A four-bedroom house on a two-acre enclosed compound has been purchased just outside Antigua, Guatemala by a newly formed corporation owned entirely by you.
2. The property will be fully furnished, including towels and linens.
3. The property will also come with four new motorized scooters and one top of the line Land Rover.
4. The balance of the purchase price, except for the cash, will be deposited into the bank account of the corporation held at Banc De Antigua.
5. Within two hours of Marie contacting the buyer, a vehicle suitable for transporting five passengers comfortably will be dropped off at the end of our driveway out on the paved road, fully fueled with $500,000.00 in cash in the glove compartment.
6. Passage will be secured for five passengers on a commercial vessel from Boston to Puerto Barrios, Guatemala. Passage will be discreet and hidden, requiring no passports. Upon arriving in Puerto Barrios, appropriate documents will be fabricated for each passenger to allow entry and freedom of movement in Guatemala under a different name. Transportation will be provided from Puerto Barrios to Antigua."

"Sound good?" asked Barger.

"Sounds good, except I did not hear anything about fruit trees and a working garden on the property," complained Moss.

"I did not ask about the fruit trees and garden. I figured that you'll need something to do once you get there," said Barger.

The Professor smiled and nodded his head in agreement. "Nice job setting all of this up. My mind just doesn't work that way. Now we will just have to wait and see whether we will ever have to actually execute this plan."

"What's your guess?" asked Barger.

Moss closed his eyes and thought a minute before responding. "Right now, I think Art is weighing the cost. I think what happens in Florida with Gene will determine what road he takes. As we know, Gene can be very persuasive."

19

Spring Break

ART ARRIVED BACK at the storage unit before he realized it. He really enjoyed being the "man in black," racing through Concord on a scooter. The second he stepped off the scooter to unlock the storage unit, Dizz suddenly appeared from around the corner.

Art froze in fear until he realized it was only Dizz. "You scared me to death! I thought the plan was that you were going to wait for me at the access panel inside Hawthorne?" said Art.

"Yeah, while you were gone I got to thinking about your sense of direction and began to question whether you would ever be able to find the sewer access in the woods," said Dizz.

"Thanks for the show of confidence," Art retorted sarcastically. "On the other hand, I was pretty worried about finding the access and getting back in."

They both laughed and Art gave Dizz a quick hug.

"Hey, hey, this does not mean we are taking the relationship to the next level," joked Dizz.

"Oh, cut it out, Dizz!"

They quickly stowed the bike and headed back to Hawthorne. Dizz was masterful in finding their way back, avoiding being seen, and easing them back into the locker room through the access panel. Within a half an hour, Art was back in his room thinking about his upcoming trip at the end of next week to Florida.

Monday and Tuesday of the next week seemed to fly by for Art. On Wednesday, Art had a meeting scheduled with Professor Silverman, his favorite music professor and academic advisor, to discuss the status of his college applications. Professor Silverman had taken a special interest in Art as a freshman and had mentored Art for the four years he had been at Hawthorne. Professor Silverman had encouraged Art to think about broadening his horizons. Even though Hawthorne was an Ivy League feeder school, he convinced Art to send a college application to the Thornton School of Music at USC and to the school of music at Berkley. When Art walked into Silverman's office, he was pacing back and forth and appeared extremely agitated.

"Professor Silverman, is everything okay?"

"No, Art, I'm afraid things around here are not at all okay. I've just about had enough of this place. I enjoy teaching and I love my students but some of the things that happen behind the scenes at this institution are despicable."

"What happened? Are you okay?"

"I'm fine, but it appears that someone in the administration of this school sabotaged your applications to USC and Berkley."

"What! What do you mean?"

"After we completed the application, I had the school overnight them out to USC and Berkley to make sure you met the application deadlines. When I called USC and Berkley today, they had no record of your applications. I went to the office to see what happened to your applications and was told not to worry about it. In fact, when I protested, I was told it was in my best interest to just drop it."

"Did they say why they didn't send them out?"

"Yes, they told me it was in the best interest of Art Jenicks and Hawthorne Academy for you to go to an Ivy League school. I'm sorry Art, I did what I could."

"I really don't like what they did, but it's not your fault. To be truthful, I probably will end up choosing an Ivy League school anyway. I am kinda leaning toward going to Princeton. Professor, you're not thinking about leaving Hawthorne, are you?"

"There isn't another school anywhere that can match the salary I receive here, but I have to admit to entertaining the thought more and more. A couple more incidents like this may just push me over the edge. I think I just need to get away from here for a little bit, so spring break is coming at just the right time."

"What are your plans for spring break, Professor?"

"I'm headed to Winter Park for some spring skiing with my sister's family. I can't wait to see that clear blue Colorado sky again and float down the hill on fresh powder. Art, are you staying here or are you going to spend it with one of the Hawthorne families?"

"I've been invited to spend it with the Taylors down at their beach house in Florida. Elisha Taylor tells me that I am going to have the best week of my life."

"Elisha? Oh, I'd be careful around her."

"What do you mean?"

"Oops, I shouldn't have said anything. Just forget I said that, okay?"

"No, what do you mean? Why should I be careful?"

Professor Silverman ran his hand across his forward and then stoked his chin. "This has to stay just between us, okay?"

"Absolutely!"

"The rumor among the faculty is that she's responsible for getting a couple of teachers fired this year. I understand that her modus operandi is to try to get favorable grades by a little flirting and if that doesn't work, she subtly lets them know that her dad is always asking for her input on the quality and performance of teachers at Hawthorne. She appears to have manipulation skills well beyond her years, if you know what I mean. I would just be careful around her, that's all."

"Thanks, I appreciate the warning. I'll be careful," replied Art, attempting to sound appreciative and look concerned.

With that, the meeting ended on somewhat of an awkward note with Art excusing himself to go study for a class. Actually, he tracked Dizz down and told him about the application fiasco. Dizz was not the least bit surprised, and was happy to give Art his little canned speech about the insidious underlying nature of Hawthorne Academy. He informed Art that he had to realize that he lived in a totally controlled environment, differing little from a medium security prison. That Hawthorne knows when you eat, what you eat, when you sleep, when your door opens, when it closes, when you leave campus, when you come back, every move on the internet, everything in your email, what you purchase, what you do in your free time. He concluded by saying that the only thing they don't know is when you take a dump, but they could probably figure that out by checking your water usage.

For the rest of the week, Art remained extremely nervous about spending time again with the Taylors. He ran into Elisha a couple of times that week. She was giddy with excitement about spring break and assured Art again that it would be the best week of his life. However, after his talks with Silverman,

Art's infatuation with Elisha and her beauty was waning, and he was growing increasingly suspicious of Elisha's flirtatiousness.

The day of departure finally arrived and a TEI Company Limo showed up midmorning at Hawthorne to take Art, Chris, and Elisha to meet Gene and Virginia at TEI's private airport. The limo drove right out onto the runway and parked beside a small jet that was being loaded with luggage and supplies.

Chris and Elisha hurried out of the limo to greet their mom and dad with hugs. Art followed politely behind and greeted Gene with a smile and a handshake. When he attempted to do the same with Virginia, she pulled him in and gave him a big hug, after which Art turned a bit red; nonetheless, he enjoyed the motherly gesture.

Mr. Taylor started talking about how they may be a little cramped on this flight since the jet was smaller. He explained that the smaller jet would allow them to land in New Smyrna Beach instead of Daytona, putting them much closer to their beach cottage.

The flight was smooth and quick with little or no personal interaction. Everyone seemed to be absorbed in their own little entertainment world while on board. That was fine with Art. It gave him a little more time to calm down and to remind himself that he was just going to relax, have a good time, and maintain a low profile around Mr. Taylor.

Once on the ground in New Smyrna Beach, they loaded into a big, white SUV and headed for the beach cottage. It was around two in the afternoon and the day was bright, warm, and clear. The SUV headed south through New Smyrna, then turned east and drove over a huge arched bridge, taking them over the intra-coastal waterway. Art was glued to the window, taking in as many of the sights as was possible; the water glimmering on the waterway, the palm trees swaying in the warm breeze, and people on the sidewalks wearing shorts, tank tops, and flip-flops.

After passing over the waterway, they rounded a curve and headed south on Highway A1A toward Bethune Beach. On the left were hotels, restaurants and condominiums located right on the beachfront. On their right, there seemed to be miles of neighborhoods filled with small quaint beach bungalows. At each stoplight parents and children laden with beach toys, towels, and boogie boards crossed in front of them, on their way to the beach.

Elisha rolled down her window so the air could blow on her face and through her hair. As the warm moist air rushed into the SUV, Art immediately caught a scent that was new to him.

"What is that smell?" Art questioned.

Elisha looked puzzled at first and then smiled. "That's right—you've never been to the ocean before, have you? What you are experiencing is the smell of the ocean."

"I think I like it," said Art, "It's kind of wet, musty, and salty, but fresh at the same time."

Elisha and Virginia laughed and smiled. "If you have never been to the ocean before, you have quite a week ahead of you," beamed Virginia.

They kept heading south down A1A until they started seeing signs for the Canaveral National Seashore. Right before entering the Canaveral National Seashore Park, they took a left toward the ocean, went about half a block, and then turned right into a large, gated compound. Inside the walled compound was an immense three-level, white stucco beach home perched on the highest point of the sand berm before the property descended down to the beach.

To the right of the three-level beach house were three matching stucco cottages lining the outside wall of the compound. Art assumed they must be used for guests and servants. On the south side of the beach house were two full tennis courts and a large pool.

"Well, Art," said Gene as they were getting out of the SUV, "how do you like our little beach cottage?"

"I guess I am confused about the definition of cottage . . . but, I like it. This place is fantastic!" said Art.

"Dad, tell him why you call it our cottage," said Elisha.

"Okay. Growing up, I lived in the Chicago area. My parents would bring our family down to New Smyrna, usually once a year for spring break to warm up. We would usually stay at one of the hotels or condos right on the beach. After a few years, my father decided that he liked the area so much that he was going to buy a place to use when we came down. I was thinking he would buy a nice condominium on the beach, but instead, he bought a little thousand-square-foot cracker-box beach bungalow about two blocks off the beach. It had concrete block walls, concrete floors and smelly sulfur tap water. He called it 'the cottage'. I loved New Smyrna, but I hated the cottage. It made me feel cheap and dirty. So, I decided when I grew up I would buy a fabulous place right on the beach and call it my beach cottage."

"How did you happen to find this place?" asked Art.

"I started tracking the beach real estate down here around, oh, I guess 2004. I knew I wanted a place close to the Canaveral

National Seashore where the beachfront could never be developed. Then, in 2008, everything came together. There were massive foreclosures of beachfront property because of the economy and there was a lot of paranoia about hurricanes. Where we are standing now used to be a Bethune Beach city street with eight little beach houses on each side of the street. Some were tiny little A-frames. I put together four little partnerships and bought up all these properties separately using undisclosed agents so as not to encourage owners to hold out and drive up the price. I paid top current market price for each place, but even that was cheap. The owners were happy to unload them to avoid foreclosure. After all the property was purchased, I folded all the partnerships into one, got the road condemned, bulldozed the crummy little bungalows and hired an architect to build my hurricane-proof cottage. The best part of this place is its location—abutting the virgin beaches of the Canaveral National Seashore. Follow me. I'll show you what I mean," said Gene.

Art followed Gene around to the south side of the house where a tight circular metal staircase ascended all the way to an observation deck on the top of the house. From the observation deck, there was a full three-hundred-sixty-degree view. To the south, it was miles of deserted pristine beach. Palmettos covered the beach berm, falling off sharply down to the sandy beach. To the west was a view of the backwaters of the intra-coastal waterway, and to the north, a view of beach houses and high-rise condominiums as far as the eye could see until they faded away in the mist rising from the surf. However, as far as Art was concerned, the best view was to the east. The sea breeze blew through his hair as he stared out, mesmerized by the beautiful blue-green ocean with the pounding roar of the waves engulfing his senses. It was like music to his ears.

"This is totally incredible!" exclaimed Art to Mr. Taylor. "I don't think I've ever been in a place that made me feel so alive and yet peaceful at the same time."

"I'm glad you approve, Art," said Mr. Taylor. "I think you and the kids are in for a great week."

Art and Gene could hear the clanking of the metal stairs as Virginia and Elisha came up the steps and urged Art and Gene to come down so they could take their traditional first walk on the beach.

"Come on. You can't miss this, Art," said Gene. "We have a family tradition that the first thing we do when we come here, even before unpacking or going into the house, is to go down to the beach, take off our shoes, and take a couple-mile walk."

They all headed down to the beach and took off their shoes, sticking their bare feet into the warm sand. Then, they headed south down the virgin beaches of the Canaveral National Seashore, rolling up their pants and wading in the cool springtime surf. Art loved the walk. He looked for shells while listening to the surf and to the Taylors talk about their memories of the beach and all the things they wanted to do that week.

Art wandered out ahead of the family and came across a large mound of sand that had been roped-off. Coming from the mound were markings that looked like giant tire tracks leading back toward the ocean.

"Hey!" yelled Art. "Does anyone know what this is?"

The Taylors all jogged over to look.

"Fantastic," said Virginia, "It looks like they are early this year."

"Early? Who?" questioned Art.

"This is where a giant sea turtle has come up and laid her eggs," said Virginia. "The trail leading back to the ocean was made by her flippers. They usually don't come ashore this early in the year. It looks like we may have to stay up one night and try to get a glimpse of another momma turtle laying her eggs."

After about a mile, they all turned around, headed back to the house, and settled into their separate rooms. Later, they met outside for an early dinner on the second-story deck overlooking the ocean. Elisha decided it would be Hawaiian night, complete with seafood, pineapple, and drinks with little umbrellas. At dinner, Virginia asked if anyone wanted to go with her to the annual Easter Sunrise Service the next morning at the 27th Street Beach Park in New Smyrna. Gene, Chris, and Elisha rolled their eyes and immediately declined.

"I'll go," said Art, ignoring the surprised looks. Art was fascinated by the invitation because it presented the possibility of getting to spend some time alone with Virginia, and maybe he would be able to ask some open-ended questions.

After dinner, they all lingered out on the deck as the sun went down and the temperature dropped. Virginia brought out blankets for them to wrap up in. While Elisha and Chris argued over plans for the next day, Art was content to snuggle in his blankets, listen to the surf, and think about his own personal journey over the last four months.

He found himself really enjoying being back with the Taylors and began to think that the professor's views were probably a bit exaggerated, to say the least. At the same time, he was wary about whether or not he was allowing himself to be seduced by luxury and opportunities and the comforts that came with wealth.

Easter Sunday

VIRGINIA CAME BY ART'S ROOM and woke him up at six in the morning to go to the sunrise service. Art quickly dressed and headed to the kitchen where he joined Virginia for homemade scones and fresh-squeezed orange juice.

"Did you make these scones?" asked Art.

"Yes, they're my mom's recipe. Do you like them?" asked Virginia

"Oh, yes!" replied Art. "These are just like... uh... I mean, they're some of the best I've ever had."

"Well, thanks, Art," said Virginia, "I'll let my mom know you approve."

"This may be a stupid question," said Art, "but what is a sunrise service?"

Virginia looked at Art and gave him a warm motherly smile. "It's extremely considerate of you to get up so early to go with me when you don't even know what you are going to. I first started going to sunrise services on Easter Sunday when I was a child living in LaCrescent, Minnesota. The Lutheran church we attended had them every year. We would dress up special, go to the service, and then go out to breakfast. After that, we would get to hunt for Easter eggs.

Virginia smiled at the memory. "Anyway, Easter is a celebration of Christ rising from the dead after being put to death on a cross. The story says that he arose from the dead early on the morning of the third day after he was killed. So, on Easter Sunday, churches schedule early morning services to celebrate his rising from the dead at the same time as the sun rises. The sunrise service we are going to is not in a church, but on the beach where we can see the sun rise over the ocean."

"Do you believe in Christ rising from the dead?" asked Art, curiously.

"I . . . well, I used to," responded Virginia. "I'm not sure what I believe anymore. I really want to believe it happened and that there is a loving God. I know there's something out there greater than us. More and more I am convinced that the design and complexity of everything around us are proof that all of this couldn't have just happened by accident."

Art and Virginia rushed to make the 6:45 service. The parking lot at the 27th Street Beach Park was packed. People were getting out of their vehicles and heading down to the beach. The attendees were old, young, and of all different races. Little girls were dressed up in their Easter outfits, old men in their suits and ties and teenagers in shorts and flip-flops. There were no chairs provided. The older people brought their folding beach chairs while the teenagers and young adults mostly just stood. Small children sat on the beach and played in the fine, white sand at their parents' feet.

The service began with a couple of young men playing acoustic guitars and singing songs that most of the attendees knew. Art and Virginia stood near the back of the crowd as nonparticipating observers, taking in the events of the morning. The ocean sky to the east was now a pink blaze as the sun illuminated the large puffy clouds on the horizon. A slight breeze came off the ocean, which was very calm with two-to-three foot uniform rolling waves, rhythmically coming to shore one by one, as if to present themselves on the beach for the enjoyment of those gathered.

Just prior to the sun's breaking through the horizon, a tall man with black hair graying at the temples stepped to the front and began to speak. He spoke about how we all, whether or not we recognize it, have an inborn desire to be connected with our Father, God, and how on our own, we futilely attempt to fill this void with things we believe will bring us satisfaction. He also talked about how it is God's desire to be Father to the fatherless and to adopt us as sons into his family. He said we come to the Father through the death and resurrection of his son, Jesus, whom we celebrate on Easter.

As if on cue, upon concluding his message, shafts of sunlight broke through the clouds on the horizon for a spectacular sunrise over the ocean.

Virginia's eyes were moist and teary. Abruptly, she motioned to Art that they were leaving. When they got back to the SUV, Art asked if she was okay. Virginia responded that she was fine; she just wanted to beat all the traffic that would be leaving the parking lot. She didn't think Art bought the explanation, but she had no desire to tell him what she was really thinking.

Virginia couldn't help wondering if she was part of the reason that Art and others were now fatherless. *How could I have let myself go down that road without thinking through the long-term consequences?*

Pulling out into the road, she told Art that she needed a good cup of coffee and knew of a wonderful little place in the old Flagler Beach downtown area. They pulled up in front of a little café called Beach Buns and went inside. The smell of freshly ground coffee beans enveloped them. Virginia ordered two cappuccinos and the two of them found a corner table by the front window where they could people watch.

"So Art, what did you think of the little sunrise service?" asked Virginia, feeling like she had regained her composure.

"I thought it was . . . " Art paused and thought for a minute, "peaceful and intriguing."

"Intriguing? That's an interesting description. What intrigued or fascinated you?" asked Virginia.

"Well, I liked the idea that if there is a God, his desire is to be a Father to the fatherless and I'm one of the fatherless who, I guess, he would adopt," said Art.

"I think that's the thing he said that got me too," said Virginia. "I never knew my father, and I always desperately wanted one. It's a nice thought to think that there is a being out there who wants to be your father and wants you for his child."

"You said earlier that you know there's something out there greater than us. Do you think it is what that guy at the beach was talking about?" asked Art.

"I don't know, Art," said Virginia. "It would really be nice if it was."

They finished their cappuccinos and headed back to the cottage. Everyone was still asleep when they returned, and Virginia and Art decided to take a little nap outside on the second deck until the rest of the crew got up.

The rest of the family didn't get up until about ten-thirty and they were served breakfast made-to-order by their personal chef.

At breakfast, Gene asked Virginia and Art how the sunrise service went. They both replied nonchalantly that it was a fascinating local event to attend; neither let on that what had been said there touched a deep wound in their lives.

"I think it's amazing that people go to church Sunday after Sunday, year after year, chasing an illusive dream. Oh, well, I guess it satisfies the masses and keeps some people out of trouble," said Gene.

Virginia decided to purposefully avoid the topic by abruptly changing the subject. "Hey, guess what? You lazy bums have almost slept the whole day away and we are in Florida! How are we going to make up for lost time?"

"I say sand castles!" blurted out Elisha. Everyone nodded their heads in agreement.

"I'll load up the supplies and we'll leave for the Islander in twenty five minutes," said Gene. He immediately headed off to get ready.

"Supplies," asked Art wide-eyed and inquisitive, "for sand castles?"

"Art, you should know by now that Gene is totally type A about everything he does," said Virginia.

"But, supplies?" Art questioned again.

"Let me explain this one, Mom," said Chris. "I think I can give him the abridged explanation while we get ready."

Art and Chris headed off to get their swim trunks. "Okay, Art, here's the quick story, otherwise you would have to put up with my mom's forty-five minute extended version. When my dad was a kid, he and his family used to come down and stay at this little condo resort called the Islander, on the beach. This was before his dad bought the infamous beach cottage. Anyway, every week the Islander had a sand-castle building competition, and my dad claims he always won. So now, he insists that we have to build sand castles at the beach by the

Islander because of the consistency of the sand. He also has this whole technique down in steps, where he digs out a giant sand pile just close enough to the water to create a moat from the surf coming in. And oh, I about forgot, the tide has to be going out during the building process. I'm sure he has already checked the times of the tides for today or he wouldn't have consented. Anyway, he really doesn't build sand castles. He builds or sculpts cars, whales, turtles, dolphins, whatever comes to mind. We help, but mostly we boogie board, tan, and eat junk food and hot dogs."

The Taylors and Art loaded into the SUV and headed up the beach to the Islander. Upon arriving, Art helped Gene unload shovels, trowels, buckets, small brooms, molds, chairs, towels, coolers, and a canopy.

Once on the beach, they set up camp at the prime spot, chosen by Gene. Gene and Chris immediately pulled out the shovels and started digging while Elisha and Virginia set up their chairs for tanning. Art joined Gene and Chris in the backbreaking digging process.

The day seemed to fly by. Virginia enjoyed watching Art get into the sand sculpting, helping Gene design and build a miniature sand tugboat. She also watched with interest as Art attempted to boogie board with Chris, but never really caught on to how to actually catch a wave. Most of the time he was being tumbled in the surf and digging sand out of his shorts.

Being with Chris and Elisha with her head clear from her many years of drug therapy allowed her to reflect on her children and her life. Looking at Chris and Elisha she realized that from a project perspective they had far exceeded expectations. When she and Gene had started working on their dream children, a lot of what they were attempting was groundbreaking work in the field of genetic engineering. Not only were they able to choose gender and eliminate genetic diseases, but they also were able to provide Chris and Elisha with the positive traits of intelligence, strength, beauty, memory and the potential for long life. She was convinced that they had gone a long way down the road to insuring their children's status and plentiful opportunities for their happiness.

However, from a family and nurturing perspective she felt that she had let her children down and had missed out on the opportunity of her lifetime to build what she was really longing for—a loving family environment. She regretted turning over the early years of child-raising to a nanny, putting them in daycares, and sending them off to summer camps and boarding schools.

The reality was hitting her that she really didn't know her children. The time she spent with them was always in vacation settings over holiday breaks where real life never really occurred. She wondered what Chris and Elisha really thought of her and Gene. She knew Gene did not share the same regrets. He looked at his children as trophies, objects that would bring him praise and display his achievements and worth for having such great kids.

As the afternoon wore on, the tide came in to the point that their beach camp and sand sculptures were overtaken by the incoming waves. They quickly packed up the SUV and then sat on the beach, watching the incoming waves surround and then slowly, but finally destroy the little tugboat.

"Ah, your masterpiece just got destroyed again, Dad," said Elisha. "You work all day just to watch the waves take it back into the sea. Doesn't that bother you?"

"I actually like the whole process," replied Gene. "As the tide goes out, it becomes a race to get it built before the tide turns. I think the pressure helps me to be more creative. Then, when it's all done, it's fun to see the ocean methodically return the sand to its originally intended natural state. Anyway, didn't you love seeing our little tugboat totally surrounded by water as if it were out to sea?"

"Intended natural state? Did you really say intended natural state?" questioned Virginia. "If it is intended, it means that someone or something intended for sand to be at the beach. You don't really mean that, do you Gene?"

"No, if you're saying some creator in his good design intended for sand to form the beach at the ocean then obviously not. I'm just saying that I like taking things where they are, reshaping them and turning them into what I desire. When I'm done with them, they can go back to what they were before."

"But, Dad, what about your work of art? It gets destroyed," argued Elisha.

"In the end, art is disposable. I guess I care much more about the whole creation process," said Gene.

Virginia hoped that Gene's statement about art being disposable was not prophetic. She was hopeful that in the end, things would go well and Art would not be perceived as disposable—as she knew numerable of frozen embryos like him were in the past, until she and Gene got it right.

The Taylor clan did not leave the beach and return to the cottage until one final massive wave completed the demolition of the tugboat. When they arrived home, everyone showered, dressed, and met on the second floor outdoor dining deck area for another gourmet meal, prepared by their private chef. Art was the last to arrive, all of his exposed skin glowing a bright pink.

"Ow!" said Chris when he saw Art. "You really got scorched, Art. Doesn't it hurt?"

"It doesn't really hurt that much, but I'm really uncomfortably hot, and my skin is tingling," said Art.

The dinner conversation revolved around the plans for the next day. Gene had to be in all day meetings in Orlando, while Elisha and Chris were planning to go to the Ponce Inlet for surfing and tanning. Virginia caught Chris's eye and nodded toward Art to indicate that they should be including Art in their plans. Chris picked up on the non-verbal clues from his mother and invited Art to be a part of their surfing adventure the next day. Virginia noticed that when Art agreed, Elisha grimaced. She could see that Elisha's grimace did not go unnoticed by Art and watched as Art did his best to mask his hurt and disappointment.

Heart to Heart

ART DID NOT SLEEP well that night, waking up every couple of hours to reapply the aloe gel Virginia had given him to soothe the sunburn. He finally fell into a deep sleep around four A.M. and did not wake up until around nine. He was hoping that the pain of his sunburn would have subsided by the time he got up. That was not the case and he realized that he would have to keep his sunburn covered for his beach day with Chris and Elisha. He went and found Virginia and let her know of his predicament. Virginia said she thought she had a solution for him. She told him to go get some breakfast and that she would be right back. By the time he was finished with breakfast, Virginia had returned with a bright red wide-brim bucket hat, a lightweight long-sleeve white cotton shirt, a pair of white cotton beach pants and a tube of titanium dioxide ointment to put on his nose and cheeks.

Art went to his room and hurriedly changed so he could meet Chris and Elisha down at the garage by ten. Their plan was to make the eight-mile trip up the beach to the Ponce de Leon Inlet on four-wheelers. When Art showed up at the garage, Chris and Elisha took one look at Art and started to laugh.

"What are you wearing, Art?" quipped Elisha in a sarcastic tone.

"Oh, ah, this is a sun protection outfit that your mother put together for me."

"Interesting," cracked Elisha as she rolled her eyes at Chris.

A pang of self-doubt and embarrassment temporarily overwhelmed Art. It was the old familiar feeling of being odd and unaccepted that he had lived with during most of his days at Hawthorne. It was a feeling that he thought he had left behind. His initial idea was to tell Chris and Elisha to go without him and stay home for the day out of the sun. As he slowly regained his composure, a spark of anger and fight rose up in side of him. He decided that he wasn't going to give into those feelings.

"Yeah, your mom has interesting taste in sun protective clothing, but I don't have any other options. Hey, are we going to get going?

Chris looked over at Elisha with a 'what are you going to do?' look, then responded with, "Ah, sure, let's get going, the surf looks good and I don't want to miss the good waves."

Chris strapped his surfboard on the back side of his fourwheeler so that it was sticking straight up. They started the engines and took off up the beach. Unfortunately for Art, the bucket hat was a loose fit and had no straps. To the disgust of both Chris and Elisha, he slowed the caravan down several times having to turn back and pick up his hat that had blown off. Art finally gave up and decided he would sit on his hat the rest of the trip.

They finally arrived at the Ponce Inlet, considered one of the best surfing spots on the east coast. The beach backed up to the Smyrna Dunes Park that consisted of acres of large white dunes with picturesque sea oats and other vegetation. Art thought the area was magnificently beautiful.

The inlet area was jammed with surfers and their female spectators. They found a spot to park their four-wheelers right next to a large group of partiers.

"Now this is really living," Chris said as he got off the four-wheeler and surveyed all that was happening around them.

Elisha smiled back at Chris and responded, "Yeah, being at the cottage with the parents was about to kill me. I really needed to get a way from Mom for a while. She has really been annoying me this trip. All of a sudden, she wants to be this loving, caring mom and it's just awkward and weird. I don't want to spend my spring break trying to help her recapture my childhood and build her idea of 'the loving family'. I just want her to leave me alone so I can have my normal, good-time spring break."

"Me too! Mom's been doing the same kind of stuff to me," replied Chris. "I don't know why all of a sudden she is doing this. She and dad have always just lived their own little lives and let us live ours . . . and at this point, I'd like to keep it that way."

Art was surprised at what he heard. He thought it was bizarre that while he was looking and longing for parents, Chris and Elisha were trying to get rid of theirs. He also thought it was strange that they were saying these things in front of him. It was as if he wasn't even there, and it didn't take long for him to realize that it was going to be that way for the rest of the day.

Chris immediately grabbed his surfboard and headed out to catch the waves while Elisha conspicuously took her time taking off her swimsuit cover-up while flipping her hair several times to attract the attention of the surfers next to them on the beach. She then set up her beach mat in their direction and slowly applied her suntan lotion. To Art, it looked like a purposeful tease. Art immediately remembered the warning he received from Professor Silverman.

Art could tell that as far as Elisha was concerned, he was unwanted excess baggage. He attempted to strike up a conversation with her, but it was clear from her responses that she was not interested and preferred not talking to him. Bored and discouraged, he decided to explore the boardwalk trail through the Smyrna Dune Park.

Walking through the dune park gave him time to think. He knew that if he stayed at the beach with Chris and Elisha, he would continue to be the invisible tagalong. He had no desire just being a spectator watching them live the lives of the beautiful people. He also thought that with Mr. Taylor being gone for the day, it may be a good time to go back to the beach cottage, where he might get the chance to ask Virginia about how to go about finding information about Dizz's donor dad.

When he got back to the beach, he found Elisha sitting on her mat talking to a couple tan, muscular surfers with sun-bleached hair. She hardly noticed or responded to him when he told her that he was going to head back to the beach cottage to get out of the sun. Art enjoyed the ride back down the beach, remembering being the man in black on Dizz's scooter, except now he was the geek in white trying to ride a four-wheeler with one hand while holding on to his hat with the other.

When Art finally got back to the beach cottage it was early afternoon. He went to the kitchen and grabbed a sandwich and a cold drink and headed out to sit under the umbrellas on the second-story, overlooking the ocean. He did not run into Virginia anywhere in the house. For the time being he was content to eat his lunch, watch the waves, and listen to the roar of the ocean.

Before long, Virginia showed up with a tall glass of iced coffee and sat down next to him. "What are you doing back here? Aren't you supposed to be at the inlet with Chris and Elisha?"

"Yeah, but I really couldn't do anything with this sunburn. Otherwise, I would have been showing up all of the surfers with my moves on the board." Art replied in a joking manner.

"I see, and how is that sunburn?" she asked.

"I think it's pretty bad. It hurt to put my shirt on this morning and I really don't want to sit back in this chair," replied Art, sitting awkwardly in his chair.

"Have you continued putting the aloe gel on?" asked Virginia.

"I've been slathering it on every chance I get," laughed Art.

"Well, I hope it doesn't ruin your vacation," said Virginia, "I imagine you will be doing some major peeling in a day or so, which may keep you out of the sun quite a bit this week."

"It's okay. I'm enjoying just being here. Besides, I've got this long-sleeve white shirt and a beautiful bucket hat, so I'll be okay," said Art with a tinge of sarcasm.

"It sounds to me like you maybe got a bit of a fashion critique from our in-house fashion snob?"

"Yeah, just a little . . . but I've decided that I won't let my lack of style stop me from enjoying the rest of the week."

"I'm glad you've figured out how to enjoy the rest of the week. What about after this week? Have you decided yet what you will do after graduation?"

"Are you referring to the plans I have for my wardrobe?" Art responded again in a joking manner.

"Not exactly," Virginia responded with an amused look, "plans for your life, like college."

"Oh, you mean real life beyond the world of fashion. I haven't yet fully decided. My trust fund has some pretty stiff economic disincentives if I don't go to college. What would you do if you were me?"

"I think I would do whatever I had a passion to do, regardless of money. If I had a desire to learn and experience college life, I'd go to college; if I wanted to write and perform, I'd do that."

"Thanks, that's good advice, but I really don't know what I want to do yet. I may just go to college to buy some time to figure out who I am."

With that, Virginia's eyes got glassy and watery. Art could not help noticing her emotional response to his comment about figuring out who he was. His confidence surged and he decided to test Virginia's response to an open-ended question.

"Are you okay?"

"Yes, I'm fine . . . I've just been over-emotional lately. I think it's from getting off some medication I've been on and probably early menopause."

"Why, when I talk with you, do I always feel like you know things about me that I don't know?"

Art could not believe that he had asked Virginia that question. It was as if, for the next thirty seconds, everything was in slow motion. Virginia stiffened, turned pale, and then broke into uncontrollable sobs. Art froze in his chair, not knowing how to handle Virginia's emotional outburst. He decided to wait out Virginia's meltdown to see whether he would get any kind of answer from Virginia.

After about a minute, Virginia abruptly rose to her feet, raised one finger in the air and blubbered out that she would be right back after she regained her composure.

• • •

Virginia rushed inside to her private bathroom. She knew that how she answered—or didn't answer—Art's question would be very revealing. Although she regretted her participation in the Jenicks Project, she knew she now had to deal carefully with the emotional health and physical safety of a real person. She was keenly aware after overhearing Gene's Arizona conversation with Eric, that if Art did not fall in line with Gene's plans, he was at risk for a removal of some sort. She didn't like it, but her first reaction was to call Gene to help her spin and fabricate an answer that would hide the truth, but at the same time be believable.

Ever since Christmas break, she and Gene had lived separate lives with very few intersecting moments. They had separate rooms, separate schedules, and had separate meal times. Their paths came together only at public functions, and at an occasional passing in the driveway.

Reluctantly, she placed the call to Gene's cell phone.

"Virginia! Is everything okay? Is there a problem?"

Through her sobbing, Virginia explained to Gene how she completely broke down when Art told her he felt like she knew things about him that he didn't know.

"And how did you respond to him?" he asked with an impatient tone.

"I didn't. I just started blubbering, excused myself, and told him I would be right back," responded Virginia.

"You certainly can't tell him the truth!"

"I know. That's why I called you. What should I say?"

"Let's say we approach this from a motherly point of view. What if you said, for some reason, you relate to him like a mother, and mothers sometimes intuitively know things about kids that their kids themselves don't know. You think you could pull something like that off?"

Virginia hesitated, "Yes, I think I can probably do that."

"I'm sure you can pull it off," said Gene. "I'm sure he's probably already picked up on your motherly concerns for him."

"Okay, I've got to get back out there. Wish me luck!" said Virginia.

Virginia took a deep breath, wiped her face dry and headed back out to the deck where Art was still waiting, gazing out toward the ocean.

"Sorry about that, Art. I just hate it when I fall apart and turn into a blubbering mess," said Virginia, pausing a moment to collect her thoughts. "I don't know if you've noticed, but I really have a soft spot in my heart for you. I think it's because I know the pain of not having a dad, and I can't imagine not having any parents. You asked me if I know things about you that you don't know. Well, I think because of what I've gone through, I do intuitively know things about you. I think it's a motherly sixth sense."

Art absorbed Virginia's explanation, caught off guard by her answer. It wasn't the answer that he was hoping for. He didn't know how to respond, but he knew he wasn't going to try to ask the question again. He was fairly certain that Virginia knew what he was really asking. He remembered what the professor had said about Virginia not really being able to do anything that would be disloyal to Gene. He decided to let things lay where they were and accept her answer without challenge.

"Thanks for caring and for understanding," said Art, "I really don't cross paths with very many people who can relate to my situation, except maybe for Dizz."

"Who's Dizz?" asked Virginia, acting as if she didn't know who Art was talking about.

"He's a kid at school. He has a mother but his biological father is a sperm bank donor. He's tried to locate his biological father through various search organizations, but so far, he's gotten no response. It really bothers him—it's like he's got a huge piece of himself missing."

Art noticed immediately that Virginia had started to mist up again. She turned her head away from him as if to brush the hair out of her face and quickly wiped her eyes.

Knowing her distress, Art decided he could not pursue any of the questions about whether Virginia could or would help him find out the identity of Dizz's biological father.

An awkward silence fell over their conversation until Virginia cleared her throat and excused herself for a menu-planning meeting with their private chef. Art was almost relieved to see her go. He spent the remainder of the day under the umbrellas on the second story deck, absorbing the beauty of the beach and napping under the spell of the sound of the ocean waves.

Enticement

BY TUESDAY, ART WAS BEGINNING to blister and peel and stayed back at the beach cottage while he watched Chris and Elisha set out to cruise up and down the beach, hitting all of the trendy little beach shops. On Wednesday, Art donned his sun protective outfit and went with the whole family on a long horseback ride down the beaches of the Canaveral National Seashore. By Thursday, the worst of the peeling was complete, leaving Art with splotchy-looking skin. However, as luck would have it, Thursday and Friday turned rainy and cold. Elisha and Chris spent the days sleeping in until early afternoon and watching movies. Art watched a few movies with them, but mostly kept to himself.

At lunch on Friday, Gene made a point to find Art and set up a time that evening to talk to Art about his future. This made Art extremely nervous. He spent most of that afternoon walking up and down the beach under an umbrella in the rain, thinking about what the Professor had told him about Gene and the Jenicks Project. He was determined to try to come off agreeable and cooperative with whatever Gene talked to him about. He didn't know for certain if the professor was totally correct about Gene, but he didn't want to take any chances.

The evening came too quickly for Art. At the end of their family dinner, Virginia disappeared and shortly thereafter came walking out of the kitchen with a huge chocolate cake with eighteen candles, singing "Happy Birthday." Gene, Elisha, and Chris joined in with the song and then insisted that Art blow out all of the candles after making a wish. Art dutifully complied. He didn't tell them his wish, but he was certain that Virginia knew that his wish was to have a family of his own.

The birthday celebration was short-lived. Once the birthday cake was sliced and eaten, Chris and Elisha quickly excused themselves to go club hopping for the night in Daytona Beach. At the same time, Gene stood up and asked Art to meet him up in his study in a few minutes for a talk. Art felt a wave of nervousness overtake him and he began to feel warm and clammy. He stayed at the table for a couple more minutes and played with the rest of the chocolate cake on his plate while the servants cleaned the table. When he felt like he'd stalled as long as he could, he left the table and slowly started up the stairs to Gene's study.

Upon reaching the top of the stairs, Art found the door to the study wide open. He could see the back of Mr. Taylor's head as he lounged in one of the two over-stuffed chairs facing the south window. Art knocked lightly on the doorframe.

"Come on in, Art," Gene said without turning to look at Art, while reaching for a drink on the end table.

Art walked slowly over to the stuffed chair that was next to Mr. Taylor's chair and sat down.

Gene's study was located in the southeast corner of the upper level of the cottage. The outside walls facing east and south were made of thick glass, which gave the office a spectacular view of the ocean and the Canaveral National Seashore to the south. It was set up more like a reading room, with bookshelves on the inside walls and a collection of large over-stuffed leather chairs and ottomans with small end tables to the side of each chair, facing the windows, allowing for a perfect view of the ocean.

"Can I get you a Coke or something?" asked Gene.

"Yes, that would be great," said Art as he stared out the window, down the coast.

"It's beautiful . . . simply a beautiful evening," said Gene, handing him a frosty can. "I think we're going to see a great sunset."

Even though it had been raining all day, the sky in the far west had become clear along the horizon. Streaks of sunlight were breaking through under the bank of clouds, giving the tops of the palmettos and the breaking waves an orange glow. The clouds in the far eastern sky were turning a vivid pink and the long shadows created by the horizontal sunshine made everything feel peaceful and dreamy.

Art stood up and stared out of the window, sipping his Coke.

"It's an amazing thing when nature comes together at just the right moment," said Gene. "Have a seat, Art, and we'll talk a while as we watch this day fade into twilight."

Art sank into the over-stuffed chair next to Gene's chair. He was shaking as he placed his Coke on the table beside his chair. He was nervous and he suspected that Gene noticed his nervousness.

"Are you okay, Art? You seem a little uptight. Is something bothering you?"

"No, no, I don't think so."

"Good, I just thought I would ask. I wanted to spend a little time catching up with you and talking about your plans for next year. Is that okay?"

"Sure, that would be fine."

"I was wondering . . . did you get an opportunity to check out TEI with the business card I gave you?"

"Oh, yeah, it's fascinating . . . ah, I mean the types of things your company does."

"Fascinating—does that mean you were interested and think it's a good service, or fascinating like strange?"

"I would say interesting and probably a good service for those who can afford it."

"Does it bother you that some can't afford it?"

Art did not really want to get into this discussion and felt like he was already blowing it with Gene. It was just too difficult to stay neutral.

"No, I guess it's not a big deal."

"You don't need to try to be nice, Art. I'm okay with you telling me what you really think."

"Okay . . . so it seems that only those already monetarily privileged have the opportunity to improve themselves and their children. It doesn't seem fair to those who can't afford it and it seems like it will further the already widening gap between the have's and the have not's. It seems like it would create a whole new area of discrimination."

"So, it's the fairness of the whole thing that bothers you?"

"Yeah, I guess it is."

"Maybe it all depends on how you view fairness."

"What do you mean?"

"Well, if fairness means equality in everything, we probably would never see any progress in the world. People strive and work everyday to be unequal, to be better than the next guy, to stand out, to achieve, and to be more than mediocre. It is those people who invent things, write things, improve things, create art; we all benefit from their efforts to rise above the norm or be unequal with the rest of us. If we insist that all things must be equal, society would stagnate or even decline. If we held off with our enhancements until we could provide them equally to everyone, it would never happen. If we have the opportunity to improve mankind, shouldn't we do it?"

"I guess I hadn't thought about it in that way before. I guess progress would stop if everything had to be fair. But, aren't you worried that the ultimate result would, by default, create a subservient class?"

"A subservient class? You sound like an old colleague of mine," Gene chuckled. "It is possible that there will be distinctions in abilities and classes. There always have been. Throughout history, classes or distinctions have arisen when groups of people have decided to distinguish themselves through improvement. And, when you think about it, the 'subservient' class, as you put it, has always been necessary to provide the basic labor force to implement improvements and advancements in the human race."

"So, you don't have a problem with society having a subservient or a service class?"

"Art, the practical reality is that it has always been that way—and for society to progress, it will need to continue."

"But does the subservient class have a choice?"

"Maybe not . . . but no matter who you are, there are limitations to your choices. I think a more important question is are they happy or satisfied with the choices they have available? If they have the choice to do what they want to do, they will be happy, satisfied, productive citizens, benefiting society as a whole."

"Sounds like you are interested in some kind of societal engineering to actually create a group of people who never have any desire or ambition to be more than servants."

"Not exactly. I would like to see a class of servants, as you call them, who have ambitions and the life desire to be excellent workers. It may sound elitist at first, but when you realize a servant class will always be needed, doesn't it make sense to have that class be happy and fulfilled in their life's work? Think of the social unrest that would be eliminated if everyone were happy with what they did in life."

"Sounds like utopia."

"Art, I really think this is the start of a golden age in regard to human productivity. We now have the ability to be the masters of our own evolutionary destiny where we can purposely improve our minds and bodies beyond just the random luck that nature granted to us through whatever our parents might have passed down to us. It's mankind's chance to finally escape the roulette wheel of life and bring our future under purposeful, rational, control! So, if it is within our power to create utopia, shouldn't we do it?"

Art's head was in a spin. His gut told him that Gene's view of the world or 'Gene's world' was all wrong, but he could not articulate why. In the back of his mind, a small voice was saying, *Protect yourself—agree with Gene and get out of there.*

"I don't know, I guess so. Yes."

"Art, we kind of got way off track here, didn't we? What I really wanted to do was talk about your plans after graduation. Do you know what you are going to do yet?"

Art was relieved that the intense discussion about societal engineering was over. He decided to try to be agreeable from here on out.

"I've been accepted at quite a few schools, but I have not made a commitment yet."

"What if I could get you into a program at Princeton that would combine an education with a performance career?"

"Sounds interesting!" Art responded with an air of excitement in his voice.

"I have connections with the group that promotes the Young Masters Tour. They would love to have you as one of their performing artists on next year's tour. Because most of the artists are still in school, the tour is intentionally scheduled over the winter holidays and school breaks. The performance schedule matches up pretty close with the Princeton academic schedule. I know the head of the performing arts department at Princeton, and he is salivating at the thought of having you in their program. How's this sounding to you?"

"It sounds very interesting. I guess I'd like to hear more about this Young Masters Tour."

"Right now they have that nineteen-year-old girl from Russia who plays the cello and a sixteen-year-old violinist from Japan. If you agree, it will just be the three of you. They are currently booked to play in London, Moscow, Paris, Tokyo, Sydney, San Francisco, and Boston. At each venue, each artist will be featured and backed by the local philharmonic orchestra. The tour will have worldwide coverage. This is the kind of thing that could really jump-start your music career. You will become a household name around the world."

Art stared out the window as the last shades of pink were fading in the eastern sky. He really liked the sound of performing around the world, the notoriety, the fame, and probable fortune, and he also liked hearing that Princeton wanted him. What he did not like was the feeling that, if he agreed, he'd be playing into Gene's plans.

"It's an incredible opportunity, Art. Does the sound of this excite you at all?"

"It sounds absolutely incredible, and I can't believe you looked into it for me. I think I am very interested."

"Good, I was hoping you would be pleased. Virginia and I knew that your trustee really wouldn't help you explore all your options like a parent would, so we thought we would look into a few opportunities. Sometime next month I will set up a meeting for you with Princeton and the Young Masters Tour so all of the details can be ironed out. I will loan you my best negotiating corporate attorney to work out your deal with the Masters Tour. He'll take good care of you. Sound good? Do you have any questions?"

"No, I'm quite overwhelmed right now. Thank you so much for helping me and for caring."

Gene stood up, indicating that their meeting was over. Art stood up to shake Gene's hand, thanking him again for all he had done.

As Art walked out of the study, a look of satisfaction came over Gene's face; his plan to become the benefactor of Art's career was taking shape. He could now envision Art, drunk with success and fame, ready to willingly embrace positive eugenics and Gene's own historical place in the movement.

Gene shut the door of the study and called Eric.

"Eric, Gene here. I wanted to give you an update concerning our project so you can report to the board."

"Good, finally some more news," replied Eric. "I'm going to need some kind of positive report from you to keep the board from pulling the plug on the public side of this project. You know they are extremely pleased with the progress of the other Jenicks brothers and are quite willing to discard Art to protect and preserve that success."

"Eric, I really need you to use your persuasive abilities on this one," said Gene. "Art is falling in right where we need him to be. He's going ahead with the career and college choices that we want and he appears to be right on track. It's only a matter of time until we can reveal his true identity to him, and his destiny as the public face of positive eugenics."

"I hope you're right, Gene," said Eric. "I will put the best possible spin on his progress. They keep reminding me that the original project was never designed for public disclosure."

"They are so short-sighted," moaned Gene. "Did they really think that they would be able to keep all of this a secret forever? What's the point of the project if you can't implement your inventions in the real world?"

"I'm not going to argue that one with you, Gene," said Eric. "You know I am in total agreement."

The conversation ended on that comment and Gene was left in his study alone, staring out the window as the last bit of pink disappeared from the clouds in the western sky. A couple of nagging thoughts still bothered him. He wanted to know what Art had really done in Boston when he said he went to the library, and he didn't like hearing the term 'subservient class' from Art. It reminded him of Moss and all those like Moss, trying to stop progress and thinking they are acting on behalf of God. He decided that once he got back on Monday, he would call in a couple of favors and have some research done on exactly where Art went on his trip to Boston.

• • •

As Art made his way back down the stairs, he was feeling very upbeat about the Young Masters Tour and attending Princeton. At that moment, he had no problem dismissing the Professor's warnings as just ramblings from an old guy who didn't get the girl and who didn't get his way years ago. He decided that he would stop by the kitchen to grab a little after dinner treat and then take one more walk on the beach before their early morning departure back to Concord. When he arrived in the kitchen, Virginia was sitting at the breakfast bar sipping on a cup of tea.

"Hi, Art," said Virginia. "How's it going? Are you looking forward to getting back and graduating?"

"I'm not looking forward to leaving this beautiful beach," said Art, "but, I am looking forward to finishing up at Hawthorne and then possibly heading off to Princeton and the Young Masters Tour. By the way, thanks for working with Mr. Taylor to help set me up with the tour. It sounds fantastically exciting!"

Virginia looked a little dazed. "Oh, sure, you're welcome, Art," said Virginia after a noticeably awkward pause that let Art know that the news was a surprise to her. "What excites you most about it?"

Art paused, still a little bit taken back by Virginia's obvious lack of knowledge, and then said, "I think it's the combined opportunity to travel and perform at the greatest music venues in the world," said Art.

"I am pleased that you have found something exciting to look forward to. It's going to be a great learning experience for you, Art," said Virginia.

Art, sensing that Virginia was struggling to act knowledgeable about what Gene had shared with him, grabbed a cookie and excused himself to take a walk on the beach.

As soon as Art left, Virginia immediately abandoned her tea and went searching for Gene. She found him still up in the third floor corner study. She walked over and stood in front of Gene, who was sitting in one of the overstuffed leather chairs sipping a spiced rum and Coke.

"What are you up to, Gene?" questioned Virginia in a stern tone.

"What's got into you? I'm just sitting here, enjoying the evening. What are you referring to?" asked Gene.

"I just had a very surprising and awkward conversation with Art. He thanked me for working with you to help set him up with the Young Masters Tour," said Virginia.

Gene quickly rose up out of his chair, "Oh no! You didn't let on that you didn't know about it, did you?" asked Gene.

"No, but I should have," said Virginia, now raising her voice. "Why didn't you tell me about this? Is this part of another one of your little manipulation schemes?"

"No, no!" exclaimed Gene. "I was just trying to help Art out with his future, that's all. I should have told you about it . . . but you know how we never talk anymore unless it's to argue. It just didn't come up. I thought you would have been okay with me giving you some of the credit for helping set this up. Art is thrilled with it!"

• • •

When Art left the beach cottage for his walk, he headed south down the beach. When he turned back and looked up, he could see Virginia and Gene arguing through the lighted study windows. This confirmed his strong suspicions that Virginia was unaware of the plans for Princeton and the Young Masters Tour. Why wouldn't Gene have told Virginia about this? Was this, as the Professor had warned, a way to set him up so he would willingly comply with Gene's plans?

Back at Hawthorne

THE TRIP BACK TO the reality of Hawthorne was uneventful except for a comment made by Chris about Dizz. During the ride to the New Smyrna Beach airport, Virginia asked Art about his favorite music genres. In his answer, Art casually mentioned that lately he had taken a liking to jazz and had been listening to a lot of Dizz's collection. Chris immediately inserted that he hated that kid. When Virginia asked Chris why he would say such a thing, he responded with a vague comment about Dizz being a "complete psycho" and an embarrassment to Hawthorne.

Art was ticked—mostly at himself for not having the guts to defend his friend.

The rest of the trip home was quiet and uneventful, giving Art time to think about the last week. He concluded that the friendship he thought he had with Chris and Elisha was a facade, probably pushed upon them by Gene. Dizz was right, the "beautiful people" were only being nice because they wanted something, either from Mr. Taylor, or maybe eventually from him. Art suspected that once back at Hawthorne his relationship would migrate back to the status that existed during his junior year—in other words, no relationship at all.

He was happy to get back to his dorm room. He felt like he had spent a week suffering in paradise, feeling awkward in about every situation with the Taylor family.

It didn't take long for Dizz to come knocking at his door, wanting a full account of the week with the Taylors. Art told Dizz he would fill him in on the happenings of the week, but first wanted to tell him about an off the cuff statement made by Chris. "Dizz, I happened to mention your name in conversation around Chris and got a pretty nasty response."

Dizz gave Art one of his classic mischievous grins. "Oh, that doesn't really surprise me. What did he say?"

"Chris actually said he hated your guts. What's that all about?"

Dizz laughed. "He probably should hate me."

"What do you mean by that?" asked Art, now extremely curious.

"If I tell you, you have to promise to keep it totally to yourself. Okay?"

"Okay."

"Well, you're aware of how I accessed the Hawthorne computer system. When I got in there I realized that I was not the only one that had hacked into the system. I found that Chris, although being brilliant, was also a lazy cheat."

"What do you mean?"

"I figured out that Chris, or someone for Chris, had positively tweaked his grades a little here and there, just enough for him to stay number one in the class."

"Okay, but why does he hate your guts?"

"Well, you know me, I like to work the system and this was an opportunity that I couldn't pass up. I figured that keeping this information secret should probably be worth something, if you know what I mean?"

"You didn't, Dizz, did you?"

"Yes, I have been successful in extracting the value of keeping that information quiet on an ongoing basis. Let's just say that Chris has been reluctantly helping me save for my college education for the last two years. He makes a nice little quarterly deposit into a brokerage account held in my mom's name."

Art shook his head in disgust.

"Hey, don't worry about it, Art. Chris can afford it, and we were never going to be friends anyway. No one is really getting hurt here. I am just helping Chris spread the wealth. Now what happened down at spring break—did you find out anything?"

Art didn't like how Dizz changed the subject, but he went ahead and filled Dizz in on the happenings of the week, his evaluation of Elisha and Chris, Gene's utopia speech, Princeton and the Young Masters Tour, Virginia's meltdown and the sunrise service.

Dizz restrained himself from his usual sarcasm and "I told you so" comments, and just let Art talk and get things off his chest.

When Art had completed his rundown of the week, Dizz remained silent for a few seconds and then asked, "What are you going to do, Art?"

"About what?"

"Are you going to follow Mr. Taylor's road map for you, or are you going to cut the strings and be your own person?"

"I can be my own person and still do the Young Masters Tour," Art responded defensively.

"You're dreaming, Art. If you do the Young Masters Tour, you'll be indebted to Mr. Taylor. You won't be able to walk away . . . he wants something from you and he's setting you up so he can get it."

"You don't know that for sure. What if he is just being nice? Isn't that possible?"

"Possible, yes; probable, no. Men like Gene Taylor are not nice out of the goodness of their heart. They are always looking for the *quid pro quo*."

"You are so negative, Dizz."

"You call it negative, but I call it street smarts. I've seen many guys with the same *modus operandi* as Gene. They don't change overnight and become saints. Trust me on this one, Art. If you do the Princeton and Young Masters Tour thing, you will have sold your soul to the devil."

"Now you're starting to sound like the Professor."

"Smart man, that one. And maybe, just maybe, the Professor has firsthand knowledge. After all, look what Gene did to him and his career when he refused to cooperate."

"Okay, okay, point taken. I hate it when you're right. Are you ever wrong?"

"Sure, but not on this one."

Gene Taylor was overwhelmed with TEI work after getting back from spring break. He placed his mental concerns about Art on the back burner for a few days, but by the weekend, they resurfaced when he was contacted by the Young Masters Tour to set up a time for contract negotiations.

Gene spent a good deal of Saturday calling to collect on favors from individuals who could provide him with research about Art, without tipping off the D.H.E. or any other agency that had a possible concern about his project.

Contacting Hawthorne was the easy call. He requested that the head of security provide him with a log of every entry or exit by Art and Dizz for the second semester. He also requested internet logs for both of them and a list of any and all transactions made by or through Hawthorne other than food purchases. Gene received the data back in less than an hour. He saw that Art and Dizz had left Hawthorne on another weekend later in the semester. He also saw that they returned together late on the same day. He reconfirmed the date that Art had told Elisha that he went to the Boston Public Library. He noticed that Dizz had left campus by himself on numerous other occasions. The other item that he found odd were records of Art leaving campus by himself when he had checked out a bike from the Hawthorne Recreation Department.

Gene contacted security to see if there was any way to track where Art had gone on his bike rides. He was told that the records indicated that Art always checked out a bike and helmet with no GPS tracking capability. He was also told that it appeared that he never took his Hawthorne cell phone on the rides. Gene requested that in the future Art only be given a GPS bike or, if that wasn't possible, that he be discretely followed to see where he went on his rides. Gene was disgusted that the tracking chip in Art's hand was defective. The tracking chip would have easily answered all of Gene's questions regarding Art's movements during the last couple of months.

Next, Gene called in his favors with a friend who had connections with NSA and the FBI. Gene was successful in getting his friend to agree to provide him with an 'under the radar' tracking report using historical video surveillance information garnered from trains, train depots, Boston city cameras and the Boston Public Library. Gene sent him pictures and profiles for each boy. Gene's source told him it would probably take him a few days to arrange a way to pull the search off without raising any red flags.

About five days later, a package was hand-delivered to Gene. It contained the tracking information on the boys for the day in question. The information showed them taking the train from Concord until they got off at the stop in Roxbury, but from there they didn't head north toward the library. The report showed that the video surveillance records for the day failed to show either boy on the Boston Public Library premises. It reported that the boys resurfaced later that day at a small pizza parlor and from there returned to the train station and back to Concord.

Gene mulled the information over in his mind. Art wasn't the kind of kid who would ever think about walking down the back alleys in Boston. He was definitely going some place with Dizz, but where? He pulled out and began reviewing Dizz's personal records, hoping to find a clue. He perused a list of all the addresses where Dizz had lived. He came across one address that he thought was fairly close to the Roxbury station, and entered the address into a map search program. Bingo! There it was, close to the spot where the boys exited the main street. The visual of the property showed it was an old, dilapidated hotel, which had a back entrance in the alley. He searched the public records, which showed the name of the owner and showed the current use as a low-income retirement facility.

This information was perplexing to Gene. What would two intelligent teenage boys be doing at a low-income retirement facility for a day? Nothing came to mind and for the next week and a half, he just let things sit, not sure what or where to look next. Then, almost in desperation, he decided to look up the public information about the facility. The information listed total occupancy, facility ratings, room size, amenities and current rent. When reading through the list of amenities, he noticed that the facility listed an information technology center offering computers and internet access.

Bingo. He knew about Dizz's run-in with the IT director at Hawthorne and the subsequent action to severely restrict his access to the system. He knew Dizz had been searching for his biological father and he wondered if the boys were somehow gaining internet access through this low-income retirement facility.

Gene called his friend in the intelligence business and asked him to provide a record of all the internet traffic from the address in question on the date he believed Dizz and Art were there. His friend told him he would get back to him in a few days with the requested information. It would arrive in the same manner as the last delivery.

Art's own prediction about his declining contact with Chris and Elisha proved true over the next couple of weeks. Elisha made no effort to either contact Art or include Art in any of her group activities. Chris, who never had really made much effort toward Art, now even barely said hello when passing in the halls. Art felt like they had completed their assignment to be nice to the pitiful orphan geek.

Art went back to spending his free time composing and hanging out with Dizz. Graduation was now only three weeks away, and Art and Dizz made plans to rent a small apartment in Boston for the summer. Art still didn't know exactly what he would do the coming year, but, to the dismay of Dizz, he was proceeding with all the plans for Princeton and the Young Masters Tour. Mr. Taylor had set up a meeting with Art a week before graduation at Hawthorne with his attorney and the attorney for the Young Masters Tour to negotiate the final terms of the contract. Art knew he would have to make a firm decision as to what he would do before signing the final contract. He thought maybe he could play the part of the eccentric, finicky, artist who would refuse to sign based on some outrageous demand, like no one attending the concerts could wear anything made from products derived from animals. He needed some way out. He decided that the coming weekend he would avoid going to the trouble of using the secret exit, take the risk, and bike down to Café Diem to see if he could get some advice. He also secretly hoped that he'd run into Marie again.

It was a fresh and beautiful Saturday morning in May and Art headed over to the rec center to check out a bike for the day. At the desk, he provided his ID and asked for a "dumb" bike. The attendant brought up his account and called over another attendant to look at the screen. The other attendant studied the screen, then told Art that all he had available were bikes fitted with GPS programs. From the desk, Art could see into the back room where they kept the bikes. He easily spotted the bike he normally checked out.

"Actually, I was really hoping to use that bike," Art stated, pointing at the bike he'd always used.

Art watched as the attendant turned and looked at the bike, and unconvincingly tried to act surprised that one of the non-GPS bikes was available. He felt a twinge of cautious concern. He remembered what Barger had said: if he had any questions or if anything at all hit him in a strange way, he was to err on the side of caution. The attendant went ahead and let him check out the bike, so Art rode off the Hawthorne grounds in a quandary as to whether to ride down to Café Diem. He decided he would stop at the Minuteman Hotdog stand, have a cheese coney, and think it through. As Art was securing the bike in the bike stand, he caught a glimpse of one of the attendants from the rec department ride by on another bike. *On a mission to repair someone's bike that had broken down?*

While he was eating his cheesy coney, he convinced himself he was just being paranoid and that as long as he had a dumb bike, there would be no harm in going down to Café Diem. He got on the bike and headed south out of Concord toward Baker Bridge. As he was getting close to Walden Pond he started burping up a bad hot dog taste so he turned off Walden Street at the pond and pedaled over to the fountain by the bathrooms. While getting a drink, Art again caught a glimpse of the same attendant out of the corner of his eye. Again he felt a cautious twinge. He now seriously wondered whether he was being followed. He decided to abort his trip to Café Diem and head back to Concord.

The thought of being followed bothered Art and he wanted to confirm his suspicions. Art rode very slowly on Walden Street back toward Concord, constantly looking in his mirror to see if he could spot the attendant following behind. He was disappointed, but at the same time relieved that he did not see the attendant trailing him. Still not totally convinced that he was not being followed, Art decided to ride his bike to Concord Academy and find an out-of-the-way place to stop and wait to see if the attendant would show up.

When he arrived at Concord Academy, Art turned into the East Gate entrance and took the road to the backside of the Athletic Center. He parked his bike by the lacrosse field, behind the Athletic Center and placed himself at the back corner of the Athletic Facility, giving him an unobstructed view down the road out the East Gate. Art only had to wait about three minutes before he saw the attendant ride by the entrance.

Art immediately hopped on the bike and headed out of Concord Academy in the other direction, back toward Hawthorne. When Art arrived at Hawthorne, he quickly turned in the bike and found another hiding spot behind a tree about forty yards from the rec center. Art waited about ten minutes before the attendant who had been following him returned. Art watched, as it appeared that the attendant on duty interrogated the returning attendant. Art had seen enough. He concluded that he was being followed, and that the only person who would have him followed was Mr. Taylor.

Gene Taylor waited four days before a package containing the internet logs for all the computers from the address in question was hand-delivered to his office. It revealed numerous hits on the DHE site by about ten of the residents. He also saw that there were numerous searches of county birth and death records for the name Jenicks. The most disturbing thing he saw was searches of newspaper archives of information about him, Virginia, Moss, DHE, and the gas explosion that killed Art's fabricated parents. Further search of the logs showed a couple searches for Jason Alexander and Boston Mercantile Bank and Trust. For a moment, Gene was frozen in shock, thinking that his twenty years of work on the Jenicks project could be in jeopardy. He quickly composed himself and began to analyze the situation.

Gene now knew that Art was aware of a lot more than he was letting on. Art must have known, by way of Dizz, that he couldn't perform those searches at Hawthorne without being detected. He guessed that Dizz must have set up some deal with the owner of the facility to access the internet using the identities of the occupants. He also knew that the fabricated birth and death records and newspaper stories were inserted into the record after the date of the searches.

Gene now understood the source of Art's verbal sparring and especially his use of the term 'subservient'. Art had obviously read some of the old editorials written by Moss objecting to scientific progress in the area of human development potential through eugenics.

What Gene couldn't grasp was what or who had prompted Art to make the searches and then, what conclusions Art had arrived at based on his searches. Gene could understand why Art would want to find out information about his parents and possible relatives. He could also see why Art may have some curiosity about his bank trustee. What he couldn't figure out was what would cause Art to do so many searches about DHE and Moss. It was possible that Art's research about himself and Virginia had led him to information about Moss and the DHE, but something about it all deeply bothered him.

Gene decided he would have to rethink his whole strategy about Art. He would have to make sure Art was totally on board before taking the risk of launching him out into the public arena.

The Raid

A DAY LATER, GENE RECEIVED an urgent call around noon from his friend with the NSA and FBI. He said it was a courtesy call to let him know what was taking place. He informed Gene that in the process of collecting the data for Gene, they had come across numerous sensitive security irregularities, leading them to believe that the owner of the housing project had been selling internet access to suspected terrorists and organized crime figures. As a consequence, the FBI and NSA were conducting a joint raid on the premises at that very moment.

Gene shared his immediate concern that neither of the Hawthorne students be named or implicated in any way. He was assured that the boys would be not be implicated, provided they were not directly involved in allowing or arranging the illegal internet access by suspected terrorist or members of organized crime.

Around two-thirty that same afternoon, Dizz received a call from his mother informing him that the authorities had conducted a raid on the Essex and had arrested Phil and removed all of the computers. She also told Dizz that it was rumored that ten frozen bodies were found on the premises. She knew that

Dizz had helped Phil set up the computer system at the Essex and was hopeful that Dizz would not be in any trouble. Dizz thanked his mom for the call, assured her that he was okay, and told her he would call her back later because he needed to get to a class.

Dizz sent a bunch of text messages to Art, all of which went unanswered. Then he went on a frantic search for Art, first stopping at his room and then going to all of the places on the campus where he thought Art might be hanging out. He finally found Art in one of the piano studios, playing away, lost in his music.

"Art! Art, we have an emergency," Dizz blurted out in a nervous, shaky voice.

Art did not immediately respond but smirked and kept on playing, thinking Dizz was messing around with him. Then, in frustration, Dizz grabbed both of Art's hands off the keyboard and held them tightly together. "Art! I'm not fooling around! We really do have an emergency situation and we need to move quickly!"

Art, now realizing that Dizz was serious, gave Dizz his full attention. He had never ever seen Dizz worried, much less in a state of panic.

"Art, the Feds raided the Essex and it won't take very long to break Phil down and find out that I was the designer and an accomplice to all of the illegal activity. Unless I disappear, I'll be going to jail as an adult for a number of things, the least of which would be defrauding the social security system. I'm afraid that's not all, when the authorities go through all of the history in the computer's memory, which they are sure to do, your searches will come to light and put you at risk."

Art, now in a state of shock, attempted to grapple with the reality of what he had just heard. His mind began to race and then jam. What would they do? What would happen to them? For a brief moment he thought about running to Virginia and Gene Taylor for help, but deep inside he knew that was not the answer. He turned to Dizz and said, "What are we going to do?"

"I think we need to get the hell out of here as fast as we can," said Dizz.

"But what about graduation?" said Art.

"Trust me, if we stay here, we are never going to see graduation," said Dizz.

"Yeah, what was I thinking? Should we just leave, walk out the front gate?" asked Art.

"No, we should go out our secret exit and head down to hide out at the professor's place," said Dizz.

Dizz asked for Art's cell phone, PACA and his student ID. Then he took both of their cell phones, PACAs and student IDs and dropped them down inside the piano that Art had been practicing on. They walked quickly out of the practice studio, trying to look as normal as possible as they made their way over to the athletic center and the locker room for their escape.

The locker room was jammed with freshman on the tennis team. Art and Dizz quickly walked out and waited until the first-years made their way outside to the tennis courts. After waiting a couple more minutes to assure there were no stragglers, Dizz and Art headed back into the locker room and over to their escape panel.

Dizz moved quickly, unscrewing and opening the panel. They crawled in and Dizz screwed the vent back into place. They quickly made their way through the tunnel of pipes to the sewer and followed it out to the ladder at the bottom of the manhole in the wood outside Hawthorne grounds. They climbed up the metal rung ladder and slowly opened the manhole. The mid-afternoon sun was shining brightly. All of their other exits had been under cover of nightfall. They would need to be extra cautious to avoid being seen by anyone in the woods or when they came out through the neighborhood on their way to Dizz's storage unit.

They jogged through the woods, constantly looking all around them. When they reached the neighborhood, two middle-school girls were riding their bikes in circles, around and around the cul-de-sac.

"What are we going to do now?" whispered Art, "wait a while and see if they leave?"

Dizz thought a moment, "I think we should just walk right out there like it's no big deal, but we have to act normal or they'll think something is wrong.

"Okay, here goes," said Dizz, "just follow my lead."

Dizz walked out of the woods nonchalantly, as if they walked through the woods all the time. He turned and started talking to Art about some made-up girl they met at the ice cream shop.

"Hey man, you really should give that girl at the ice cream shop a call. She was watching you like a hawk, and I loved the way she kept giving you that little half smile."

"I ...ah . . . ah . . . " said Art.

"Oh, come on man, don't act like you didn't notice," said Dizz.

"Well, I guess I kinda noticed," said Art, trying too hard to play his part.

"Okay, okay, I can take a hint. I won't bug you about it if you don't want to talk about it. But, I'm betting you call her," said Dizz.

By that time in the conversation, the boys had walked through the cul-de-sac and past the girls as if they didn't even exist. The girls looked at the boys, then at each other, rolled their eyes, and kept riding in circles. Dizz had pulled it off.

About two hundred yards down the street, Dizz turned to Art and said, "You are really bad at pulling a con. Fortunately, those middle-school girls just thought your awkwardness was from embarrassment."

"Sorry, Dizz, I'm just not a good liar," said Art.

They quickly made their way to the storage unit where Dizz kept his scooter. Dizz only had one jumpsuit and helmet. Dizz rummaged through the nearby trash and found an old trench coat and stocking cap that someone had thrown away in their moving process. He convinced Art to put them on and pull the stocking cap down so no one would be able to recognize him. After suiting up, they took off on the scooter, buzzing their way through Concord and on down to the Professor's house in Baker Bridge.

The Search

GENE WAS STILL AT WORK when he received a frantic call from Eric.

"Gene, do you know what is going on?"

"I know a lot of things that are going on. What specifically are you referring to?"

"I just got a call from one of my inside contacts on the DHE board."

"And, and . . . go on," said Gene impatiently.

"And I guess Art has been implicated in some kind of illegal activity, granting terrorist access to the internet. They also said that based on additional information they have garnered in the matter, they believe Art is now a threat to National Security, and you know what that means."

"No, No, this can't be happening! You need to let them know immediately that Art's not the guy . . . it is Dizz, I mean, Edward Benson. Tell them that Art has nothing to do with this."

"They know all about Benson. They are saying that both Art and Benson know too much. Gene, they have authorized a removal. Even as we speak, they are heading to Hawthorne to attempt to extract them without making a scene."

"Do the boys have any idea that something has happened?"

"NSA shows a call being made from Benson's mom to Benson at Hawthorne about two hours ago, informing him of the raid on the retirement facility that Benson was associated with through the owner. This guy's an ex-boyfriend of hers, and he spilled his guts about everything almost immediately based on a promise of leniency."

"I assume that Hawthorne is cooperating?"

"What choice do they have?"

"Eric, thanks for the call. Promise me that you will let me know when you hear anything more."

"Sure, Gene, no problem. Gene, I'm really sorry I had to break this to you."

"No problem, Eric. It is what it is."

Gene sat in his office for a few minutes staring out his window at the trees that lined the lake at TEI Corporate Headquarters. It was clear to him that twenty years of his work could vanish in one afternoon.

Gene called Virginia and told her about the raid and the probable fate of Art and Dizz. He also told Virginia that, if for some reason Art contacted her, or managed to show up at the house, to call him right away. In the back of Gene's mind, he was hoping he could somehow broker some kind of deal to save Art. Realistically, he knew he would need to either have Art in his possession or special knowledge of his whereabouts to effectively bargain with the DHE and NSA.

Virginia took the call extremely hard. She told Gene to call her with any news. Realizing she would probably never see Art alive again, she felt the overwhelming weight of responsibility of helping to set events in motion that ultimately placed Art in this position. She wished she had never been involved with the Jenicks project. She wished that she would have never used her talents and skill to help design the Jenicks brothers, and she wished she had never met Gene and fallen for his caring facade.

Dizz and Art rode the scooter around the backside of the Professor's farmhouse and stowed it in one of the small outbuildings. They went to the back door and knocked several times, but no one was home.

"We should have stopped at Café Diem first, to see if the Professor or Barger were there, said Art.

"I don't think so," said Dizz. "Believe me, the way the two of us looked riding on the scooter attracted enough attention. All we needed was a café full of customers to see us ride up and talk to Moss. When the feds come looking for us, they'll be asking everyone in the area if they've seen a couple of guys who look like us. No, we just need to hang out here, in one of these sheds, until this Prof guy shows up."

A small contingency of NSA and FBI officers showed up at Hawthorne and made their way to the main office. After they identified themselves as FBI agents, they informed the headmaster who they were looking for and demanded his immediate and full cooperation. They further informed the headmaster they would tour the grounds posing as potential corporate donors.

They first went as a group to McLaren Hall to search Dizz and Art's rooms. Two agents stayed behind to search their rooms, while eight other agents split out in pairs to search the grounds. After coming up empty, they headed back to the main office and demanded that the head master provide them with current GPS location of Art's and Dizz's student ID cards. They also demanded to review the campus surveillance records for the day. The headmaster reluctantly consented.

They tracked down the student ID cards along with their cell phones and PACAs. Finding them stashed in the bottom of the piano was indication that the boys were aware that they were in trouble and were on the run.

Review of the surveillance records revealed that Art and Dizz left the piano studio and went to the athletic complex. From there the trail went cold. The records revealed that they never left the athletic complex. This prompted an all out search of the athletic complex.

Moss and Barger rode in on their bicycles around five o'clock. Art raced out to greet them when they came around the backside of the house. He quickly introduced them to Dizz and then with the help of Dizz frantically attempted to explain their current emergency and how they escaped from Hawthorne.

After listening, Barger looked intensely at Moss. "We need to put our exit plan in motion. Now."

Moss nodded grimly, and Barger got back on his bike and headed back to Café Diem to have Marie make the necessary calls. Inside the kitchen, the Professor told the shaken boys to grab something to eat. "Listen carefully. We'll be leaving tonight, after dark. It's only a matter of time before the Feds exhaust their search of Hawthorne and start pulling up satellite imagery to track you." He looked at both of them, the gravity of the situation settled on his face. "Which means no one leaves the house. Clear?"

Back at Hawthorne, the agents were becoming more and more frustrated. How hard could it be to locate a couple of teenage boys at a private prep school? They demanded that the headmaster allow them to access the building plans for the athletic complex. After a thorough review, they discovered what Dizz had found earlier, that there was a way off the grounds through the sewage system by way of the access panels in the boys' locker room.

The headmaster confirmed that at one time Dizz had hacked into the Hawthorne computer system and would have had access to all of the school's building plans.

After hearing this, the agents hustled back over to the Athletic Center. They quickly found the loose access panel and shoe tracks from the access panel to the drain sewer. With this new discovery, they called for satellite surveillance imagery to be pulled and reviewed from mid-afternoon forward. The agents also called for trained tracking dogs to be delivered. In the event the boys were still on foot, the dogs would find them.

Barger peddled full speed into Café Diem. He hopped off his bike and rushed breathlessly through the back storage room and up to the front counter where Marie was working. Still out of breath, he motioned for Marie to come back to the storage room. Marie quickly followed him back.

"Dad, what's happening? You look really intense."

"You know that emergency exit plan I have been working on for Moss and us? Well, something has happened with Art that is causing us to have to implement it immediately."

Marie was stunned by what her father told her. They had gone over and over the plan in detail countless times, but the reality was far different. Barger saw her shocked face and gently hugged her, reassuring her that things would be okay. Marie responded with a teary smile.

"Dad, I'll make the call and then meet you back at the Professor's house as soon as I close down the Café."

"Thanks. I love you honey. Things are really going to be all right. Okay?"

Marie shook her head and gave her Dad one more big hug before he headed out the door to ride back to Moss's farm.

A call came through to Gene while he was still at his office. It was Virginia.

"Gene, did you hear anything yet?" asked Virginia

"Eric just called to say that the agents believe the boys are on some kind of motorized scooter, but they haven't figured out which direction they are heading," answered Gene.

"Oh, Gene, I can hardly bear this! I am totally exhausted from worrying about Art and what they will do to him if they find him. I am going to take a sleeping pill and try to get some sleep, but promise me you will call me as soon as you hear anything, okay?"

"Okay, Virginia, I promise," said Gene. "I'm staying at the office, just in case I can help. Remember, these guys have access to every piece of surveillance technology you can imagine. It's just a matter of time before they find them."

Virginia took the sleeping pill and laid down on the couch in the study. The medicine was effective almost immediately, and Virginia quickly fell into a deep sleep.

Upon running into a dead end at the storage unit, the lead agent called in and requested immediate access to satellite photos of the area from that afternoon that might reveal the direction the boys headed on the cycle. While waiting for the information, they questioned the storage unit manager who was able to provide them with a vague description of the scooter, and the black jumpsuit and helmet that he had seen Dizz wear when he rode the scooter.

Marie arrived at the farmhouse right about at dusk, bag in hand, and only a slight tremor in her voice giving away her nervousness as she detailed the plan. Within the next hour, one vehicle would be dropped off out on the paved roadway, and the other vehicle and the driver of the first vehicle would leave immediately in the second vehicle.

Barger and the Professor quickly briefed the boys. Then they called the boys over to the back door and handed them a pair of their shoes and told them to walk out to the river's edge, sit down in the Adirondack chairs, change into the shoes and walk back to the house.

"Why are we doing this?" questioned Art.

"We are just providing a little misdirection to possibly slow the Feds down a bit," answered Barger. "They'll more than likely have tracking dogs, so we'll make it look like you might have escaped down the river."

"I like it!" announced Dizz with a smirk.

The boys grabbed the shoes and headed out to the river's edge.

After the boys got back, Marie went over and gave her dad a big hug.

"Have you removed the chips yet?" asked Marie.

"We won't do that until right before we leave, just in case we accidently set off the tamper-proof system in the process of removing a chip," said Barger. "We're pretty sure that the temperature readings from the chip are the trigger. Once you remove a chip, the temperature falls to room temperature, which we believe will trigger the tamper alarm."

Clearly fascinated, Dizz asked, "How are you going to avoid the temperature change when you take it out?"

"Follow me," said Barger. Marie, Art, and Dizz followed Barger back to the kitchen. Laid out on the kitchen table were surgical tools, gauze, and bandages. Attached to the two chairs at the table was what looked like a mechanical arm holding a small metal tube. Attached to the tube were a small battery and a digital temperature read out.

"Wow!" said Art. "How does this all work?"

"It's really very simple," said Barger. "We will use a surgical punch that is first heated to about ninety-nine degrees to remove the chip. We'll immediately place the chip in the metal tube, which contains water heated to 98.6 degrees. The battery heater will maintain that temperature for about three days.

The mechanical arms are prepared with one hundred different movements and are on a program to randomly trigger the time and amount of movement. If for some reason an alarm is set off and they check our location, they will see that we are in the house at the table, hopefully making normal movements."

"How do you think of all of this stuff, Dad?" asked Marie in admiration.

"Fear is an incredible catalyst for creativity," said Barger.

Gene's pacing and thinking yielded a thought. He remembered that Art had done a lot of research on Moss. What if Art had figured out where Moss lived and actually made contact with him? What if Art and Dizz were hiding at Moss's little farmhouse down at Baker Bridge? Maybe that's where Art went on his day trips with the bike. Maybe that's why Art always checked out bikes with no GPS capability so his movements could never be tracked. Moss would have probably warned him.

Gene estimated that he could grab a vehicle and make it to Moss's old farmhouse in less than thirty minutes. He called down to the TEI transportation department and asked if there were any vehicles available that he could use. The on-duty manager wanted to call a limo and driver, but Gene insisted on him bringing over whatever vehicle was immediately available. The manager said that all he had in the underground garage was a small company panel van.

"Drive it over ASAP," Gene demanded.

• • •

It had been about forty minutes since Marie had shown up and announced that the vehicles should arrive sometime within the next hour. Both Barger and the Professor had begun to fidget and pace back and forth, occasionally walking back to the kitchen to see if everything was ready to go. Then, two sets of headlights appeared out on the paved road near the end of the driveway. The driver of the first vehicle quickly jumped out, hopped into the second vehicle, and the first vehicle quickly disappeared.

As soon as the taillights vanished, Barger and Moss bolted out the front door and ran down the driveway to check out the vehicle and its contents. They both sighed in relief as they realized that everything, including the cash, was in order and perfectly matched the agreed-upon specifications.

As Art, Dizz, and Marie watched, Barger and the professor sprinted back to the house. Once inside, the two men headed for the kitchen to extract their chips.

The removal went very smoothly, with both men removing the other's chip and depositing it immediately into the heated water inside the metal tube. Once the removal was completed and both men were bandaged, the whole group quickly proceeded to the vehicle and loaded up. Moss and Barger insisted on carrying Dizz and Art from the house to the vehicles piggyback-style in order to avoid leaving either of the boy's shoe prints.

They were just getting into the SUV when they noticed a pair of headlights approaching in their direction. Barger quickly instructed Art, Dizz and Marie to get down on the floor of the back seat so they would not be seen.

• • •

Gene turned off of Old Concord road onto Fairhaven. As he approached Moss's farm, he noticed a vehicle parked out on the road. He pulled up slowly in front of the vehicle and stopped in front of it blocking its way. Gene got out of the van and walked slowly over to the man seated on the driver's side of the SUV.

"Hello, Gene," came the calm, reserved voice of the Professor out of the driver's side window. "What are you doing down here in Baker Bridge?"

"Hi, Derrick, long time no see," responded Gene as he peered through the window of the SUV. "I'm down here looking to find a young man and save him from a disaster."

"A disaster? Sounds serious, Gene."

"Yes, it's very serious business. Serious for him and for anyone who may be with him. I don't suppose you have possibly seen a couple young teenage boys around here, one named Art and one named Dizz?"

"Doesn't ring a bell," the Professor responded, looking away from Gene.

Gene now squinted in the darkness, trying to make out who was with Moss sitting on the passenger side. "Barger, is that you?"

"Hi, Gene," replied Barger, nodding his head in acknowledgement.

"You haven't seen any young boys hanging around here have you, Barger?"

"Nope," responded Barger in a matter-of-fact fashion.

Gene attempted to stick his head through the driver's side window to see if anyone else was in the SUV. "You know, Derrick, you never were a very good liar. I'm betting that not only have you seen them, but that you are attempting to disappear with them. I'll make a deal with you, Derrick. If you hand Art over to me, I'll let you drive away from here without placing a call to the authorities. I won't tell them that I've been here, seen you or talked with you. However, if you insist on playing dumb, I'll have to make the call and all of you will have to live, or should I say deal, with the consequences."

Art started feeling clammy and sick to his stomach. He understood the consequences of Gene's ultimatum. He knew that he was probably the only one who could make this right.

Moss continued to stare straight ahead for a few seconds and then turned and locked eyes with Gene. "Even if I did know where he was, I wouldn't hand him over to you. God only knows what you would do with him."

"Come on, Derrick. You make me sound like a monster. Regardless of what you think of me, you know I have way too much invested in Art to let anything happen to him. Art will be much safer with me than he will ever be with you. If he doesn't come with me now, he will be hunted down and eventually disposed of with the rest of you. If you turn him over to me, I'll be able to protect him and you will have a fighting chance of getting out of here alive."

Art stayed curled up in a tight ball on the floor of the SUV next to the passenger side back door as he listened to the conversation. He didn't like what he was hearing, but he knew Gene was right. If he didn't go with Gene, it would be like signing a death warrant for all of them. If he went with Gene, the Professor, Barger, Dizz, and Marie would at least have a decent chance of getting away. Beads of sweat were forming on his forehead, his breathing was becoming shallow and his gut was in a knot. He wasn't going to be the cause of his friends' deaths. He knew what he had to do. He motioned to Dizz and Marie to stay down. He opened the back door and walked around the back of the SUV to the driver's side.

"Mr. Taylor," said Art with a trembling voice. "I'll go with you, but you have to promise that you will keep your word about letting Mr. Moss and Mr. Barger drive away without notifying the authorities or letting them know that you ever saw or talked to them."

"Art!" pleaded the Professor, "you don't have to do this, you are not responsible for what happens to Barger and me, and who knows what Gene will really do. We can still make a run for it. We may still be successful in getting out of here."

"Art," interrupted Gene, "I promise you I will keep my word about Moss and Barger. What Moss is saying about getting out of here is insane and he knows it. If I call you in, you don't have a chance of getting even ten miles from here."

Art looked over at the Professor. Their eyes met for a moment and without a word communicated that they cared for each other and that this was good-bye. Even though he had known the Professor for a very short time, Art would be forever grateful to the Professor for risking his life to provide him with answers and for giving him the freedom to consider his own desires.

Emotion overwhelmed Art as his eyes welled up with tears and began to run down his face. He turned his gaze away from the Professor and told Gene he was ready to go. Without looking back, Art walked over to the TEI van and climbed into the passenger seat. He kept his head down buried in his knees, not being able to look up at the Professor and Barger sitting in the SUV. He could somewhat hear the ongoing conversation between the Professor and Mr. Taylor but couldn't make out what was being said. The next thing he knew, the SUV backed up and pulled out around the van and passed by his window. He sat up and watched in the rearview mirror as the taillights of the SUV, and his freedom, disappeared into the night. He knew he had done the right thing for his friends, but he realized that he would continue to be Gene's science experiment. He wondered if he would ever be allowed to just be himself and fulfill his own destiny, not the destiny that Gene had scripted for him.

Gene walked back over to the van and opened the driver's side door to speak to Art. "I promised them I would stay here at least fifteen minutes before leaving to assure them I would not follow them. Barger also told me that I really should get rid of the evidence in the shed behind the house. Art, do you know what he was talking about?"

Art nodded his head, "Yeah, Dizz's scooter and our clothes are in there."

"I see," responded Gene. "Why don't you get out of the van and we will walk over to the shed and get the scooter and the clothes and stow them in the van. It's supposed to rain tonight which should wipe out our tracks, but the van is much heavier and I don't want any of the van's tire tracks on Moss's property."

Art reluctantly got out of the van and went and helped Gene retrieve and load the scooter. They also gathered up Dizz's black jumpsuit and helmet, and the trench coat and stocking hat that Art had worn on the trip down. By the time they got everything loaded, the fifteen minutes had passed and they began their trip back to Gene's home.

Art felt extremely awkward and somewhat afraid riding in the van with Mr. Taylor. He felt like he was a captured spy that had been caught working for the wrong side. What would

Gene do with him now? Would Gene really be able to protect him? What would be required of him by Gene to warrant ongoing protection?

Gene broke the awkward silence. "Art, you did the right thing back there. Now it becomes extremely important to your well being that you continue doing the right thing going forward. I have not completely thought this out yet, but for your continued safety, none of what just took place at Moss's farm ever happened. Do you understand?"

Art swallowed hard, "Yes, sir, I understand."

"I will have to work on the complete story, but for now, as far as anyone else is concerned, including Virginia, this is what happened. You went to Boston a couple times with Dizz. You did a little research on the internet trying to find out more about your parents. You had no idea that Dizz was involved in anything illegal. Dizz came to you in a panic today about the raid on the Essex and told you that you too could be implicated in the illegal activity he was involved with. He convinced you to go with him and run from the law. Once you got down to the storage shed your head cleared and you realized that you had no reason to run because you had done nothing illegal. Not knowing exactly what to do, you let Dizz go his own way and you came to our house for help and to figure things out. When you got to our house, you rang the bell but got no response so you decided to just wait at the front gate until someone got home. That's the story we'll start with. You got it? Any questions?"

"I got it. It seems simple enough and fairly close to what happened," replied Art, not knowing exactly what Gene really knew.

"Good, you stay with that simple story and I will run interference with the authorities."

The Awakening

VIRGINIA'S DEEP SLEEP WAS STIRRED by the distant sound of one of her favorite songs. The song repeated several times and then stopped. Virginia drifted back to sleep until the song interrupted her again. This time she sat straight up and listened to the song repeat several times. It sounded like one of her old cell phone ringers.

Virginia opened her eyes to total blackness. Still groggy, she realized that she was wearing a sleeping mask that she didn't remember putting on when she laid down on the couch. What's more, she was in a bed wearing a pair of pajamas.

The music played again. She removed the sleeping mask from her face in order to find the source of the music and was blinded by the bright morning light flooding through large wooden windows that were surrounded by atrociously bright, orange paisley curtains. She was confused and felt anxious. When her vision cleared, she saw the source of the music: an old flip phone looking something like one she had used years ago. Virginia opened up the phone and said, "Hello?"

"Virginia, where are you?" responded the voice on the phone.

"Gene, is that you?" asked Virginia, "Any news on Art?"

"Gene? Who is Gene, and who is Art? Virginia, this is Aaron, Aaron Taylor. Where are you? You were supposed to be here a half an hour ago."

While Aaron was talking, Virginia looked around. She was not in her house. She was in the apartment where she had lived in Boston prior to marrying Gene.

She heard Gene's voice on the phone again, "Virginia, Virginia, are you there?"

"Yes," Virginia replied in a flat monotone.

"I have been waiting for you at Starbucks for the last forty-five minutes. Did you forget that we were going to meet and go over our testimony one more time before getting on the plane to DC?" asked Aaron.

Virginia did not answer immediately. Her head slowly cleared until she was finally fully awake. It then hit her all at once, "Oh my . . . Oh . . . this is unbelievable, has it all been a dream?" asked Virginia in an astonished tone.

"Has what been a dream? What are you talking about?" asked Aaron.

"I think I've just had the most realistic, vivid, dream that I've ever had in my life. You and I were—"

Aaron interrupted her, "Virginia, forget about the dream, we need to go over our testimony. We need to have our act together to be able to counter any of the moralistic dribble that Moss throws at the committee. We really need to convince them that there is a vital need for a new Department of Human Enhancement."

"Moss, he was in the dream too, and you had changed your name to Gene, and we were—"

Aaron interrupted impatiently, "Virginia, not now! You can tell me all about your crazy little dream later. Right now, you need to get out to Logan so we don't miss our flight. Look, we are probably not going to have any time to go through our testimony prior to the hearing and we can't discuss this on the plane. Virginia, your testimony is critical. You have the knowledge and the credibility to sway the committee in the right direction. I am really counting on you. Do you know what you are going to tell the committee?"

There was a long pause of dead air.

"Virginia, are you there?" questioned Aaron.

"Yes, yes, I'm here," responded Virginia.

Once again, Aaron pressed, "Do you know what you will tell them?"

Virginia, still confused and uneasy about the whole situation, sat on the edge of her bed looking out of the window of her apartment into the bright Boston sunshine. Then she responded emphatically, "Yes, Gene, I know exactly what I am going to say."

"Come on, Virginia, I'm not Gene, this is Aaron."

Virginia closed the flip phone, thinking to herself, *Yes, I know exactly what I am going to say.* She gazed at the orange glow streaming through the paisley curtains, then closed her eyes and began to formulate a plan....

Virginia felt her shoulder being nudged and Gene's voice urging her to wake up. After several more nudges that approached shakings, Virginia finally opened her eyes to see Gene bent over her staring at her intensely. She immediately noticed that she was lying on the couch in the study.

"Virginia, sorry to wake you up, but you wanted me to let you know when I had news about Art."

Virginia sat up on the couch. She was still groggy from the sleeping pills and was very confused. Had she not already woken up, or was this another false awakening?

Apparently Gene could see the puzzled look on her face and decided that she was not yet fully awake. "Virginia, are you okay? I'm sorry for waking you up, but I knew you would want the latest news about Art."

"I think I'm okay now," Virginia said as she stretched and yawned simultaneously. "I thought I already woke up . . . I was back in my apartment in Boston before we were married. It seemed so real."

"It's probably just your sleeping pills doing a number on you. You really are awake now and I have some news about Art."

"Is he dead?" asked Virginia in a panicked tone.

"No, he's very much alive. Actually he's in the kitchen making a sandwich."

"He's here? Is he okay? How did this happen?"

"He realized that there was no reason for him to run and try to hide from the authorities because he had done nothing wrong. He left Dizz in the middle of his attempt to run and came here for help. He was waiting outside at the front gate when I came home. He said he rang the bell several times but no one answered. You must have been sleeping."

"What happens now? Is there a risk that DHE and DARPA will shut down the 'ART' side of the project?"

"Oh yeah, there is always a risk, and crap like this always increases the risk. However, I think I can do enough damage control by individually lobbying the board members and closely managing and monitoring Art from here on out."

"Gene, are you really going to continue to control every little detail of his life so you can make sure to accomplish your goals for the project? Haven't you had enough of playing god with someone's life?" Virginia turned her back on Gene and walked briskly out of the study, slamming the door behind her. She almost ran down the hall into the kitchen where she found Art and gave him a big motherly hug.

"Oh, Art, I can't tell you how relieved I am to see you here. I feel terrible that I didn't hear you ring the doorbell. How long were you waiting out by the gate?"

"Oh, ah, I really don't know. I kinda lost track of time. It's been a crazy day."

"Are you okay? I was so worried that something bad was going to happen to you."

"Yeah, I'm fine, really, I'm doing okay."

"How did you make it here all the way from Concord?"

"Oh, I walked and hitchhiked a little."

"Well, I'm glad you are okay. I think you should stay here a few days until all of this confusion gets straightened out. You can stay in the guest room back by the pool."

Art looked deeply into Virginia's eyes. "Thanks, Virginia. I don't know what's going to happen from here and I really appreciate your concern for me and for helping me out like this."

Virginia was relieved that Art was safe for now, but she knew his continued safety and possible existence would depend on his ongoing cooperation with Gene's plans. It made her sick to think about where her life's journey had taken her. She wished that her false awakening had been real and that she could go back in time and take action to prevent what had taken place with Art, Art's brothers, and Moss. Alternatively, she wished she could somehow protect Art and at the same time expose the hideous things she and Gene had done, and then just disappear. And maybe, just maybe she would figure out a way to do just that.

• • •

Virginia showed Art to his room and helped him settle in. After Virginia left, Art sat on the end of the bed with the lights turned off, staring out the sliding glass door at the lightning of the approaching storm and listening to the crashes of thunder. He wondered whether the Professor, Barger, Dizz and Marie actually got safely away. He wondered if he would ever see them again. He wondered what Gene would now require of him.

Somehow, someway, regardless the cost, he would figure out a way to take back his life.

Questions to Ponder

1. In the book, Gene Taylor states that it is a waste of valuable time and resources for a parent to struggle with trying to determine their child's natural gifts and talents. Do you believe this is true?
2. What, if anything, entices you about the possibilities of human engineering and pharmaceutical applications? Long life? Advanced athletic abilities? Specific, enhanced gifts and talents?
3. Would you categorize what was done to Art as limiting or enhancing?
4. By engineering human beings, do we take away freedom from future generations? If so, in what way?
5. What skills would be lost if future generations were engineered to be free of virtually all life's problems?
6. In his inaugural address, a United States president stated that we must "restore science to its rightful place, and wield technology's wonders to raise health care's quality"? What does this mean, and is it being implemented today?
7. Should we place limits on our creativity in the area of biotechnology? Why or why not?
8. What happens to freedom, equality and democracy in an engineered world? Would it create new areas of discrimination?

9. What do you believe is the definition of "good health"? Does it mean free from all suffering? Absent of pain and disease? Should the definition include good looks, talent, vitality, athleticism, and high intelligence? Should the concept of good health include having all of our needs (and perhaps even whims) satisfied?
10. Should the findings of science be deemed the highest truth and off limits to religious and personal views, moral premises, tradition, and policy?
11. How do we control the possible destructive aspects of biotechnology? Who should decide what is good and what is destructive?
12. Are you the sum of your genes? Do genes define who you are? If not, then what makes you unique from the rest of humanity?

For additional discussion questions suited for classroom and/or in-depth individual study, please feel free to contact the author at THEAWAKENINGBOOK.NET.

For more information on this topic, see the links below.

The Center For Bioethics and Culture Network
www.thecbc.org

The President's Council on Bioethics
www.bioethics.gov

The Hastings Center—Bioethics and Public Policy
www.thehastingscenter.org

The National Human Genome Research Institute
www.genome.gov

Center for Human Life & Bioethics
www.frc.org/get.cfm?c=CENTER_LIFE

The Center for Bioethics & Human Dignity
www.cbhd.org

American Society For Bioethics + Humanities
www.asbh.org/about/purpose.html

Bioethics.net—The American Journal of Bioethics
www.bioethics.net

The Kennedy Institute of Ethics
kennedyinstitute.georgetown.edu/index.htm

Kennedy Institute of Ethics Library
bioethics.georgetown.edu

Institute on Biotechnology & The Human Future
www.thehumanfuture.org

National Catholic Bioethics Center
www.ncbcenter.org

Acknowledgement

THE GENESIS OF THIS BOOK was born out of a request made by my son to help him research a biotech debate for his high school biology class. Little did I know that the research would be the catalyst for this book. Thank you, Taylor, for asking for my help!

Writing a book is incredibly time consuming and my family has been extremely gracious, putting up with me saying things like "just a minute, I'm on a roll" or "do I have to go to that, I was going to work on my book". Thank you, Jody, Brie, and Samantha for your loving patience and understanding!

Books are not written without help; at least this one wasn't. I have been blessed with help on all sides. My wife Jody has read rewrite after rewrite and patiently listened to my wild ideas. My daughters Brie and Samantha have given me invaluable input. My sister-in-law Trudy, and her two sons Ben and Jesse, have gifted me with their valuable time along with their encouragement and counsel. In addition, I am sure that my friend Lance is delighted that I will not be asking him to read yet another rewrite.

I have also been exceptionally blessed with very good editors. In the early stages, Carol Richards provided the essential early editing to keep this book headed in the right direction. In the later stages, Barb Lilland adeptly prodded me during the rewrite process and provided her superb editing skills to clarify and sharpen the story. Thank you, Carol and Barb, for all of your hard work and direction.

TGATTCATC